THE SWEETEST KISS

"Have you ever been kissed before, Spotted Wolf?"

"Not often," he muttered. "And not for a long time."

His expression was incredibly gentle and his eyes glowed like the embers of a slow-banked fire. A peculiar warmth spread through Jennifer, extending outward until it permeated her entire being and made her feel weak as a kitten.

Jennifer wondered if her feelings showed in her face but the thought held no real concern for her. His gentle strength had calmed her, completely dispelling her fears until they scattered like leaves in the wind. "The kiss was my way of thanking you for saving me from Three Fingers."

His head lowered until his lips hovered mere inches above hers. "You do not place enough value on yourself. Surely your life is worth more than one kiss." His mouth covered hers then, in a kiss so sweet that it literally stole her breath away.

DANGEROUS GAMES   (0-7860-0270-0, $4.99)
by Amanda Scott

When Nicholas Barrington, eldest son of the Earl of Ulcombe, first met Melissa Seacort, the desperation he sensed beneath her well-bred beauty haunted him. He didn't realize how desperate Melissa really was . . . until he found her again at a Newmarket gambling club—being auctioned off by her father to the highest bidder. So, Nick bought himself a wife. With a villain hot on their heels, and a fortune and their lives at stake, they would gamble everything on the most dangerous game of all: love.

A TOUCH OF PARADISE   (0-7860-0271-9, $4.99)
by Alexa Smart

As a confidence man and scam runner in 1880s America, Malcolm Northrup has amassed a fortune. Now, posing as the eminent Sir John Abbot—scholar, and possible discoverer of the lost continent of Atlantis—he's taking his act on the road with a lecture tour, seeking funds for a scientific experiment he has no intention of making. But scholar Halia Davenport is determined to accompany Malcolm on his "expedition" . . . even if she must kidnap him!

Comanche Sunset

Betty Brooks

Zebra Books
Kensington Publishing Corp.
http://www.zebrabooks.com

ZEBRA BOOKS are published by

Kensington Publishing Corp.
850 Third Avenue
New York, NY 10022

Zebra and the Z logo Reg. U.S. Pat. & TM Off.

First Printing: February, 1998
10 9 8 7 6 5 4 3 2 1

Printed in the United States of America

Dedicated to Virginia Hughes

Sister, friend, and laughmaker
God smiled on us when he sent you our way.

One

Spring
1871
West Texas

The full moon rose high in the sky, its pale light shining down on the stark ruggedness of the Apache Mountains, washing silver over the stunted cedars and gnarled oaks that clung to the dry canyons and ridges.

The moonlight, however, did not reach the warrior sheltered by a shrub with low spreading branches. He had been there for hours, motionless, unmoving except for his eyes, grass green eyes that were intense and watchful as he scanned the fort below him.

Spotted Wolf had pinpointed the building he sought moments after he arrived, yet still he waited. It was essential that he learn everything possible about the habits of the soldiers.

He knew them now, every move, every chore, yet still he waited. Until the soldiers sought their rest, he could not chance leaving lest the enemy spot his movement.

That time would come soon though. Spotted Wolf

had learned the White Eyes' way of keeping time and knew the hour of ten neared.

Then the bugler sounded taps. As the mournful strains filled the air, it was joined by the distant answering cry of a coyote.

Yip, yip, arooo. Yip, yip, arooo.

The warrior moved then. And as he stood, he heard a deadly rattle. A chill washed over him, as though he'd been drenched in ice water.

He reacted swiftly, sliding his knife from its sheathe as he spun around, and in one swift, reflexive stroke, he struck at the rattler, slicing its head from its body.

As he watched the reptile die, he felt a burning sensation in the back of his thigh, and the truth sank in. He had moved too slowly. Even now, the rattler's deadly venom was moving rapidly toward his heart.

He fumbled his headband loose and bound it tightly across his thigh above the wound. His steel blade gleamed in the moonlight as he pressed the knife tip against the bite in his calf.

Unflinching, he slashed across the wound, once, twice, three times. Then he sheathed his bloody weapon. For the moment, he'd done all he could.

Sparing another brief look for the snake, a big one, as thick as his arm and twice the length of his leg, he moved quietly up the hillside.

By the time he reached the crest of the hill, his heartbeat sounded like war drums in his ears, but he knew he couldn't stop. If there was any chance of cheating death of its prize, he had to keep moving.

He cast a regretful look at the thick walled building below that he'd watched for so many of the white man's hours. He had meant to slip into the fort, to reassure the prisoner behind those barred windows that he had not been forgotten.

But the gods had intervened.

He had to leave now, before the poison kept him from going. If he could reach his mount, the buckskin would take him home. He must at least try, because his mission was vital; the future of his people depended upon it.

He *could* not fail.

And yet he had.

Two

Fort Davis was located at the mouth of a box canyon near Limpia Creek where there were ample quantities of wood, water and grass for grazing animals.

Built in 1854 to protect travelers from the Indians, the fort had been abandoned during the Civil War. The buildings were assembled in an irregular fashion up the canyon, as were the officers' quarters, which consisted of thirteen large, single-unit dwellings for families. Four multi-unit quarters had been built for bachelors.

Although the single-unit dwellings appeared alike when seen from the front, those occupied by higher ranking officers had additional rooms in the back.

It was in one of the larger dwellings that Major Walter Carlisle resided with his niece. And, since Jennifer Carlisle's bedroom was at the back of the house, she knew the dim light cast by the flickering candle in her room would remain undetected by the sentries who patrolled the area.

Jennifer was seated on the edge of the four-poster bed. Excitement flushed her cheeks, glittering in her blue eyes as she slid a black leather boot over her right foot.

But the other occupant of the room didn't share

her elation. In fact, the creases between Clara Boseley's brows revealed her extreme anxiety.

"Don't go, Jenny," she pleaded, keeping her voice low so it wouldn't carry beyond the room. "You don't have the least notion of what you're getting into. If you're right, and I'm not saying you are, then you could be in danger."

"I *am* right," Jennifer said. "I just have to prove it. Anyway, do you really think I could just crawl into my bed and actually go to sleep knowing Lieutenant Carter and One Eye are up to something devious?" There was exasperation in her tone.

"Do you really think I have no more gumption than that?" Without waiting for an answer, she reached for the other boot.

"You have too cotton-pickin' much gumption," Clara complained. "But if either of them see you . . ."

"They won't see me," Jennifer declared, sliding the other boot onto her left foot. "Now stop fussing, Clara, and help me get ready."

She seated herself at the vanity, scooped her copper colored curls off her shoulders and twisted them into a knot. Securing it at the nape of her neck with long, brass hairpins, she looked at her friend again. "How do I look?"

"Like a woman dressed in a man's clothes," Clara retorted smartly. "You won't fool anyone."

"I'm not trying to fool anyone," Jennifer said impatiently. "I'm trying to keep from being seen."

Settling a black hat atop her head, she looked into the vanity mirror and appraised her image. Clara was right. Nobody would mistake her for a man. Her features appeared too fragile, and the thick, dark lashes framing her blue eyes were too long. Yet those were minor differences, covered eas-

ily by the darkness. It was the swell of her breasts
that gave away her gender, that, and the roundness
of her buttocks.

"Be honest, Clara," she said, finding herself in
need of reassurance. "If I stay out of direct moonlight, the dark breeches and shirt should blend with
the shadows."

"I suppose so," Clara conceded reluctantly. "But
I still don't like it. And if your uncle finds out, he's
going to be angry."

"He isn't going to know. And you promised to
help me, Clara. You know you did."

"I only said that 'cause I thought you'd change
your mind. But now . . ."

"A promise is a promise." Jennifer opened the
wardrobe and lifted a holstered revolver from a
hook inside. Wrapping it around her waist, she settled it against her hips and fastened it securely.

"Jennifer!" Clara gasped. "You aren't going to
take that *thing* with you?"

"This *thing* is a pistol, as you well know," Jennifer
chided gently. "And of course I'm going to take it.
You told me yourself that I would need protection."

"But a gun . . . Jennifer! You might shoot yourself
with it!"

"Oh, for God's sake! Don't be a complete fool,
Clara! I'm not a child. I'm twenty-two years old. Pa
taught me how to use a weapon the moment my
grip was strong enough to hold one." She adjusted
the gun belt one more time, settling it firmly around
her hips. "I guess I'm ready. Do you remember what
you're supposed to do?"

"Do?" Clara's rising voice squeaked. "You said I
wouldn't have to do anything! Jennifer, I'm the
world's worst coward. You know that!"

"For heaven's sake, you don't have to *do* anything,

except cover for me if my uncle wakes up, which is highly unlikely. He's usually dead to the world the moment his head hits the pillow."

"Oooh. What if he's restless tonight? What if he wants some coffee, or something like that? And if he finds you gone . . ."

"He won't. And even if he did get up, he wouldn't come in here."

"Then why do you need me here? I could be home asleep, instead of worrying my head off about you and this fool's errand."

"Clara, nothing is going to happen. You're only here in case of an emergency, like a fire or something."

Clara rolled her eyes.

Jennifer sighed heavily. "There won't be a fire, Clara. That was just an example. You'll be perfectly safe in here. Just crawl into bed and stop complaining. I'll be back before you know it."

"I wish I had never agreed to this," Clara sulked.

"I don't mean to sound testy," Jennifer said, trying to curb her impatience. "It's just that there's so much at stake here." She squeezed her friend's shoulder. "Aren't you the least bit curious? Lieutenant Carter and One Eye see each other every day. Why would they need to arrange a meeting outside the fort? And in the dead of night, too."

"I don't know. And furthermore, I don't care."

"Well, I do. They're up to no good. And I intend to be at that meeting."

"I can see you won't be dissuaded, Jenny. But please don't go alone. Take Roddy with you."

"I can't do that, Clara. Rodney is *your* beau. He barely tolerates me. He thinks I have mush for brains. Anyway, two people make more noise than one."

Jennifer slid a long leg over the window sill.

"Wait!" Clara grabbed Jennifer's arm. "Don't do this. Tell your uncle what you overheard. Let *him* handle it."

"He wouldn't believe me." Jennifer had already approached her uncle several times to complain about Lieutenant Carter's avid pursuit, but her uncle had shrugged aside her complaints, dismissing them as a young man's natural desire for the company of a beautiful woman.

Jennifer found herself in an untenable position. As the fort commander's niece, she was expected to be polite to his officers. Yet it was her aversion to Carter that had sent her racing for shelter into a storage room when he entered the Suttlers' store. Hidden from view, she had overheard the conversation whispered between Carter and One Eye, the Kiowa scout employed by the cavalry.

It had been a brief conversation, only a few words to settle on the place and time of their meeting. But Jennifer's curiosity had been aroused. There had been something furtive, secretive, about the two men's encounter. They were up to no good and she was determined to ferret out their secret, to discover if the fort was at risk.

"Loosen my arm, Clara," she whispered. "And don't worry. I'll be back before you know it."

Reluctantly, Clara released her, and Jennifer climbed through the window, hurrying down Officer's Row toward the six stone barracks that housed twelve companies of soldiers.

Keeping to the darker shadows of the alleyway, Jennifer continued on, past the laundry, the blacksmith shop and the hospital until she reached the large, multi-unit that housed the bachelor officers.

A crackle sounded in the darkness and Jennifer

froze, her fingers closing over the butt of her revolver. She gripped the weapon while her narrowed gaze searched the shadows for danger, sliding down the length of the long building, then back again.

There was nothing. No movement.

She sighed with relief and slid the weapon back into its holster.

Sharply, the sound came again.

Her heart pounding, Jennifer looked up at the nearest window. The sound had come from within. Relief flooded through her when she realized it was only a restless sleeper. The sound had been nothing more than the crackling of a cornshuck mattress.

She waited, watched, listened for some sound that would tell her she'd been discovered. Then, satisfied that she was alone, she turned her attention to the large monolithic rocks scattered over the mountain.

Her gaze swept the moonlit rise that loomed high above the fort, black and ominous. Once she reached its mantle of sheltering rocks, she would remain hidden from prying eyes.

Keeping low to the ground, she darted from shadow to shadow until she reached an open space that extended over a hundred feet. Then she dashed toward the nearest rock, fearing the shout that would signal the discovery of her presence. But silence reigned. She was safe.

Jennifer worked her way up the steep rise, intent on reaching the leaning rock on the other side of the mountain. Since Carter and One Eye would be traveling by horseback, they would take the road that wound around the mountain instead of the much shorter and steeper path that Jennifer followed.

As she reached the peak, she paused momentarily and studied her surroundings. She could see the leaning rock in the moonlight far below. And the horses waiting nearby told her that she had miscalculated somehow. The meeting was already under way.

She crept closer, moving silently, until she heard the sound of voices. And then she settled down to listen.

". . . . not so sure he'll go along with that," Lieutenant Carter said. "He set the price. You knew that. And if you weren't prepared to go along with it, you should have told him then."

"I apologize, *señor*. How could I know the *Comancheros* would not agree to meet your terms?"

Jennifer was startled by the Mexican's voice. She had not expected a third man. And yet there he was, silhouetted in the moonlight, his bulky shape concealed by a large poncho. But where was One Eye?

Her question was answered when he moved next to Carter.

"Dammit, Chavez!" Lieutenant Carter exclaimed. "The shipment of rifles has already left Galveston. How in hell do you expect me to stop them now?"

Rifles! Oh, God, Jennifer thought. Lieutenant Carter was worse than a bounder. He was a traitor, a Judas, selling out his own people for a few pieces of gold! She clenched her fingers, making two fists. If she could only leave now, hurry back to the fort and rouse her uncle. But she dared not. If there was more, she had to hear it, to learn as much as possible.

"Why should you stop them, *señor?*" the Mexican Chavez asked. "The Comancheros are willing to pay for the rifles. All you need do is take the gold that is offered."

Lieutenant Carter swore vehemently. "You're a

thief, Chavez! A lousy, dirty thief! You'd slit your mother's throat if there was gold in it."

When the Mexican spoke, his voice was hard. "And you would not? You, who delivers rifles into the hands of your enemies? No, do not look innocent, *mi amigo*. We both know what the Indians, the Comancheros will do with the guns."

So that's what it was all about! Jennifer had heard officers from the fort talk, knew they were puzzled about how the Indians had gained possession of new rifles while the soldiers had to contend with worn-out weapons. This was the answer.

The lieutenant was worse than a traitor, he was a murderer. But he was not alone. One Eye was with him, perhaps acting as the go-between, and yet, they were not alone in their dealings. Carter didn't have the intelligence or the contacts to pull together something like this. They were following someone else's orders.

Whose? she wondered. Could it be someone in the fort? Someone who had enough power behind him to make Lieutenant Carter serve as his flunkey?

Jennifer waited impatiently for the men to conclude their dealings. She watched the exchange of gold take place, watched them mount their horses and ride away. Only then did she leave her hiding place and begin the return journey over the mountain.

She had only gone a short way when she heard the soft nicker of a horse. She immediately dropped behind the shelter of a boulder and waited, her heart thumping heavily beneath her rib cage.

Silence hung over her like a dark cloud as she waited, huddled behind the boulder for several agonizingly slow moments until finally, the soft whinny came again.

The sound was quickly muffled, making Jennifer wonder if her presence was suspected. She gripped the butt of her pistol. Slowly, she drew it from the holster.

Thud!

The sound that broke the silence was like a clap of thunder to her ears. She peeked around the boulder.

A buckskin horse with a lowered head nudged something on the ground. Senses alert, Jenny edged around the boulder and stepped out into the moonlight, her gaze glued to the *thing* on the ground.

It was not a *thing*. Not a mere inanimate object. It was a human form . . . a man, naked except for a loincloth and the moccasins on his feet.

An Indian.

A wave of horror washed over Jennifer.

What in the name of God was a savage doing so close to the fort?

Three

Jennifer spun on her heels to run, to race away as fast as she could to the safety of the fort. Then she hesitated, looking back at the Indian. He lay unmoving, completely motionless.

Was he as harmless as he appeared?

The buckskin whinnied softly and nudged the Indian again, but the man remained still. Was he dead? If so, she could leave, guilt-free. But if not . . .

Jennifer was no stranger to death, not since her parents had been shot down before her eyes. Nevertheless, she did not relish the idea of being alone with a dead man. She liked the idea of being alone on the mountain in the dark with a live Indian even less.

Her hesitation was brief. Jennifer could not easily ignore the suffering of others. But experience had made her cautious. And it was with pistol in hand that Jennifer cautiously approached the crumpled form.

The moonlight illuminated his bronzed flesh, making his features easy to see. She guessed his age to be around thirty, or perhaps a few years more. His shoulder length black hair was tied at the back of his neck and held with a leather thong, making his face appear long and angular.

The bear-claw necklace hanging around his neck emphasized the muscular width of his chest. The loincloth did little to cover his naked, bronzed flesh.

The horse whinnied again, nudging the man at its feet once more, but the Indian remained motionless, as still as death.

He *must* be dead.

She prodded the Indian with the toe of her boot, testing for some kind of reaction. But there was nothing, no movement.

Her tense muscles relaxed. The Indian was definitely dead, which led to a multitude of questions. Why was he here on the mountain? Could he have been spying on the fort? If so, for what reason? And what on earth had happened to him? Could he have encountered the lieutenant or One Eye?

Jennifer quickly discounted that possibility. When the traitors left the rendezvous, they had taken the road around the mountain. The Mexican, Chavez, might have killed the Indian, but how? She hadn't heard the sound of a shot.

Perhaps he had used a knife.

She bent closer. There was no blood. At least none that she could see. And if the Indian had been stabbed to death, surely there would have been blood. Lots of blood.

Her narrowed gaze slid down the length of his body. A rag was tied around one of his legs, but a stab wound there wouldn't have been fatal.

She poked the rag with the barrel of her pistol, trying to slip the steel between fabric and flesh, but found she could not. The rag was bound tightly around the flesh the way a tourniquet would be.

A tourniquet? an inner voice inquired. *Why would he need a tourniquet?*

She jabbed the rag again.

"Ka."

The sound was weak, but it jerked her upright. Jennifer stared at the Indian, saw his eyes were open and focused on her.

Oh, God! He *wasn't* dead.

Horror washed over her, but her reaction was instinctive. Jennifer raised her weapon, the barrel pointed straight at him. "Don't move!" she said shakily.

"You have no need to fear me," he said weakly. "My strength is almost spent."

Although his use of the English language startled her, Jennifer remained wary, watchful. Her gaze clung to his, her fingers gripping the pistol so tightly that her knuckles showed white. "What are you doing here?" she asked harshly.

He sighed, as though weary beyond belief, rolled his head to the side and closed his eyes.

She leaned closer. "What happened to you? Are you ill?"

He made a sound that might have been a laugh had it not been so weak and humorless. "Are you offering me help? I am a savage, and you are fearful. But you need not run, only to wait. The rattler's poison will soon take me from this land of the living."

"A rattlesnake?" She shuffled a little, looking down at her feet for the loathsome reptile. "Where is it now?"

"Dead." The word was harsh, as venomous as the poison that coursed through his veins.

"But you . . . the rattler is deadly; its venom is poison!" Her fear of the warrior had completely evaporated, swept away by the surety of his fate if he didn't receive help immediately. "How long ago did it happen?"

"Why do you ask? Do you wish to watch me die?"

"Don't be absurd!" she snapped. "I wouldn't leave a dog to die such a death without trying to help."

He was silent for a long moment, studying her as though trying to determine if she spoke the truth. Then he said, "The bugler was blowing taps."

Taps! That was at ten o'clock! More than an hour ago. Too long. He was probably beyond help. "Did you try to suck out the venom?"

"It is on the back of my leg, beyond my reach."

Although her efforts would probably be in vain, Jennifer said, "Roll over on your stomach. Maybe it's not too late."

Turning seemed to exhaust him. Once done, he sucked in a sharp, rasping breath. Jennifer stared soundlessly at the wound revealed by the pale moonlight. It gaped blood where he had slashed across it.

"Where's your knife?" she asked huskily, pushing a copper colored curl from her face. As a child, she'd watched her father try to help a nearby farmer who'd been bitten by a rattler.

It had been too late for the farmer, and perhaps it was too late for the Indian. But she could do no less than her father had done.

The Indian's hesitation was barely perceptible, only a moment's delay before he withdrew the blade and handed it to her. "My life is in your hands."

She was already well aware of that fact, and didn't like it one whit.

Bending closer, she made a slash directly above the one he'd already made, then, stooping low, placed her mouth over the wound and sucked hard. She spat away the blood, praying it contained part of the venom as well. She repeated the action, twice, three times, four times more, until she was satisfied that she'd done everything in her power to remove the venom for him.

Then, gently, Jennifer shifted the Indian onto his back again and met his eyes. "You need a doctor," she said grimly. "I'll return to the fort and rouse Captain Evans. He's the fort doctor. It shouldn't take us long to get back here and . . ."

"No doctor," he whispered. "No one must know I am here."

"You'll die without help," Jennifer protested. "I've done as much as I can."

"My death is still an uncertainty, woman, unless you reveal my presence to the yellow legs."

"What do you mean?"

"They would take me prisoner. Have you ever been inside the walls of a prison?"

"Of course not!"

His lips curled wryly. "The mere thought horrifies you. As it does me. If it is my fate to die, then let it be here instead of behind the bars of the White Eyes' prison."

His words stabbed at Jennifer, causing a curious knot of sympathy to lodge in her throat. Although his words were those of an educated man, he was obviously an Indian. That fact alone would guarantee his imprisonment if he was found so close to the fort.

"I sympathize with your plight. But there is nothing more I can do for you. Except, perhaps, to bring you some water. And some quinine." Quinine would help assuage the fever that would surely come. "Or a poultice. A tobacco poultice might help draw out the poison."

His expression was stoic. "I will accept whatever help you can offer, so long as you keep silent about my presence here. If I live, I will offer you thanks. If I die, then so be it."

His calm acceptance of his fate troubled her deeply as she made her way back to the fort. When the crunch of gravel outside the livery alerted her to the presence of others, she skirted the building, keeping to the shadows. In a matter of moments, she reached the neat square house where she lived with her uncle and climbed through the open window to her bedroom.

"Thank God you're back!" Clara exclaimed, throwing back the bedclothes and sliding from the bed. "What took you so long?"

"Was I very long?" Jennifer asked, waiting for the girl to ask her about the secret rendezvous. But Clara didn't ask. In fact, she seemed to be angry.

"Yes you were!" Clara snapped, crossing the room and pulling her shawl from the back of a chair.

"Where are you going?" Jennifer asked.

"Home!"

"Did something happen?"

"Your uncle knocked on the door and I almost fainted with fright."

"Oh, Clara, I'm sorry." Jennifer took her friend's hands. "I didn't dream . . . he always sleeps straight through."

"Well, someone came to the house," Clara said grudgingly. "And then your uncle knocked on your bedroom door and called out for you. I told him you were asleep, and he said he was going out on patrol and would be gone most of the night."

Jennifer patted her friend's hand. "And you handled the situation beautifully. I'm so proud of you. Do you want me to walk home with you?"

Clara placed her hand on her chest. "If I can fool

your uncle, Jennifer, then surely I can make the short way home alone."

At the door, Clara finally asked, "Did you learn anything?"

Jennifer pretended to stifle a yawn. "I'll tell you all about it tomorrow. Right now I'm so tired I can hardly keep my eyes open."

Grasping the doorknob again, Clara pulled the door open. "What time do you want me to come over?"

"How does ten sound?" Jennifer asked.

"Ten sounds good. See you then."

Moments later Clara was gone and Jennifer hurried around to gather up whatever she could think of that might be of help to the Indian. Then, after bundling the supplies into a pillowcase, Jennifer left the house again and headed back up the mountain.

Four

Coyote Man was late arriving at the large oak tree where he was supposed to meet Spotted Wolf. He felt slightly alarmed to find the place deserted. He told himself that his friend had only been delayed, that soon he would ride up the creek and shout a greeting.

As time passed and his friend did not appear, Coyote Man's apprehension increased. It wasn't like Spotted Wolf to be late for a meeting. And, since he was, something must have happened to prevent his arrival.

His errand had been a simple one: to spy on the fort where Cloud Dancer was being held prisoner. But when the bluecoats were involved, nothing could be taken for granted.

Although it was highly unlikely, considering Spotted Wolf's skill at remaining undetected, he might have been seen.

Coyote Man decided to wait no longer. He would go in search of his friend.

Halfway up the mountain, uncertainty began to plague Jennifer. She had been raised on a farm in southeastern Texas, and was unaccustomed to Indians, but she had heard oldtimers tell stories of Indian massacres where entire families had been wiped out. Of forts being overrun and everyone killed. But those days were long gone. Except for a few renegades, like Quanah Parker and his bunch, who refused to accept defeat, most Indian tribes were now on reservations.

Jennifer had expanded her minimal knowledge of Indians and their plight through Chicago newspapers a few months ago while visiting her maternal grandparents after the death of her parents which had occurred about a year ago.

One paper had run a continuing story on Quanah's mother, Cynthia Ann Parker, who had been captured by Indians at the age of nine. The tragic story had torn at the hearts of many readers, including Jennifer's. Cynthia Ann had lived among the Comanche for more than twenty-five years. She had married an Indian and borne him three children.

Cynthia Ann's return to white society occurred the way she'd left it, through a raid. Jennifer couldn't remember the year, but the place had become lodged firmly in her mind. Pease River. Pease. It was a battle that took the woman from her Indian family, except for the babe in her arms, forever. It was said that she never smiled, and that she attempted to return to them many times.

Jennifer swallowed around the lump that always lodged in her throat when she thought of Cynthia Ann's poignant story. When she had mentioned it to her uncle one day, he'd snorted and said it was a bunch of hogwash, a story made up by the newspapers to gain sympathy for the Indians. But when Jennifer had pressed him for details, he had refused to supply them.

It was a sad situation, Jennifer knew. But better minds than hers were working on the Indian problem. Perhaps, in time, a solution would be found. She was only one person, could do little for the Indians as a whole, but she might be able to help the one on the mountain.

Jennifer thought of Cynthia Ann as she hurried to the wounded Indian. In the final accounting, home, lineage, even race, were all relative. Every man was human, and the Indian needed her.

Snap!

The sound caused Jennifer to jerk around, her heart jumping wildly as she scoured the area for whoever or whatever had made it. Nothing moved on the slope. She listened carefully. Nothing. Only silence.

Deciding that she had been mistaken, Jennifer hurried on her way. She passed the spot where she'd left the Indian, then stopped, puzzled.

He was gone. But how? He was too weak to move, much less leave the area. The horse. The buckskin was no longer there. But how had the Indian mounted?

She heard a soft scraping sound coming from the direction of the tall, leaning rock where the rendezvous had taken place.

"Hello," she called softly. "Are you there?"

When the Indian left the shadow of the leaning rock, he took her by surprise. She hadn't expected him to be standing upright.

Suddenly, she realized it was a different man, unwounded and untamed. Quickly, she reached for the pistol strapped across her hips.

The Indian leapt toward her, wrapping steel fingers around her wrist and squeezing hard while the other hand effectively held her captive. Tears of pain stung Jennifer's eyes as the gun clattered to the ground, kicked away by her captor.

She saw a spark out of the corner of her eyes, a steel blade. She screamed, a loud, piercing sound that was quickly muffled by the Indian's hand over her mouth.

"Mmmmmpppph!" she cried, struggling violently to escape.

"Ka!" a harsh voice rang out.

Jennifer's gaze skittered toward the sound. It was the warrior she had tended. He sat atop the buckskin, almost hidden among the shadows. His utterance, however short, caused her attacker's hand to stop. He responded in a short, guttural exclamation. Then, slowly, as though with great reluctance, the knife was lowered.

Trembling, Jennifer tried to keep her fear from showing. Another word from the mounted man and Jennifer's captor uncovered her mouth. She licked dry lips as she turned to face the two men, her chin jutted forward as her flashing eyes went from the mounted warrior to her attacker.

The latter was short of stature, his hair midnight black. His face was a dark mask of anger that carved his bold featured face into an ugly mask with deep, down slashing grooves.

Swallowing around her fear, Jennifer forced herself to speak calmly. "Why have I been attacked when I came to give you aid?" Despite her efforts at control, there was a slight quiver in her voice.

"I did not expect you to return," the injured warrior replied gravely. He swayed slightly in the saddle, then pulled himself straight again.

The other warrior grunted and Jennifer caught the glint of the steel blade of his knife. She looked quickly at the mounted warrior who spoke sharply to his companion.

"Didn't I say I would come back? I always keep my word." She stepped backward. "But since you no longer need me, then I'll just leave and . . ."

"*Ka!*" the short Indian snarled. Then, in heavily accented English, he added, "You will not leave!"

"I . . . I . . ." She swallowed hard, backing away from the Indian who advanced slowly toward her. "I only c-came to h-help your friend. N-Nothing else."

"Leave her!" the mounted Indian said, his voice low and uneven. He spoke in English, apparently for Jennifer's benefit. "She is but a woman and can do nothing to stop us from leaving."

"She is the enemy. She must be silenced, Spotted Wolf."

The man called Spotted Wolf was silent for a long moment, then, "She must not be harmed, Coyote Man. She will be of use to us if we are seen leaving this place."

As Jennifer's gaze flickered between the quarreling warriors, her indignation sparked with fear. How dare he use her in such a manner, when she had tried to help him? Then, considering the shorter Indian's harsh features, fear won out. Coyote Man wanted to kill her.

She retreated, trying to watch both men at the same time. Jennifer was positive her reflexes would be faster than Spotted Wolf's. It was the other Indian, Coyote Man, who would prove to be the more dangerous one, especially since he had melted into the shadows.

But there might be a chance to escape from them. And Jennifer knew that she had to at least make the

attempt. She spun on her heels to flee . . . and was
stopped by a wall of flesh.

"Get behind me, Jennifer!" She recognized the
voice immediately. It belonged to Lieutenant Carter.
"The Indian is mine!" He brandished a pistol. "Get
off that horse, Indian. We're about to have us a conversation."

Spotted Wolf showed no reaction to the lieutenant's presence, almost as though he'd known the
man was there. Was that why Coyote Man had
melted into the shadows?

Realizing that Carter was unaware there were two
men, she said, "He's not alone!" Even as she spoke
the words, she realized she had uttered the warning
too late. Coyote Man emerged from the shadows
suddenly, his knife in hand.

"Run, Jennifer!" Lieutenant Carter swung his gun
around. "Rouse the fort!"

The Indian's knife sliced through the air with a
whooshing sound, the blade thudding into Carter's
chest. The lieutenant staggered and looked down at
the knife that was buried in his flesh, then turned
disbelieving eyes on Jennifer. His mouth worked, as
though he were trying to form words, but no sound
issued from his lips. His legs buckled and he crumpled to the ground.

"Oh, my God!" Jennifer shrieked, her eyes wide
with disbelief. "You killed him!" For a second, absolute horror froze her to the spot. She was unable
to flee. Nor was she able to tear her gaze from the
lieutenant, from the dead eyes that remained open,
staring sightlessly up at the velvety, star studded
night.

Then she ran. Before she'd taken ten steps, Coyote Man snagged her wrist with iron hard fingers
and jerked her to an abrupt halt.

Struggling, Jennifer screamed until the Indian slapped his hand over her mouth. *Survive! Survive! Survive!* The word pulsed through her veins, sounding in her mind with each beat of her heart. Her thoughts tumbled furiously as she faced the ferocious warrior who seemed intent on ending her life.

What had Spotted Wolf said before? She searched her memory for the words. *She will be of use to us if we are seen leaving this place.* Yes, that was it! That was her way out. Ceasing her struggles, she hung limply in Coyote Man's arms and mumbled against his hand.

"Release her!" Spotted Wolf urged his horse closer.

Tightening his grip, Coyote Man spoke harshly in the guttural language he'd used earlier.

"I said, free her." Command radiated from Spotted Wolf's voice. Angrily, Coyote Man flung Jennifer aside.

She fell as if she were dead weight, breaking her fall at the last minute with her hands. She looked up at Spotted Wolf.

"I can help you," she said hoarsely.

"How?"

"Gold."

"We have no need of White Eyes' gold," Coyote Man muttered.

"How much would your people pay for your release?" Spotted Wolf asked.

"Anything you asked. My uncle is a rich man; he would pay anything, any amount of gold, for my *safe* return."

"How do I know you speak the truth?"

Jennifer straightened her shoulders. "My uncle is Major Walter Carlisle. Everyone knows of his wealth, his . . . importance."

Seemingly unimpressed, the two Indians spoke together at length in their own language. She understood nothing, but throughout the conversation, Coyote Man gestured wildly and Spotted Wolf held strong and firm.

She began to relax.

Then Spotted Wolf's arresting gaze fell on her. Jennifer froze.

"You say Major Carlisle will pay anything?" Spotted Wolf asked.

"He will." She raised her chin a degree higher. They were going for it. "I promise. Name your price."

"Then so be it." He nodded at Coyote Man who jerked her toward his horse.

Oh, God, no! They weren't going to release her!

She struggled wildly, kicking out, striking the warrior in the softness between his legs. With a muffled exclamation, he dropped her, covering his groin area as he fell to his knees.

Jennifer struck the ground hard, then rolled away from the warrior and leapt to her feet. Before he recovered, she was up and running, racing away as fast as her legs would carry her.

She was conscious of the Indian taking up pursuit, but didn't take the time to look behind her. She ran across the mountain, realizing if she went down he would catch her quickly. Her only chance was to get to the densely wooded area, to hide from her pursuer. Her legs pumped frantically as she ran, deaf to all other sounds except the frantic beating of her heart, her lips peeled back in a grimace of pure terror.

When she finally reached the wooded area, she sought a place to hide, knowing that was her only choice. She ducked behind the large trunk of a cedar and slumped there, sweating and gasping for breath. Her mouth was dry, sour. Her throat burned and her chest ached. But at least she was safe . . . at least he hadn't found her.

Even as the thought occurred, hard fingers grasped her upper arm and whirled her around to face the Indian who seemed intent on killing her.

One Eye, the Kiowa scout for the U.S. troopers, sat loosely on his horse, seeming more intent on the high, scattered clouds that were painted scarlet from the rising sun than on the cavalry column that rode to meet him.

Major Carlisle was aware of many sounds, of jangling bridle chains, creaking saddle leather and the thud, thud, thud of many hooves pounding against the sandy earth. But surprisingly, there was no sound of conversation among the troopers. They were tired, he knew, but something else, perhaps the threat of battle, inhibited discussion.

As they reached the scout, Major Carlisle said, "The horses need a rest, Captain. So do the men. We'll stop for fifteen minutes."

He listened to Captain Brady pass the orders to Lieutenant Sanchez, who passed it on to Sergeant Willis.

"Prepare to dismount!" Sergeant Willis's hoarse voice was loud enough to reach the furthermost soldier.

As the troopers began to dismount, Major Carlisle urged his mount closer to One Eye. "Well?" he inquired. "Any sign of them?"

"No sign." The scout looked at Carlisle. "Maybe Private Jordan see ghosts. One Eye see nothing. No horse. No Comanchero. Nothing."

Captain Brady reined in beside them. "Private Jordan is a good man, Major. If he says he saw Comancheros, then he damn well saw them." He dismounted and turned on his heel, staring back at the column of troopers. "Yo, Jordan!" he shouted. "Get your butt over here."

Major Carlisle permitted himself a smile. Captain Brady had that effect on the men. He would order and they would obey. He wasn't unnecessarily harsh in his dealings with them. He had worked hard to earn their respect. And it had paid off.

Brady was a good man, a career soldier. The second son of a wealthy rancher. He didn't waste time crying over the fact that his older brother would inherit the family holdings. Instead, he had entered West Point and begun a military career. Didn't pay very much, but Brady didn't seem to mind. He was a good man to have around. Especially if you needed someone to watch your back.

"You wanted me, Captain?" Jordan asked.

"Yeah," Brady said. "Tell us again what you saw."

"Well, like I done told Corporal Hooker, I was coming back from town, ridin' over the mountain there . . ." He pointed at the mountain rising in the distance. ". . . when I saw them. Comancheros. They was close, not more'n a half a mile away and . . ."

"How do you know they were Comancheros?" Captain Brady interrupted.

"Don't really know they were, Captain. Ain't no way of knowing for sure. Thought they might be, though, 'cause they was several of 'em wearin' serapes and big sombreros, and when they seen me, heard 'em shout and point at me, they turned tail and lit out in the other direction. Now why in hell do you think they'd do that? Me, I was only one, and they was a bunch. I figured they didn't want me to know who they was. Coulda killed me for sure if they was of a mind. But they didn't and that left me wondering why."

Captain Brady turned his attention to One Eye again. "And you say you can't find a sign of them?"

"Nothing," One Eye said, studying the sky again, seeming to dwell on each cloud floating there.

What in hell did he find so interesting up there anyway? Major Carlisle wondered. Then the answer suddenly dawned on him. "Has the wind been blowing hard?"

One Eye's lips twitched momentarily, then quickly firmed again. "Big wind. Move sand around. Hide trail good. Nothing left."

Major Carlisle sighed with exasperation. "Why didn't you say so before?"

A slight curl of the mouth preceded the scout's words. "You no ask."

Anger surged through Major Carlisle. One Eye was about as helpful as a turd on a stick. If a replacement could be found, then the Kiowa would be replaced.

It was a weary bunch of men who rode into the fort several hours later. Dismounting in front of post headquarters, Major Carlisle handed his reins to the corporal and entered his office to see if there was anything that needed his immediate attention.

After ascertaining there was nothing so important that it couldn't wait until later in the day, he went home.

Although he'd expected Jennifer to be awake, the house was silent. She had probably had a restless night with Clara sleeping over.

He opened the door to his bedroom and stepped

inside, closing it firmly behind him. He shucked his clothing and crawled between the sheets.

Moments later he was sound asleep.

Five

She ran swiftly through the forest, keeping far enough ahead that he had no hope of reaching her. Wait, he shouted, but no sound issued from his lips. Even so, she paused momentarily, looking back at him, her laughing eyes meeting his for a mere moment before she hurried onward.

Stay! His lips formed the words, but again, no sound escaped them. He felt a deep fear at that moment, a horror of what would come if he did not stop her from her headlong flight. And yet, how could he when she would not heed his silent warning? Her midnight dark hair flowed around her like a living thing as she ran, obviously unaware of the danger that lay ahead of her.

Then suddenly, the forest was behind him. He was in a clearing, creeping toward a small cabin. He felt a curious foreboding . . . didn't want to go farther but his feet refused to obey his command to cease their forward movement.

Why did he feel such dread? Such a horror going on? What fearful thing lay waiting for him in that cabin, a place that looked innocent enough, surrounded as it was by a profusion of wildflowers in every color imaginable? Even the vivid array of colors that would, under ordinary circumstances, have brightened his day could not lessen his dread for what lay inside.

He didn't want to recognize it . . . the thing that caused him such dread, such total fear. He refused to give voice to his terror, the absolute horror of knowing.

Yet he knew it was no use. He would see it, as he had done many times before. Even now his feet continued to carry him forward, to that abhorrent thing that caused him such fear. He opened his mouth to scream, to give vent to his rage, his terror, his absolute certainty of what lay ahead.

But it was no use. He continued forward, knowing he must see, must know.

He was at the door. And strangely, it had become slanted, narrow. He tilted his body slightly, knowing he could not enter the house without doing so.

And then he stepped inside into a black hole and he was falling, falling, falling. . . .

"Ooooff!" The muffled sound left Spotted Wolf at the exact moment his breath whooshed out of his body. He lay stunned, his ears ringing, his lungs burning for air. And then his chest rose, contracting as he sucked air into his lungs again. With it came particles of dirt, and judging by the pungent smell of it, grass.

A sharp exclamation somewhere above him caught his attention and he blinked, then opened his eyes. His vision was blurry, vague, seeing nothing more than a huge blob of yellowish brown.

Realizing that he was on his stomach, staring at a patch of dried grass, he rolled over and squinted against the glare of the mid-morning sun.

A creak of saddle leather and a sudden movement in his peripheral vision jerked his head around. Coyote Man was dismounting from his horse. *"Hihites,"* he said, kneeling beside Spotted Wolf.

"Ida-ha. Che-ida-ha," Spotted Wolf replied. And he *was* cold. So terribly cold. It should not be so, he

reasoned. This was the season of *Tah-arch*, Summer, and the sun blazed down with its usual ferocity. But it appeared to have lost its heat.

"He has a fever," a feminine voice said.

Looking beyond Coyote Man's left shoulder, Spotted Wolf saw a woman watching. He wondered momentarily why her hands were bound, why she glared so hatefully at them, then comprehension suddenly dawned. She was a captive.

"Can you understand me, *Indian?*" she asked, her red-rimmed eyes focused on Coyote Man, her lips tight with anger. "Your friend is trembling. He has a chill brought on by fever, a fire in his body. It has weakened him. There is no way he can continue this journey."

Coyote Man's countenance was grim. "I fear you are right, woman. Spotted Wolf is too weak to ride alone."

"You could camp here," she suggested eagerly. "I could ride back to the fort for help and . . ."

"No! You will ride with him."

Her lips curled with contempt. "You are a fool if you believe I would help either one of you."

"You will if you wish to live." Coyote Man's words effectively silenced the woman.

Spotted Wolf felt a curious surge of pity coupled with a good degree of shame for the woman. She would not be in this situation had she not returned to the mountain to render him aid.

Jennifer's fear increased as she watched the warrior stride toward her, but she knew better than to allow him to see that fear. She'd heard Indians despised fear, that those who begged for mercy would receive none. Courage was respected.

Oh, God, she silently cried. *Help me to at least give the appearance of courage.*

She shrank away from Coyote Man as he unfastened her bonds, jerked her off the horse and settled her on the buckskin. Moments later, Spotted Wolf was seated before her and her arms were pulled around his middle and bound tightly with the leather cord again.

It would be an impossible position to maintain for very long, she knew, and quickly informed her captor of that fact.

"Those who savor life find strength to endure," he replied harshly.

She made a choked sound that she quickly stifled.

"Do not be foolish and attempt escape," Coyote Man warned, fastening a noose around her neck. "The other end of this rope will be in my hands. And so will your life."

Then, with the reins and her tether caught tightly in one hand, he mounted the paint and urged it forward. Jennifer felt the noose tighten around her neck.

Panic-stricken, she tapped the horse with her heels until it gave a forward lurch. She made a grab for the pommel to steady herself but it was beyond her reach.

Those who savor life find strength to endure. Remembering her captor's warning, she gritted her teeth and shoved herself closer against Spotted Wolf's heated back, gaining enough reach to grip the pommel with her bound hands.

Then they resumed their journey across the plains.

The commotion outside the stockade caught Cloud Dancer's attention and he slowly straightened his old body. His weary gaze lifted to the patch of blue sky beyond the high, narrow window. He longed to be free of his prison, wanted to walk again among the mountains, to breathe the fresh air that was unpolluted by civilization. But he could not. He was confined to this one room, shackled by a chain fastened to his cot.

He had been imprisoned for two weeks now. The longest two weeks that he had ever lived. There was nothing to do but pace the empty cell and wonder when the White Eyes would come again with their questions, endless questions that would never be answered.

At least not by him.

The commotion became louder. He heard shouts, then the sound of running. He rose to his feet and the chain shackling him to the cot clanked noisily. It dragged at his leg as he crossed the room and looked through the window that faced post headquarters. He rarely looked through that window, preferring the one that faced the mountains.

But raised voices, excited shouts, meant something was amiss. And if the bluecoats were disturbed, there was a good possibility the cause of that disturbance might be of interest to him.

He gripped the bars tightly and stared across the parade ground to the post headquarters where several troopers had gathered together. They appeared to be watching Captain Brady and Private Jensen, two men Cloud Dancer had come to know since his confinement at the fort.

Although Cloud Dancer couldn't distinguish their words, Private Jensen's tone was anxious, perhaps even fearful, and he continually pointed toward the mountain throughout the conversation.

Captain Brady appeared grim as he spoke harshly, spewing out his words like bullets from a repeating rifle. The moment he finished speaking, Private Jensen spun on his heels and took off at a run, headed toward the houses on Officers Row.

Cloud Dancer smiled grimly. Something was afoot all right, and whatever it was, the bluecoats were not pleased about it.

He wondered momentarily if the source of disturbance should worry him, then shrugged the thought away. He had enough to worry about already. The bluecoats were becoming more insistent with their questions with each passing day. How long would they continue with mere words? How long before they decided to try other means to make him divulge the whereabouts of the Comanche stronghold?

No matter what their methods were, he would not answer. Nothing, not even the threat of death, would ever make him betray his people.

Nothing!

Bang, bang, bang!

The sound shattered Major Carlisle's sleep and jerked him upright in bed. "Oh, God," he muttered, "what in hell is causing all that racket?"

Bang, bang, bang!

The noise came again, and with it, the answer to his question. It was the door. Someone was knocking, or rather, banging on the damned door!

"Jennifer!" he yelled. "See who's at the door!" Intense pain streaked through his temples and he stifled a groan.

Bang, bang, bang!

Dammit, why didn't Jennifer answer the door?

Sliding his long legs to the floor, he reached for his breeches, pulled them over his hips and fastened them.

Bang, bang, bang!

"I'm coming!" he snapped. "Keep your damned shirt on!" Although he knew the visitor couldn't possibly hear him, Major Carlisle found a measure of relief in verbalizing the complaint.

Moments later, he yanked open the door and stared at the trooper who stood waiting outside. "There's been some trouble, Major Carlisle, Sir," the young private said. "You're needed at post head-quarters."

"Why?" Carlisle barked. "What is so damned important that Captain Brady can't handle it?"

The trooper gulped and backed away. "It's a body, sir," he whispered. "The Captain thought you ought to be told right away."

"What?" Carlisle roared, wincing at the sound of his own voice. "Speak up, man! What does Captain Brady have to do with this?"

"He sent me, Sir," the trooper said, in a slightly raised voice. "Thought you'd want to know . . . about the body on the mountain." He backed away from his commanding officer. "Lieutenant Carter's body."

"Lieutenant Carter is dead?" Carlisle studied the trooper from beneath beetled brows. "Dammit Private! Explain yourself! What happened to him?"

"We don't know yet, Major, Sir," the private said, backing away. "The doctor hasn't looked at him yet. But there was a puncture in his chest that looked like a stab wound."

Major Carlisle sighed deeply. "And you said it happened on the mountain?"

The trooper nodded his head. "That's where he was found."

"Dammit," the major swore. "Too bad. Lieutenant Carter was a good man. He'll be sorely missed around here." He pushed his fingers through his graying hair. "Tell Captain Brady I'll be with him shortly."

"Yes, Sir!"

The trooper saluted smartly then turned on his heel, intent on reporting back to Captain Brady. "Wait!" Major Carlisle said. "Have you seen my niece?"

"No, Sir!" the trooper replied. "She might be with Clara Boseley though. They spend a lot of time together."

The major knew that. In fact, Clara had stayed overnight with Jennifer. It was she who answered when he had knocked at his niece's door last night. He looked toward the Boseley residence. There was no sign of anyone about, but there was nothing unusual in that. The two young women were probably inside the house, either baking sweets or quilting, or perhaps gossiping together in the usual manner of women.

Nevertheless, he felt a nagging worry that refused to be ignored. He was determined to find his niece, just as soon as he left post headquarters.

Six

Time passed slowly for Jennifer, who dared not relax a muscle. Not when the Indian seated before her on the horse became weaker with each passing moment. It took every ounce of energy she possessed to hold him upright.

The sun was relentless, a white, hot ball hanging in an azure sky, blazing down on earth that was already parched from months without moisture.

Wearily, she rested her forehead against Spotted Wolf's back, shading eyes that felt abraded by the ever present wind. How much longer would they continue to travel across this barren terrain? Oh, God, how much longer?

Until we reach the Comanche stronghold.

At that moment, even the Comanche village would have looked good to her. At least there she might be allowed to rest.

And you might not. You might wish yourself in the desert again, holding Spotted Wolf on the horse.

Oh, God, what did they have in mind for her? Why hadn't she told someone about the Indian? She had possessed the opportunity to do so, had been afraid of speaking out, had known that Clara would object. But no. She had kept silent, had returned to the mountain, believing in her ignorance that the treachery of the Indians was mere fiction, fabricated by greedy white men. Jennifer had believed the newspaper stories she'd read in the East! Had swallowed every damn word they printed.

How could she have been so gullible? She was living proof of their treachery. She had pitied the snake bitten Indian, had done everything she could to help him. And this was her reward! To be abducted, taken away from her home against her will.

Jennifer's blood boiled with anger, yet she couldn't sustain that emotion. Not when it took so much energy just to stay upright in the saddle.

Where was that damn stronghold, anyway?

She looked around Spotted Wolf's body and realized the landscape was slowly changing. Were those blue hazy shapes rising in the distance mountains? She squinted, hoping to bring them into focus, but they remained no more substantial than an early morning fog. Even so, Jennifer felt they must be mountains, which probably meant they would soon reach the stronghold. That thought, which had moments before been a welcome one, now sent fear surging through her.

Somehow, even though she hadn't admitted it to herself, Jennifer had felt certain the cavalry would rescue her before they reached the elusive stronghold.

A sudden lurch unbalanced Jennifer. She realized the horse had stumbled, probably stepped in a gopher hole. Although the horse quickly regained its balance, the damage had already been done. Jennifer couldn't hold the double weight upright. Spotted Wolf was sliding sideways, dragging her with him.

They toppled from the saddle together, striking the ground with enough force to send a choking breath whooshing from Jennifer's body. A sharp pain streaked through her left shoulder and her head snapped back, striking something hard. Then, Jennifer knew no more.

When she regained her senses, Jennifer remained motionless, listening to the silence around her. It was absolute. No, she quickly corrected herself. Not really. There was a sound; a soft, crackling sound that she could not identify.

Opening her eyes to a narrow slit, Jennifer allowed them to widen slowly. She was in a cavern. It was small, measuring no more than ten feet in circumference, yet large enough to afford them shelter.

The dry, musty smell that was usually prevalent in most caves had been replaced by another. Coyote Man had used mesquite to make the fire that burned within a small circle of stones.

Jennifer attempted movement and a white hot pain flared through her left shoulder. She bit down on her lower lip, stifling a moan, hoping to remain unnoticed by the warrior who bent over his companion.

Coyote Man, alerted by the stifled sound, shot her a brief glance before returning his attention to his injured friend.

"Please. Can't you loosen these bonds?" Jennifer despised herself for pleading with her captor. But what good would suffering in silence do? And, she consoled herself, if he could be persuaded to loosen her bonds, she had a much better chance at freedom.

She might as well have saved her breath for all the good it had done. The Indian ignored her as though she were of no more consequence than a fly on the wall. Merely an annoyance to be dealt with at his leisure.

And how would he deal with her? Oh, God, what did he have in mind? Now that they were no longer on horseback, would he torture her? Perhaps ravish her? Both thoughts were so horrible that she refused to allow her mind to dwell on them.

Instead, she turned her attention to her surroundings, to the limestone walls which were the color of thick cream. The thought of cream, thick, freshly skimmed, caused a sharp pang of hunger.

How long had it been since her last meal?

Too long, she decided.

Her stomach growled and her feeling of hunger increased. She thought about the meal she had prepared last night, pictured the thick slab of steak resting on her plate near a pile of creamy mashed potatoes. She hadn't been hungry then, had left most of her food on her plate, a fact that she chastised herself for now.

Why hadn't she minded her own business? She had been so foolish in her desire to expose Lieutenant Carter and One Eye, his partner in crime. She had made a dreadful mistake that would cost her dearly.

Oh, God, how could she have been so stupid?

The ache of her cramped muscles took up all her attention as she tried to shift positions to ease the strain. But it was impossible. She was trussed up like a turkey at Thanksgiving.

She glared at Coyote Man, her fear mingled with anger. She couldn't help but notice how the flickering firelight shining on his chiseled features gave him a sinister appearance.

Spotted Wolf's sudden cry claimed her attention.

She watched him tossing restlessly in his delirium. *"Ka! Nei mah-tao-yo! Kiss!"*

Coyote Man spoke softly to his companion in the language they shared. Then, he pulled the stopper from a water gourd and poured water on a small cotton rag. He brushed the dampened cloth across the feverish man's forehead.

Jennifer saw Spotted Wolf's eyes flicker open. *"Cona,"* he muttered. *"Ur-ate, ur-ate."*

"He-be-to." Coyote Man held the water gourd against his friend's lips and tilted it so that a small amount dribbled into his mouth.

"Serena," Spotted Wolf whispered. *"Ner-pa-cher . . ."*

"Hein ein mah-su-ite, Hites?" replied Coyote Man gruffly.

Serena. It was the only thing Jennifer could understand. Serena. A woman's name obviously. But who was she? And why did Spotted Wolf speak her name in his delirium?

"Serena," Spotted Wolf muttered again. *"Ein mea-dro . . . Kiss, kiss!"* He flung his arm out and struck Coyote Man across his nose. The warrior jerked his head back abruptly, then grasped his friend's flailing arms until he became still again.

Although subdued, Spotted Wolf continued his restless muttering. *"Noo-be-er . . ."*

"His temperature is too high!" Jennifer said grimly. "He won't last through the night if it remains that way."

Coyote Man pinned her with glittering black eyes. "Do you know of such things, woman?"

There was no thought of hesitation. Jennifer held the warrior's gaze as she uttered the bold faced lie. "Of course I do."

The Indian's expression was inscrutable as he

crossed the distance between them. And all the time his black eyes bored into hers as though he were attempting to read her innermost thoughts.

He bent over her. "I will release you, paleface, but if Spotted Wolf does not survive the night, then your life will be forfeit."

The words sent a chill through her. Jennifer realized then that she dare not fail. The quinine in her pocket would help, but would it be enough to break the fever?

The moment she was free, she knelt beside Spotted Wolf and placed her right palm against his flushed cheek. Oh, God, he was so hot! His temperature was much higher than she had imagined.

Realizing she must act swiftly, she reached for the quinine in her pocket. As she leaned closer, her long coppery curls brushed against his bare chest, his eyelids fluttered and then opened.

Jennifer sucked in a sharp breath, staring at him in shock. His eyes were not dark as she had imagined. Instead, they were an impossible shade of green.

But how could that be? Even as she asked the question, the answer came to her. His parentage was mixed. Only one of his parents was Indian.

The knowledge that he was a half-breed brought a small measure of relief. Since one of his parents was white, then surely he would be sympathetic to her plight. He would surely help her. If he survived.

Oh, God! He *must* survive.

"Serena," Spotted Wolf muttered hoarsely, reaching up to touch her hair with one trembling hand while the other one gripped her forearm with surprising strength. *"Ner-pa-cher."*

"I'm sorry." Jennifer spoke softly. "I don't understand you." She looked up at Coyote Man. "What does he want? And who is Serena?"

Coyote Man remained silent.

The grip on her arm tightened, and Jennifer turned her attention to the feverish man again. "You're going to be all right," she soothed. *Oh, God, if she could only be sure of that!* "Coyote Man!" Her voice was sharp, commanding. "Hand me the water gourd."

Coyote Man was quick to comply. Jennifer lifted Spotted Wolf's head and trickled a small amount in his mouth, watching his throat as he swallowed thirstily.

"That's enough for the moment. You can have more with the quinine." As she uncorked the bottle, Spotted Wolf closed his eyes and began to mutter words that she could not understand.

Except for the one word; the name he continued to mumble. Serena. Serena. Serena. Then suddenly, he lapsed into unconsciousness again.

Jennifer became frantic. She had to wake him, to administer the quinine. "Wake up," she said insistently. She held the bottle to his lips. "Wake up, Spotted Wolf. You need to take some medicine."

Although he remained motionless, she pried his lips apart and forced the quinine into his mouth. The liquid dribbled out again and trickled down his chin.

Jennifer's thoughts whirled frantically. She had to find a way to lower his body temperature. Ice would be good. Or snow. But there was none. Cold water might work.

She looked across at Coyote Man. "We need to cover him with cold water."

He reached for the water gourd and shook it gently. "There is not enough. I will go to the spring and fill the gourd again."

"No. That's not enough. He needs to be under the water. Is there a stream nearby? Or a river?"

"No stream," Coyote Man replied. "No river. Only a spring. Very small." He held out his arms and made a circle, not more than three feet in circumference. "Not deep," he added. "Very shallow." He held his hand a few inches above his ankles to measure the depth.

"That won't do," she said quickly. "We need to get all of him wet, and we need to keep him that way until the fever breaks. We must take him to the spring."

He considered her for a long moment, then reached for the leather thongs that had bound her.

"What are you doing?"

"You cannot be trusted," he said gruffly. "Give me your hands."

"But my hands need to be free!" Jennifer insisted. "How do you expect me to look after him without the use of my hands?"

Coyote Man ignored her protests. After jerking her hands together, he bound them securely, then looped the noose around her neck. With the end of her tether gripped firmly in his fist, he lifted Spotted Wolf into his arms, handling the grown warrior as though he weighed no more than a babe in arms, stretching him gently across his right shoulder.

Jennifer's lips tightened with anger as Coyote Man left the cave, leaving her to follow or be strangled to death, whichever pleased her more.

The spring was only a short distance from the cave, a walk of no more than ten or fifteen minutes. When they reached it, Coyote Man lowered Spotted

Wolf to the ground and turned to release Jennifer. Then he sat back on his haunches to watch her attend the unconscious man.

Sensing the coldness of the warrior's gaze, and feeling threatened by it, Jennifer cupped her hands and scooped handfuls of cold water over Spotted Wolf's fevered skin. But it was not enough, she knew. The water was cold, might have been effective if she could have devised a way to keep it on him. But that would require something she didn't have. A thick towel or blanket, something large enough to cover him, or at least a good portion of him.

Although she had no wish to expose herself to the men, Jennifer realized she had no choice. She stripped off her heavy shirt and dipped it into the spring, conscious of the fact that the lacy chemise she wore did little to hide the swell of her breasts.

As she laid the wet garment across Spotted Wolf's chest, his eyes jerked open and he stared up at her with those brilliant green eyes.

"Serena," he muttered. "Are you a vision . . ." He broke off suddenly and jerked his head back and forth, his eyes flickering wildly. "I forgot about Cloud Dancer! Serena? I promised him. I . . ."

"Shush," she soothed gently, pushing the dark hair back from his forehead. "Don't worry about a thing. It's all been taken care of. But you must have the medicine I brought you." She uncorked the bottle and forced the bitter quinine into the warrior's mouth. "Swallow it down. It will help the fever."

"Water," he whispered.

Coyote Man was beside her then, leaning over the other warrior with the canteen. After swallowing only a few drops, Spotted Wolf drifted into unconsciousness again.

Jennifer continued to apply the cold, wet shirt to

his skin, dipping it often into the spring since his heated flesh dried the cloth out so quickly. But despite her efforts, the fever continued to rage unchecked, making her wonder if the wound had become infected.

That thought jerked her eyes toward Coyote Man who squatted on his heels a short distance away. "Come here!" she said sharply. "You sponge him off while I look at his wound."

The warrior silently obeyed the command, making it obvious she was in charge at the moment. He dipped the shirt into the spring again and again, wetting it thoroughly before spreading it across the injured man's chest.

And as Coyote Man kept the cooling liquid on his friend's heated body, Jennifer unwound the binding that covered his leg. When the wound was finally exposed, she sucked in a sharp breath. The flesh was puffy, the edges of the wound raw. But what concerned her the most was the puss seeping around the edges.

It *was* infected. There was no doubt in her mind now. But what could she do? She had no medical training, no healing drug with which to treat the wound.

Medicine!

Oh, God, she had forgotten the tobacco! It was not medicine, but she knew of cases where a tobacco poultice had drawn the infection from the wounds.

Dipping her handkerchief into the cool spring, she washed the wound, then covered it with a tobacco poultice. Then she took over the water applications again, hoping that her efforts were not in vain.

Jennifer continued to administer to the sick warrior, ignoring the pain of her left shoulder, concentrating instead on applying the cold water against his flesh over and over again.

Time passed, an eternity, and he showed no sign of improvement. And then, suddenly, his teeth began to chatter. Alarmed, she knelt closer, placing her palm against his cheek and found his skin much cooler.

"Pick him up," she ordered Coyote Man. "The fever has subsided now and he has become chilled. He needs warmth so his lungs won't become infected."

Coyote Man obeyed her orders silently. Then, with quickened strides, he carried Spotted Wolf to the cavern, glancing occasionally at Jennifer who trotted along beside him, ready to lend a hand should it be needed.

The thought of trying to escape never entered her head. Not until they were back in the cavern again. And by then the opportunity had been lost.

Seven

A fire was kept burning to keep the cold night air at bay, but the heat from the flames barely reached Jennifer as she leaned against the limestone wall, legs drawn up, arms wrapped around them, keeping vigil over the sick warrior.

She had been successful in her attempts to lower his temperature, but even so, knowing how quickly his body heat could rise again, she dared not relax her vigilance.

It was quiet in the cave, no sound, except for the crackle of flames eating away at the wood. But outside the cave the night was a veritable orchestra of sound. Leaves rustled in the wind, and there was a flutter of wings. An owl screeched in the distance, a poignant cry as it went about its business of hunting.

A slight movement in her peripheral vision startled Jennifer and jerked her gaze in that direction. In the darkness, Coyote Man was only another shadow among those that flickered in the orange glow cast by the firelight.

Jennifer ignored him, turning her attention to Spotted Wolf again. Was he warm enough? she wondered. Although he lay close to the fire, it was burning low.

Realizing the wood needed to be replenished, she unfolded her shaky legs, rose to her feet and added a large chunk of mesquite, watching the resulting flames spit and spark as they ate at the wood.

Jennifer leaned closer to the fire. Its warmth felt good against her bare shoulders and breasts covered only by her lacy chemise. She remained there at length, rubbing her upper arms briskly to distribute the heat.

Perhaps her shirt had dried out. She ran her hand down the garment she'd hung over a protruding rock and uttered a sigh of relief. It was warm from the heat of the fire. She slid her arms into the sleeves when Spotted Wolf uttered a moan and began to toss restlessly again.

She knelt beside him and felt his cheek. Her eyes widened with alarm. His skin was cold. She ran her palm across his chest. Cold. In his weakened condition, his lungs could become infected. He needed a blanket, some kind of covering, but there was none to be had. Nothing large enough to even cover his chest except her shirt.

His teeth began to chatter, and Jennifer realized she had no choice. She slid the shirt from her shoulders and spread it over his chest and shoulders, frowning down at him. How long would it take his flesh to warm? He muttered hoarsely and pushed at the shirt, exposing his cold flesh again.

"Be still," she murmured, covering him again. "You have to keep warm."

He pushed the shirt aside again and Jennifer tugged it back in place. Before he could cast it off again, she slid her arm beneath his shoulder and lifted his upper body, cradling his head against her shoulder and rocking gently to quiet him while she held the shirt against him.

"Serena," he muttered. "Sere . . ."

"Shhhhh," she comforted. "Be quiet."

He settled down again, making her wonder if he found comfort in the sound of her voice. She hummed softly and continued to rock back and forth, hoping to ease his restless state. She had to keep him covered, couldn't take a chance on anything happening to him. He must recover. And when he did, perhaps he would be grateful enough to send her home again.

She continued to rock him and hum a lullaby until he fell into a deep sleep. Then she lowered him gently and resumed her position against the wall. She wrapped her arms around her knees, hugged them tightly and tried to relax her tired muscles.

The night creatures had become quiet, she realized. The wind had grown calm, and the leaves no longer rustled. Everything was still, making the crackling of the fire seem especially loud.

Jennifer yawned widely. She was so tired that it was hard to continue her vigilant watch, so she rested her chin against her knees while trying to support the heavy weight of her eyelids. She sighed deeply. The crackle of the fire was familiar, somehow comforting.

She yawned again. God, she was so sleepy. And her eyes were so tired, the lids so heavy. She would close them, just for a minute. Yes. It felt good to rest them, felt good to shut out the cold world. But a minute was all she would allow. No more. *Can't take the chance of going to sleep. Need to keep watch over Spotted Wolf. Make him grateful enough to send me home.*

Jennifer yawned again and felt the tension draining away. And as she relaxed, so did her mind. Her thoughts drifted slowly, to another place, another time . . .

That particular day had been like many others. By the time Pa had finished the evening chores, Ma had had supper waiting on the table. They didn't know yet what was to come, didn't know of the horror that would end their lives, and change their daughter's so drastically.

Jennifer would never forget that day. No matter how long she lived, it would haunt her.

Just in from the fields, Pa had been cleaning up in the wash house at the back of the four room cabin. Ma had just taken a pie out of the oven and had set it on the window sill to cool in the night air.

Beside the square table, Jennifer had stood with pitcher in hand, pouring milk into tall glasses that had once belonged to her father's mother.

Suddenly the door had flung open. Jennifer tried to identify the dark-haired intruder. Even then she had felt no real fear. Not then. The fear had come moments later when the pistol spat flame and painted the blouse that Ma wore a deep ruby red.

Jennifer had screamed then, the sound long and piercing. It had brought Pa into the kitchen. He burst through the door, shoving her out of the way while the pistol he carried had delivered death to the man who'd slain his wife.

But the intruder hadn't been alone. While Jennifer's mind had tried to deal with the fact that her mother was dead, two more men had shoved their way into the room, their guns already blazing.

If Jennifer had reacted quickly enough, Pa might have been saved. But she hadn't. She had stayed on the floor beside her mother, unable to move, unable to do anything at all.

And then came the silence. The terrible, horrible silence.

Jennifer's senses had come alive. Her nostrils

twitched, assailed by the acrid smell of gunpowder and below that, the coppery scent of blood.

Oh, God, her mind had screamed. *The blood! All that blood!* There was blood staining Ma's kitchen floor. Ma's blood. Pa's blood. And blood from the two dead men who had defiled their home.

Only two of them.

The other one had stood in the middle of the kitchen, a wide smile of triumph spread across his face. "Guess you won't be needin' this farm after all," he growled.

Jennifer then knew what it had all been about. Tom Harris, owner of the Circle H ranch, had been after the farm for years. The sixty acres Pa owned had been all that stood between the Bar H and the river. Since Pa had remained firm in his refusal to sell, Harris had apparently decided to obtain the farm by other means.

That knowledge had washed over Jennifer as she lay on the floor with the blood of her parents staining the faded boards around her. The gunman had apparently discounted Jennifer as no threat and he then slowly turned his attention to her, a bad mistake on his part.

She had wrenched the pistol from Pa's hand and squeezed the trigger, having no need to take aim since he was such a big target. There had been no way she could have missed. The pistol had boomed and the gunman flinched.

His eyes had widened as he stared at her. Then his knees had buckled as he crumpled to the floor, falling across one of his cohorts, the hired gunman who had killed Ma.

Jennifer had cried then, bitterly, her shoulders heaving with sobs until she heard sounds that indicated both her parents weren't dead after all.

She had looked at Pa then, had heard his rasping whisper. "You stop that cryin', girl."

"Pa! Oh, my God!" She had crawled quickly toward him. "I thought you were dead."

"Ain't yet," he had muttered. "But I'm done for, Jenny girl."

"No," she had whispered, wrapping her arms around herself. "Don't say that, Pa."

"Gotta say it. An' you gotta face it." His blue eyes had a glazed look about them. "Give me your Ma's hand, Jenny."

Tears had dimmed her eyes as she'd placed her mother's work-roughened hand in his much larger one.

"Good." He had coughed and blood had bubbled from the corner of his mouth. "I couldn't go easy without your Ma beside me."

"No," she had sobbed. "Don't say that, Pa. You're going to live. You can't leave me alone."

"Ain't got no choice, Jenny. Besides, would you want your Ma to go by herself? We been together for nigh on to thirty years now. It wouldn't be right for her to go on this last journey without me." He had attempted a smile that didn't quite come off. "Go to Chicago, Jenny. To your Ma's people. Your Grandma is a hard woman but she'll do right by you." His lips had tightened. "But don't you sell the farm, girl. Else I'll come back and haunt you."

Those were his last words to her spoken over a year ago, a promise to haunt her if she sold the farm. And she hadn't sold it. She had gone east to live with her grandparents. But life in the city had not been to her liking. She'd considered her grandmother's friends useless. Teas and endless parties seemed frivolous pastimes for a woman who had lived on a farm where every hand was kept busy throughout the day. A letter from her uncle had prompted her to appeal to him. He had agreed to her request and she had joined him at the fort.

"Serena."

The word jerked Jennifer into awareness, and she reacted swiftly, blinking back tears of remembrance as she hurried to kneel beside Spotted Wolf.

"You are real. Not a ghost. And not Serena."

Her lips curled slightly. "Yes. I am real." As she remembered why she *was* there, the smile died away slowly. "It's a good thing I *was* here too, Spotted Wolf." She realized that she must emphasize the point while he was weak enough to listen. "Coyote Man didn't have the slightest notion what to do for you. If I hadn't been here, you might easily have died."

"What are you called?" Spotted Wolf asked.

"Jennifer," she replied. "Jennifer Carlisle."

"Carlisle," he muttered, his green eyes darkening suddenly. "Yes. I remember now. Your uncle is a man of influence."

"Yes," she agreed eagerly. "He's an officer at Fort Davis. His circumstances are such that he can afford to pay well for my safe return."

She deliberately emphasized the fact that her uncle was a man of means, knowing that, if saving Spotted Wolf's life wasn't enough to sway Coyote Man, then surely the gold he would gain by her release would make the difference.

"Yes. You told us that, just before you ran away." He closed his eyes and turned away, as though he were deliberately shutting her out.

Jennifer felt as though she'd been kicked in the stomach. She told herself she was being foolish, he was tired, hadn't meant her to feel rejected, and yet, she couldn't convince herself of that fact.

She resumed her original position against the wall, pulling her knees up and wrapping her arms around them.

Things will work out, you'll see. Her mind uttered the reassurance, but her heart refused to listen. There was a cold knot in her stomach, a frozen mass that coiled tighter and tighter with each passing moment.

Jennifer remained that way, staring fearfully into the dwindling fire as it slowly burned away, leaving nothing but coals and ash as a reminder of the warmth that was once there.

The early morning sun filtering through the entrance of the cave woke Spotted Wolf. He blinked against the sunlight playing across his eyelids and moved his head to evade the bright shaft of light.

Staring up at the limestone ceiling, he wondered what he was doing there. But his confusion was only a momentary thing, gone as quickly as it had come. He remembered everything that had happened, remembered the snake, the resulting fever and the woman who had tended him so carefully.

He pushed himself upright and the dark fabric that had covered his upper body fell away. He shoved it aside before realizing what it was: the shirt the white woman had been wearing.

She was asleep in the back of the cavern, her limbs free from restraints. Puzzled, he looked at Coyote Man, who returned his look.

The two warriors had no need to speak. No questions uttered, no answers given. It was obvious Coyote Man had been keeping watch throughout the long night. There was no way the captive could have slipped past him.

It was Coyote Man who broke the silence. "You are better, my friend," he said, speaking in the Comanche language.

"Well enough to continue our journey," Spotted Wolf replied in kind. "I am sorry for the delay."

"You need not apologize. It could not be helped."

"We must continue with haste," Spotted Wolf said. "There is much to be done if we are to gain Cloud Dancer's release."

Coyote Man nodded his head. "But first we must eat. The woman's body is weak. It has not the strength of ours. And she would be no good to us dead."

"Wake her," Spotted Wolf said gruffly. "I will see to the horses." He left the cavern, taking with him a picture of her, huddled against the cavern wall in the flimsy white thing she wore for an undergarment, probably cold since she'd given her shirt to keep him warm.

Somehow, that thought didn't set well with him. Not at all.

Clara Boseley lay huddled beneath the covers in her bedroom. She'd just wakened from a horrible nightmare where Jennifer was held captive in a bordello somewhere south of the border.

It couldn't be so, though. That couldn't be where Jennifer was. It was only a nightmare, something conjured out of nowhere, caused by the guilt she felt for not having revealed the truth about the last time she had seen Jennifer.

But how could she tell them? she wondered. Nobody would believe Lieutenant Carter had been a traitor. They might believe it of One Eye, but if she told what she knew, then he would surely retaliate. There was no telling what he would do to her.

No. She couldn't divulge her information.

Anyway, she consoled herself, she knew very little about the whole thing, nothing really of consequence. She couldn't be expected to divulge something that she had no knowledge of. Jennifer would understand that.

If she came back. If Jennifer was still alive, that's what she would expect Clara to do. Wouldn't she?

Oh, God! Jennifer might be suffering untold horrors! And she, her best friend, was doing absolutely nothing to help her.

But what could she do?

Nothing. Not one single, solitary thing, without putting her own life in danger.

Better to wait awhile longer. Jennifer would be found soon. She just *had* to be found!

Clara pulled the covers over her head, trying to shut out the normal sounds of morning. She could hear pots banging in the kitchen, knew her mother would be coming to wake her soon. She wouldn't get up though. She'd tell her mother she had cramps. And it wouldn't really be a lie. Her stomach *did* cramp. It cramped with fear for Jennifer and fear that One Eye would somehow discover that Clara knew about the secret rendezvous and come for her.

"Oh, God, please help me," she muttered. Then she added quickly, "And Jennifer too, of course."

Then, closing her eyes, she forced every thought from her mind and soon fell into a restless sleep.

Eight

The soft sand muffled the rhythmic thud of horses' hooves as they moved through the dry wash. Jenny had no notion of how long they had been riding; she only knew it seemed to be forever. She had an acute ache in her buttocks that moved continually up her spine to jar her teeth.

She shifted positions, trying to ease the ache, and the movement shoved her rounded buttocks closer against the warrior who rode behind her.

"Be still, woman!" Spotted Wolf snarled, obviously in an evil temper.

Jennifer tightened her lips. The warrior had shown no sympathy for her plight. The ungrateful wretch! It would be a cold day in hell before she ever lifted a finger to help him again.

Her head throbbed with pain and the merciless sun caused shimmering heat waves to dance before her eyes. Her tongue was thick, her mouth dry. She glanced skyward, her hopeful gaze finding the sun. It seemed not to have moved since the last time she had looked; the day had hardly begun.

Coyote Man urged his mount up the bank of the dry wash, and the buckskin lurched forward, trying to keep abreast of the paint.

Unbalanced as they were, it would be a simple

matter to shove Spotted Wolf from the buckskin. If she could succeed alone on the horse, she might be able to elude her captors.

She measured the distance between the two horses. The buckskin she rode on was much sturdier than the paint and might have more staying power. If push came to shove perhaps she could . . .

As though he had guessed the direction her thoughts had taken, Spotted Wolf's hand tightened around her waist. "You would be foolish to try anything, paleface," he said harshly. "It is true my body is weak, but I know how your mind works. You cannot fool me. Even if you managed to elude me, you could not escape Coyote Man. And the penalty for trying would be severe."

A chill swept through her and she was swift to make a denial. "I-I don't know what you mean," she muttered. "I had no such thoughts in my head."

"That is good." He slumped wearily against her as though the warning had taken the starch out of his large, muscular frame.

They were crossing the *Llano Estacado,* the Staked Plains, a place Jennifer had heard only a few white men had dared to venture. She scanned the terrain, hoping to find something to use for landmarks, something to help her find her way back to the fort when she managed to escape from the Indians.

As she most certainly would. Somehow.

They couldn't always be alert, couldn't watch her every single moment of every single day. A time would come for her, and when it did, then she would escape. And then she would have to make her own way back home.

If she could find the way back.

She couldn't allow that word though, that *if.* She *would* find her way home.

Jennifer examined the area around them. There was nothing to use for a landmark. Nor in the distance as far as she could see. The vast terrain was dotted here and there with barrel cactus, catclaw bushes and mesquite trees. Yet there was nothing to set one cactus, or one bush, or one mesquite tree apart. Not one thing to use for identification.

She licked her parched lips. The heat was so intense that there was little life to be found in this harsh land. Nothing except scorpions, snakes, lizards, horny toads and Gila monsters. She shuddered at the thought. How, she wondered desperately, could she hope to survive there, let alone find her way back home?

Despair clutched at her as they made their way across the scorched, unforgiving earth. The hours seemed endless, yet the warriors showed no sign of stopping to rest.

And during those long hours, Jennifer worried constantly, worried that Spotted Wolf, weakened from the fever, would succumb to a state of unconsciousness again. If that happened, then she would be left to the mercy of Coyote Man. She shuddered at the thought. Spotted Wolf might be no less savage than the other warrior, but there was a slight chance that he would feel some obligation, however mild it might be, for her help in his recovery.

Realizing such thoughts could lead to insanity, Jennifer forced them away. Time passed, she had no way of knowing how much, and still they rode on, across a prairie that stretched as far as the eye could see.

Jennifer felt numb from the long hours in the saddle and wondered if they would ever reach their destination.

When the horses suddenly stopped, she thought

the warriors had decided to rest them until her gaze
dropped lower and she realized they were on the
rim of a great chasm that centuries of wind and
water had etched into the high plains.

There, spread out more than a thousand feet below them, was a vast, multicolored valley where water
flowed and vegetation was abundant.

Jennifer realized then that they had reached the
Comanche stronghold that her uncle was so desperately trying to find.

How could they descend into the valley? she wondered.

Did they actually mean to travel down that steep,
perpendicular path that wound below?

Her question was quickly answered as the buckskin took the first lurching step down the steep
slope. Jennifer clutched the horse's mane tightly,
her knuckles showing white from her grip.

"Easy," Spotted Wolf muttered. "You will come to
no harm from the descent."

You will come to no harm from the descent.

The words, probably meant to comfort, echoed
in her mind, reminding her there might be harm
waiting for her below. She had been so eager to
reach the valley, and yet now, she was fearful of doing so.

It seemed an eternity before they reached the
wide valley at the base of the cliff. And even then,
Jennifer realized, the journey was not over. They
rode parallel to the cliffs as they continued down
the canyon for miles until the village finally came
into view.

Jennifer's blood chilled at the sight.

She didn't know exactly what she had expected,
but it certainly hadn't been a village of that size.

Jennifer had been given to understand the renegades constituted a ragtag band of only a few warriors who refused to stay on the reservation as they had been ordered. But it was obvious from the size of the village that the cavalry had no idea what they were up against.

Jennifer saw more than a hundred tepees built in a wide circle that spread across the valley.

As they rode closer to the village, Jennifer thought the cone shaped hide dwellings with their tops blackened from the smoke of many fires resembled miniature mountains.

Jennifer's ears were suddenly assailed by a cacophony of sound. Dogs barked, fierce, throaty sounds that were reflected in the faces of the people who came toward them. There were hundreds of them, people who appeared to be looking at her.

Her eyes darted from side to side, trying to look at something else other than those savage faces with eyes that seemed to glare at her. She looked instead at the large animal skins that were pegged to the ground, looked at the long strips of fresh meat drying on the racks out of reach of the dogs.

Oh, God, how would she ever be able to leave this place? How? When there were so many of them! Even the cliffs rising on both sides of the valley were like walls to a prison cell.

People were still pouring from the lodges and several children were running toward them, crying out in loud voices, *"Hihites, hihites!"*

"Hihites," the warrior seated behind Jennifer responded.

Jennifer tried to make herself as small as possible, hoping to remain unnoticed for a time, but it was an impossible feat. Her bright hair, if nothing else, made her highly visible to people who were used to seeing only dark hair.

Spotted Wolf guided his mount among them and Jenny shrank closer to him, preferring the familiar to the unknown.

The other warriors stood back, showing little interest in the new arrivals, yet Jennifer felt their indifference was only a pretense. The women though, had no need to hide their curiosity. They converged on the riders, babbling in shrill voices in a language Jennifer found unintelligible.

Some of the women wore shapeless buckskin dresses that hung to mid-calf, while others wore a combination of buckskin and brightly colored fabric. Some of them wore their black hair twisted in coils at the nape of their neck, while others wore them in braids.

As they came closer, Jennifer saw the expressions on their faces. There appeared to be no sympathy for the newcomer, no pity for her plight. There was only loathing and disgust for the paleface who had come among them.

Fear was a hard knot coiled tightly within her belly. While at the fort, she had overheard the troopers speaking in low tones about a white woman who had been recovered from the Comanches. She had told of being repeatedly raped by the warriors during her time of captivity, and of the burning sticks the women of the tribe had applied to her flesh. In another instance, the troopers said, where gold had been exchanged for a white woman, she had been returned with her nose sliced off, leaving two gaping holes where her nostrils had been.

Jennifer had tried not to believe such horror could exist, had thought they might be stories invented to make the settlers fear the Indians. Until now. Until this very moment when she looked into the crowd of savages that surged toward them.

Oh, God! she silently cried as a shudder rippled through her slight frame. *Am I destined to suffer such a fate?*

"Hold your head up!" Spotted Wolf commanded sharply from his place behind her. "Do not allow them to see your fear."

Instantly her chin jutted forward and, trying to hide her cowardice, she lifted her gaze higher, looking beyond the crowd, focusing on the Comanche woman who stood apart from the others, lingering near a tepee decorated with coyotes in every conceivable position. She looked at the painted coyotes. They were remarkably well done. Her attention returned to the woman.

There was nothing fierce about her. Instead, she appeared almost fragile. She was small, barely reaching five feet with a maiden's slimness. Her hair gleamed beneath the sun like a raven's wing and, as they drew closer, a slow smile parted her lips, a smile of welcome.

For one brief moment, Jennifer actually thought the smile was for her and her own lips curved slightly in return. But her hopes were quickly dashed as she realized the woman was staring at something beyond her, at Coyote Man, who urged his mount closer, then stopped beside her and vaulted from his mount with the litheness of a mountain lion. He touched her cheek with his rough palm and his fierce countenance suddenly gentled.

Jennifer was dumbfounded as she perceived the warmth in his face. His voice was low and husky as he spoke to the young woman whose face suddenly glowed with an uncommon beauty. Then he guided the woman into the tepee and closed the deerhide flap behind them.

Spotted Wolf's mount would have stopped beside

the paint had he not urged the buckskin forward, toward a lodge very similar to the one Coyote Man had entered. The only difference that Jennifer could see was the markings on the hide covering. Instead of coyotes, there were moons and stars and geometric designs.

Although Jennifer realized Spotted Wolf had not yet regained his strength, he showed no sign of his weakness as he dismounted, then reached up and plucked her from the saddle.

The moment her feet were on the ground, the crowd closed in around her, reaching out with their hands and tugging at her bright hair, pulling at the loose shirt that covered her upper body.

Hearing the fabric tear, Jennifer cried out, "Stop! Please, stop! Leave me alone!" Her fear was almost overpowering as she pushed at the grasping hands while shrinking closer to the warrior at her side.

"*Ka ta-quoip, Mah-ocu-ah!*" he ordered harshly, gripping her upper arm and pushing her roughly toward the lodge. "Silence your tongue, woman!" He shoved her inside the dwelling, then spoke again, his voice taking on a different tone, a much softer one. "*Asa Mah-ocu-ah!*"

A small, aged woman with silvery hair twisted into a knot at the nape of her neck, rose slowly to her feet. Her eyes were fastened on Spotted Wolf. "*Nei ner-too-ahr! Nei ner-too-ahr!*" she exclaimed softly.

Her deeply creased, sunbaked face was the same color as the beaded doeskin dress she wore and, although her expression was impassive, her eyes glittered as she placed a hand disfigured by arthritis against Spotted Wolf's cheek. "*Hi, nei ner-too-ahr!*"

"*Hi, Ner-be-ahr,*" he replied. "*Nei te-bitze utsa-e-tah.*"

The little woman smiled then, and when she did, the creases in her skin deepened. "*Kiss, nei ner-too-*

ahr," she said, turning her attention to Jennifer, who stood beneath the smoke hole where the sun's rays turned her tangled curls into a fiery blaze. *"Cona!"* she exclaimed. *"Ma-be-quo-si-tu-ma!"*

"What did she say?" Jennifer asked, her gaze flickering between the woman and Spotted Wolf.

"My mother called you Woman of the Burning Hair of the Head."

"Oh." Jennifer looked at the old woman and attempted a shaky smile. "My name is Jennifer," she said. "Jennifer Carlisle."

"You are whoever Star Woman wishes you to be," Spotted Wolf said roughly. "If it pleases her to call you Woman of the Burning Hair of the Head, then you will answer to that name. Obey her in all things and you will not be treated harshly." He turned his back on her then, obviously intent on leaving her alone with the old woman.

"Spotted Wolf!" she cried out in panic. "Don't go, please!" She might as well have kept silent for all the good it did her.

As though he'd already washed his hands of her, Spotted Wolf exited the lodge and strode briskly away, seeming intent on putting distance between them.

Jennifer looked at the old woman, and tears suddenly blurred her vision. She blinked quickly, unwilling to allow the old woman to see her weakness.

"Ein mah-suite mah-ri-ich-ka, Ma-be-quo-si-tu-ma?"

Star Woman's words seemed to pose a question, but Jennifer had no idea what it was. "I don't understand you," she murmured, shaking her head in the hopes that the women would understand the gesture if not the words.

"I asked if you would like to eat," the little woman said in perfectly good English.

Jennifer was so surprised at Star Woman's use of the language that she found herself unable to answer, and merely nodded her head.

The old woman pointed toward a spot on the earthen floor beside the fire. "Sit there. I made rabbit stew for the evening meal. It should be ready to eat." Although the old woman used the English language, there was no doubt in Jennifer's mind that she was an Indian. That meant Spotted Wolf's green eyes had come from his father.

Star Woman left the lodge and Jennifer took advantage of her absence to rest herself. She sat down beside the cold fire pit and took in her surroundings.

It was a small but spotless dwelling. A chest woven from rushes had been placed against the conical wall and a pile of furs which served as her bed were spread over a thick mat of willow branches. Brightly painted clay pots occupied a space beside the trunk and several hide bags bulging with supplies were hung from lodge poles. One of the hide bags, a particularly long one, had an open end and the object protruding from it resembled the handle of a hunting knife.

Jennifer's gaze narrowed. She rose to her feet when she realized a knife would do little to help her situation. If she killed the old woman, then she would most certainly seal her fate. There was no way she could escape the valley alone. Her only hope lay in being ransomed for gold by her uncle.

Nine

Spotted Wolf entered his lodge and stretched his weary body on the buffalo hide mat that served as his bed. The rushes beneath it rustled slightly as though they'd recently been replaced. He didn't wonder about that though. Although he lived apart from his foster mother, Star Woman, she made certain his needs were seen to. He wasn't the least bit surprised when she entered his lodge moments later carrying a bowl of rabbit stew in her small hands.

"I didn't expect you, Little Mother." He spoke in the Comanche tongue. "You should not have put yourself to the trouble of preparing my meal."

"When has it ever been trouble for a mother to prepare food for her son?" she asked. "Now eat your food, then speak to me of your appreciation."

More than happy to oblige, Spotted Wolf used his fingers to shovel a large portion into his mouth. "Mmmm, delicious," he grunted, reaching toward the bowl again. He paused suddenly, remembering the paleface woman he had left with Star Woman. "Is the woman alone in your lodge?"

"Of course. She cannot leave the village without being noticed." Her expression was suddenly thoughtful. "You seem worried about her." When he remained silent, she said, "Do not worry about her hunger. The bowl of stew she is eating will fill her belly even if the taste is not to her liking. I am wondering, though, why you are concerned with her welfare. Is she not a captive?"

"Yes," he said. "But it is due to her efforts that I survived the bite of a rattlesnake." He explained the circumstances, ending with, "A great debt is owed to the woman."

"It is a debt that must not be repaid," she said shortly. "The woman cannot be allowed to go free unless her people agree to the exchange. Cloud Dancer must be freed from the White Eyes' prison. A debt owed to a white captive cannot be allowed to come before the needs of our medicine man. He is of the People and the People come first."

Her dark eyes glittered. "But you did not need this old woman to remind you. It is a thing you have always known." Since there was no one to see the display of affection, Star Woman kissed her foster son's cheek and left him alone to consider her words, something that he would do many times during the days that followed.

Jennifer had just swallowed the last mouthful of rabbit stew when the old woman returned. "The stew was delicious," she said, putting the bowl aside. "Thank you for bringing it."

The woman nodded her silvery head, silently acknowledging Jennifer's words of appreciation. Then, seating herself on the stack of hides, she began her own meal.

Jennifer wondered what was expected of her. Should she keep her seat until the old woman said otherwise? She wasn't left to wonder long. The mo-

ment the last bite of stew was gone, the old woman
turned her attention to Jennifer again.

Was her gaze more stern than before? And if it
was, what had caused the change? The old woman
hadn't been exactly welcoming before, but she
hadn't been hostile either. What had happened during the time the old woman was absent? Where had
she gone?

Jennifer was provided with the answers when the
old woman began to speak. "My son tells me you
are responsible for saving his life."

On the point of speaking, Jennifer was silenced
by a wave of the woman's arthritic hand.

"Although you will be rewarded for your efforts
on his behalf, you may not consider the debt paid."

"My freedom is enough," Jennifer said eagerly.

"We cannot guarantee your freedom!" Star
Woman said sharply.

"But—but I want nothing else," Jennifer protested. "Only my freedom."

"Be careful of your words, *Ma-be-quo-si-tu-ma*.
There are many ways to repay you besides granting
your freedom."

"What else would I want?" Jennifer asked.

"To be left unmolested by the warriors of the
tribe. To be kept safe from the torture the other
women would inflict on you. To have your workload
made less by half. If I were in your place, all these
things would be desirable to me. I would consider
any debt, however great, to be paid for any of those
things. If you were to choose one, which would it
be?"

Jennifer's eyes were wide with horror. Was her
imagination working overtime or was the old woman
asking her to choose one of the horrible things she

had listed? And that one thing would be excluded from her life here in the village.

Oh, God! It was too horrible to even consider!

Star Woman waited for Jennifer's answer. But how could she give her one?

"Do-do I have to decide right now?" Jennifer asked shakily.

"No," the old woman replied. "Not now. You may consider the choices for awhile."

Jennifer's horror was so great that she wanted to take her mind off her situation for awhile. Hoping the old woman would be willing to converse with her, she said, "How did you come to learn the English language?"

"Many of my People know the language of the White Eyes." The woman's eyes betrayed no softness as she apprised Jennifer of that fact. "Especially those of us who have lived on the reservation."

"You lived on a reservation?"

"For a time. Everyone in this village, except for the youngest children, were there for a time, sent by the bluecoats." Her mouth curled with contempt. "But they cannot keep us there. Quanah is a strong war chief. And . . ."

"Quanah Parker?" Jennifer interrupted. "Is this his village?"

"So you have heard of Quanah Parker."

Although Star Woman didn't confirm or deny his presence in the village, Jennifer felt that he must be there. And perhaps he could be appealed to for help.

"With Quanah and Spotted Wolf to guide our People, we will elude the bluecoats," Star Woman said. "They are both men of strength who can lead the other warriors to victory. It was Quanah who founded this stronghold. It is a place unknown to the White

Eyes. They cannot find us here." She turned away, stooping over to pick up the used bowls.

"Enough talk," she said. "The sun has not yet left the sky and there is work to be done, a feast to prepare, to celebrate the return of those who were lost to us." She handed the bowls to Jennifer and pointed to the water jug.

"Wash the bowls," she commanded sternly. "And make sure they are clean, then peel the vegetables in that large basket beside the chest. And do not leave any peel or you will be severely punished."

The old woman's words, as well as the tone, sent a chill over Jennifer. Would Star Woman really punish her for so simple a thing? Jennifer tried to put the thought out of her mind, telling herself that it was ridiculous, that the old woman was only making threats. But somehow, she couldn't quite convince herself of that fact.

Unwilling to allow her thoughts to dwell on her fate, Jennifer tried to make conversation. "You said the celebration was for those who were lost to you. Do you mean Spotted Wolf and Coyote Man?"

The old woman raised a dark brow. "Did you see any others return with you?"

"No."

"Then why do you waste time asking foolish questions?"

Jennifer's lips tightened. She didn't think she was going to like living with the woman. But then, nobody had asked her preference. Nor, she suspected, would they be likely to do so.

Several hours later, Jennifer sighed with relief and seated herself on the earthen floor. She looked longingly at the sleeping mat, but since there was only one, she realized the old woman would be sleeping there.

With a heavy sigh, she leaned back against a lodge pole, pulled her knees up and rested her head against them. She could hear the thrum, thrum, thrum of many drums beating a welcome for the men who had returned to the village and the throbbing sound kept time with her beating heart. But her fear of being mistreated was not as great as it had been. The old woman had seemed pleased with her work, although she had given no indication of that fact, neither by word or deed.

Perhaps captivity among the Comanche would not be as bad as the old woman had indicated.

Which will you choose for payment? The old woman's words surfaced in her memory, causing fear to surge anew. If a choice must be made, then it would be to avoid rape at the hands of the warriors. The heavy workload she could deal with, and the punishment dealt out by the women could be suffered as silently as possible. But to be raped repeatedly was unthinkable.

Suddenly the hide flap was pushed aside. Jennifer's heart leapt with fear, remembering the old woman's words. Had the choice been taken from her hands? Had the first warrior come, intent on ravishing her? Were others gathered outside the lodge, waiting their turn?

As a large shape entered the lodge, Jennifer stifled the scream that threatened. The shadows were too dense to see clearly, but she knew it was a man who'd entered. Her heart beat rapidly as she shrank against the hide wall, fearing the worst from the newcomer.

Then as he stepped into the light that shone through the smoke hole and she saw him clearly, she drew in a breath of relief.

It was Spotted Wolf.

"You frightened me," she whispered shakily. "I didn't know it was you."

He remained silent as he reached for her, wrapping strong fingers around her wrist and pulling her to her feet.

"What are you doing?" she demanded.

"Come with me," he commanded.

They crossed a short space and were about to enter another lodge, almost twice the size of his mother's, when a thickset warrior with wide shoulders suddenly appeared out of the darkness.

"Ein nodema Ma-be-quo-si-tu-ma?" he grunted.

"Ka!" Spotted Wolf said shortly. *"Ka nodema!"*

Reaching out quickly, the warrior curled his fingers around a long hank of Jennifer's hair. *"Heepet ein mu-su-ite?"* His black eyes glittered. *"Pihet-eh-samon tuh-huh-yet?"*

"Ka!" Spotted Wolf said again. *"Ka nodema!"* Shoving Jennifer into the lodge, he quickly followed her and closed the entrance flap behind them.

"What was that all about?" Jennifer asked.

"He wanted to trade thirty horses for you," Spotted Wolf replied. He pushed her toward the sleeping mat across the room. "It is late and I am tired."

"So am I," she replied, stretching out on the sleeping mat with a heavy sigh. When he sat beside her and removed his moccasins, she jerked upright. "What are you doing?" she asked.

His expression was inscrutable. "You have no need to fear me, Jennifer Carlisle. You will come to no harm through me."

"Then why did you bring me here? I thought you meant for me to stay with Star Woman."

"That was my intention," he admitted. "But during the celebration, Three Fingers made his intentions known. That is the only reason you are here now." He stretched out on the sleeping mat and sighed deeply. "Now be silent, woman. I have had too little sleep for more days than I wish to count."

"What is going to happen to me, Spotted Wolf?" she asked. "Star Woman said . . ."

"Go to sleep!" he ordered.

"But I don't know what is going to ha . . ."

He raised himself on his elbows and glared fiercely at her. "Is it your wish to have another warrior guard you?"

Another warrior? *Oh, God, no!* "No," she whispered shakily. "It's just that I can't sleep when I don't know what is going to happen to me."

Spotted Wolf sat up and reached for his moccasins.

"What are you doing?" she asked quickly.

"Leaving. I will sleep elsewhere. Two Knives has been sleeping well enough the last few days. He can guard you adequately enough. And perhaps he will not mind your flapping tongue."

"Two Knives? Oh, no, Spotted Wolf!" she protested. "Stay here. I promise to be quiet." To prove she was telling him the truth, she stretched out on the pallet again and held herself tensely, afraid to move lest he leave the tepee and send the man called Two Knives to guard her.

She would have preferred being left alone, but if she must have a guard, then let it be Spotted Wolf. At least he was too tired, too drained from his recent illness, to treat her badly. But another warrior was an unknown factor. She could not take a chance on what he would do if left alone with her.

Her relief was great when Spotted Wolf stretched out beside her again. She swallowed back the panic that was almost overwhelming. Although he was unconcerned by his nakedness, she could not so easily dismiss it. Not when he was so close. His heat, his maleness, seemed to encompass her.

Jennifer felt certain she wouldn't be able to sleep. She lay beside him tensely while the drums outside continued to beat out a steady rhythm. Time passed and her muscles relaxed, her body began to unwind, and finally her mind drifted into oblivion.

Ten

Although Star Woman proved to be a hard task-master, she allocated the work fairly, leaving as many chores for herself as she gave to her new slave.

And Jennifer *was* a slave. If she hadn't realized it that first day in the village, she was certainly made aware of it when the old woman woke her early the next morning.

"*Savate erth-pa!*"

The voice had been shrill enough to disturb Jennifer's slumber. She tugged the blanket over her ears to shut out the noise and attempted to return to the arms of Morpheus.

"*Savate erth-pa!*" The words were accompanied by a sharp nudge against her rib cage. "*Savate erth-pa, Ma-be-quo-si-tu-ma!* Get up you lazy girl!"

Jennifer groaned as she recognized Star Woman's voice. Pushing the blanket down, she blinked at the little woman who stood over her. "What time is it?" she muttered, realizing almost immediately how ridiculous the question was. The Indian woman would have no knowledge of time.

Star Woman's dark eyes glittered brightly as she dipped her hand into a leather pouch hanging at her waist and pulled out a long chain. Dangling from the end was a watch. The old woman's face was expressionless as she opened the face and peered at the timepiece.

"The time is ten minutes after seven o'clock," she said in a solemn voice. And then she smiled.

Star Woman actually smiled!

So what if it *was* only a mere twitch of the lips, gone as quickly as it had come. That small movement of her lips went a long way toward lifting the heavy burden of fear Jennifer had worn like a mantle since the night she'd been taken captive.

And it was the reason she scrambled so quickly out of bed and reached for her boots. She wanted desperately to please the old woman who seemed at that moment not unlike Grandma Nell. In that smile Jennifer had detected a hint of warmth, and where there was warmth, so might there be compassion.

"I'm sorry to have slept so late," Jennifer apologized. "I suppose Spotted Wolf is waiting impatiently for his morning meal."

"My son had no need to wait. He ate with me more than an *hour* ago."

The way she emphasized the time had Jennifer's lips curling softly. "I am sorry. I'll do my best to see you aren't bothered in the future."

The old woman frowned. "It is always a pleasure to prepare my son's meals, but it is your duty now."

Something in Star Woman's voice made Jennifer wonder if she should apologize for depriving her of her pleasure. Instead, she decided to change the subject. "How did you come by the watch?" she asked curiously.

"My *Ner-co-mack-pe* gave it to me. Many years ago."

"*Ner-co-mack-pe?*" Jennifer inquired, pushing the toes of her right foot into a boot. "I don't know

the word. Was your son, Spotted Wolf, the one who
gave it to you?"

Star Woman's eyes glittered in her tanned face.
"*Ka!*" Her voice held a wry humor. "*Ner-co-mack-pe*
means husband. My husband gave it to me many
years ago. He took it from a White Eyes, along with
his scalp."

Jennifer's movements stilled as a shudder rippled
through her. She tried hard to pretend the old
woman's words had not affected her in any way.

But they had disturbed her. Badly. Jennifer had
detected no sympathy for the murdered man who
had originally owned the watch, but she had detected the malicious amusement in the old woman's
voice, an amusement caused, she was almost certain,
by the fact that her words might distress the white
captive.

Jennifer tried to eat the bowl of mush Star Woman
handed her, but found it hard to choke down even
though her stomach was empty. Then the old
woman began to list her duties for the day, a list
that seemed endless; she was obviously going to be
a hard taskmaster.

The first item on the list was the preparation of
food.

The meat that had been left drying over the racks
throughout the night must be made into *pemmican*
each morning. And, although Jennifer had no idea
what the food was, she did not ask, knowing that
she would learn soon enough.

Silently, she followed Star Woman toward the
brush arbor where several women were already hard
at work.

As they entered the shade, the women looked up
at Jennifer curiously, then most of them returned
their attention to their work. Except for two of

them. One, an old woman bent with age whose face
was liberally sprinkled with pockmarks. The other,
a younger version of the first.

"You are late this morning, Star Woman." The
malicious glance the older woman cast at Jennifer
made it obvious why she spoke in English. "Did your
slave detain you? If she were mine, she would not
be allowed to do so."

"She is lazy," commented the younger woman.
"You should beat her." Picking up a stout stick that
lay nearby, she offered it to Star Woman.

"Thank you for your kind offer," Star Woman
said, "but the captive is new to our ways, and can
be forgiven this one time. If she gives me trouble
tomorrow, I will accept your stick to beat her with."
She pointed to a spot several feet away where two
women sat apart from the others. "That is your
place, *Ma-be-quo-si-tu-ma. Taih-kay Mah-ocu-ah* will
show you what to do."

One of the women from the designated group
motioned Jennifer toward her. "Sit here beside
me." As Jennifer settled down beside the woman,
she realized her hair was dark brown instead of
black as she had first imagined.

"I saw you gathering wood for the feast last evening, but didn't dare speak to you until given permission." She scooped dried fruit from a nearby
basket and placed it in the hollowed out circle of a
large rock.

"This is their version of a pestle. Use the stone
mortar to grind the plums." She returned her attention to the brownish mass that she'd been
pounding.

"What are you grinding?" Jennifer asked, seeing
no reason why they couldn't converse as they worked
together.

Apparently the Indian women had no objection either, since they paid no further attention to Jennifer and her companions.

"Pecans," the brown-haired woman replied. "Did you know Star Woman referred to you as Woman of the Burning Hair of the Head?"

"I know. Spotted Wolf told me what it meant. My name is Jennifer though. Jennifer Carlisle." She spared a brief look at the woman. Her complexion had been darkened by the sun to such a degree that, if it hadn't been for the lighter brown streaks in her hair, Jennifer wouldn't have known she was a white woman. "Have you been with the Indians very long?" she asked.

"Several years. So many that I lost track. They call me *Taih-kay Mah-ocu-ah*. It means Crying Woman because I cried a lot at first. But my name is Helen Stewart." She looked curiously at Jennifer. "They say you saved Spotted Wolf's life."

"You should've let him die," muttered the dark-haired woman who was seated on Helen's left side. "He's a traitor to his own kind."

"Don't mind Sarah," Helen said in a voice so low that her words couldn't possibly carry to the circle of Indian women. "Her owner is a cruel master."

"He beats me every night," Sarah said bitterly. "So I won't have the strength to resist when he rapes me. And every night, when Cruel One is asleep, I lay in that lodge of his and look at that knife that killed my husband. It would be so easy for me to kill the bastard, but I'm afraid of what they'd do to me. If only I had the courage to do it. Oh, God," she whimpered. "If only I had the courage!"

"Stop it, Sarah!" Helen ordered sharply. "Don't you dare start crying now. Walks With a Limp is just waiting for a reason to beat you again. Just keep on

working. Do it, Sarah!" she commanded. "Pretend
that dried meat is Cruel One's head. Beat it hard
and fast 'cause we gotta get it done in time or
there'll be hell to pay."

During the whispered exchange, Helen hadn't
missed a beat with her grinding stone. Her hands
continued to work steadily, seeming to be apart
from her mind that obviously pitied the other
woman who had been so badly mistreated.

"I'm sorry, Helen. But you know how hard it's
been for me." Sarah's voice seemed calmer now.
"My life ended the day my Samuel died. You know
that, Helen. Even if I could escape from the Comanches, there's nothing for me back home. Nothing at all. My parents were dead long before Samuel
came into my life. And now he's gone too."

Jennifer could hear the tears in Sarah's voice and
knew a change of subject was needed. "I gather
there's a purpose to what we're doing, Helen."

Helen gave her a quick smile. "We're preparing
the mixture for *pemmican,*" she explained. "The
pounded fruit and nuts and meat will be mixed with
tallow and marrow fat. Then the whole mess will be
stuffed into clean buffalo gut and sealed with
melted tallow. Stored that way it will keep for years."

That day a bond was formed between Helen and
Jennifer. They were aware of it, and so was Sarah,
who seemed resentful of that fact.

When the last of the *pemmican* mixture had been
stuffed into the last gut and sealed with tallow, the
women left the brush arbor and gathered armloads
of fresh hides. Then they took a trail that wound
through a thicket of cedars.

"Where are we taking the hides?" Jennifer asked.

"To the river," Helen replied.

Jennifer's footsteps quickened. Perhaps she would

be given a chance to bathe while they were there. Soon she was kneeling on a large flat rock that reached over the water, scrubbing animal hides beneath a blazing sun. The black shirt and trousers that had seemed so sensible the night she'd donned them had proven to be the worst thing she could have worn, since the dark fabric absorbed and held heat. But when she'd left her bedroom that night, she'd had no notion that whatever she chose to wear would remain her only apparel for so long a time.

She scraped the limp, wet hide against the rock, only half listening to Sarah's constant complaints about her life since she'd been among the Indians.

As the afternoon passed, Jennifer's back began to ache. How much longer would they continue to work? She looked toward the western sky, and saw the high, scattered clouds painted scarlet from the setting sun.

"Not much longer now," Helen said, as though reading Jennifer's mind. "You'll be expected to finish the hide you're working on, but the others will have to wait until tomorrow." She looked past Jennifer to the stack of hides there. "How many more do you have?"

"Too many," Jennifer replied. "But this one is almost finished. Do you think we'll be allowed to bathe before we leave here?"

Helen shrugged. "That depends on Star Woman."

When Jennifer finished the hide, she stacked it beside the others she had scraped and crossed the flat rock to where the Indian women were congregated. Star Woman looked up as she approached.

"I would like permission to bathe," Jennifer said, trying to sound humble, even though she did not feel that way.

Star Woman's eyes glittered knowingly, but there

was nothing to give away her feelings. "You have worked hard today, *Ma-be-quo-si-tu-ma*," she said, nodding her dark head. "You may bathe. Not because you have worked hard, for that is expected of you. I am giving permission because you smell like a *cha-na*. And I would not have my son offended by your smell."

The other women laughed spitefully, making Jennifer wonder what a *cha-na* was. She had only just decided she'd rather not know when Sarah's voice intruded. "She said you smell like a hog, Jennifer!" Sarah seemed to take some sort of perverse satisfaction from sharing that bit of knowledge.

"I imagine she's right," Jennifer said. Even though her voice was calm, she felt humiliated by the old woman's words.

Although Jennifer would have liked privacy for her bath, she realized it would not be forthcoming. For that reason she decided to bathe in her undergarments.

Before she was finished with her bath, Star Woman had become impatient and ordered her out of the water. Jennifer pulled her clothing over her wet garments and followed the old woman back to the village.

"Your last duty of the day is to prepare my son's meal," she said gruffly. "Unless, of course, he requires something else from you."

Something else? What else could he require of her unless . . . No! She wouldn't even consider such a thing. Spotted Wolf would require nothing except his evening meal. If he had expected more, then he would have said so last night.

Jennifer parted from the old woman and entered Spotted Wolf's lodge, expecting to find him there. But it was empty. She heaved a tired sigh and sank down on the earthen floor, wondering what she was supposed to prepare for his evening meal.

Her gaze roamed the dwelling and stopped on several large hide bags that were stored beside a woven chest. The food supplies must be there, inside either the bags or the chest. She pushed herself upright and groaned as her muscles protested, sore from the strain of hard work. And there was a knot between her shoulder blades that would benefit from a good massage.

She smiled grimly at the thought. A massage was out of the question. There was food to be prepared. She stooped over the chest, ignoring the surge of pain the action caused, opened it and looked inside. Hides. She lifted one of them and realized it was a fringed buckskin shirt. Probably used when the weather was cold. She lifted another hide garment. Breeches. Beneath them were several pairs of moccasins.

Closing the chest, she opened one of the hide bags. It contained dried herbs, but no food. Not even one small root vegetable. Each bag was opened in turn, yet none of them contained the food she sought.

How then, was she supposed to prepare a meal?

Realizing Star Woman must be consulted, Jennifer turned toward the entrance and stumbled over the corner of the willow branch foundation that supported the sleeping mat. She righted herself immediately, but the hide bed looked so soft, so inviting. If she could stretch out for a moment, the ache in her muscles might ease.

Jennifer stretched out on the sleeping pallet and sighed deeply. Oh, God, it felt so good! She sighed again. She'd had a long, hard day, but it was finally over. At least nearly. There was still the evening meal to prepare, but first she would relax another minute . . .

"Jennifer, wake up!" The voice that reached into her sleep was hard, angry. And it was accompanied by an equally hard shake.

"Wha-what's happening?" she muttered, opening eyelids that seemed impossibly heavy.

Spotted Wolf stood over her, his expression one of anger. "Nothing is happening, woman."

"Then why did you wake me?" she complained.

"The reason is obvious. I have come home from a long hunt, and not only do I find a cold fire pit, but there is no meal prepared to fill my belly."

His words swept away the cobwebs of sleep. She sat up and stared at him furiously. "So you are hungry?"

"Of course I am hungry!"

"Well so am I," she said grimly. "But there is nothing in this lodge that even remotely resembles food. How do you expect me to prepare something that is not there?"

"Star Woman would have provided what was needed," he said sharply. "All you needed to do was ask her."

"I know," she admitted, feeling her anger begin to melt away. "And that was my intention. But my muscles were aching and there was a hard knot between my shoulder blades and I guess . . . well, I just decided to stretch out for a few minutes before I asked her."

He frowned down at her. "Your shoulder muscles are probably knotted up from the unaccustomed strain. Turn over on your stomach."

Although she was surprised, she flipped over and lay her head on her arms. She felt the pallet give as he knelt beside her, felt his hands kneading the place between her shoulders, working the stiffness out of her muscles, and she expelled a long sigh of relief. "Oh, God, that feels good. So good." His movements stilled and she said quickly, "Don't stop, Spotted Wolf. Please don't stop. Not yet. Just a little more."

"No." His voice sounded strange.

Jennifer sighed and turned over, her blue eyes suddenly widening with shock.

Spotted Wolf had untied his breechcloth, leaving nothing to cover his naked flesh.

Eleven

When Spotted Wolf had entered the dwelling, hunger was uppermost in his mind. But there had been no meal prepared to warm his belly, to give his body the energy it required. And the woman who should have prepared his meal was asleep on his pallet. Having realized that she must be exhausted, his first reaction had been to allow her to sleep uninterrupted. But when he'd approached his sleeping pallet and gazed down upon her delicate features, made even more fragile by the fiery curls that framed her face, he'd found himself drawn to her in a way he didn't like to think about.

That was the reason he'd woken her so abruptly. He'd meant to make her prepare his meal, but the obvious pain she was experiencing had swayed him. He had massaged her shoulders, had listened to her small moans of pleasure and his body had reacted in a way that angered him. But he had managed, somehow, to control that part of his body that was so responsive to her, had managed to leave her alone so that he could ready himself for sleep.

"Wh-what are you d-doing?" she asked weakly, turning her head away quickly and covering her eyes as though his manhood was a weapon, something fierce to behold.

Puzzled by her demeanor, he looked down at himself and saw nothing to cause her alarm. That part of himself was obeying his command to remain quiescent. Why then, did she turn away from him, as though fearing she would be struck blind if she did not? Was it because he had removed his breechcloth? Perhaps she had never beheld a naked man before. That might account for her reaction. As a Comanche warrior, he was comfortable with his nakedness, but perhaps she, with her White Eyes sharply edged code of conduct, was not.

Was she a virgin? he wondered suddenly. Almost immediately he knew it must be so. Although he'd known many women, he'd never made love to a virgin before. Nor, he reminded himself, did he intend to do so now, even though his member had stirred at the thought.

Quickly bringing it under control again, he seated himself beside her on the sleeping mat. "Don't!" she cried out, shrinking away from him.

He sighed deeply. "Must we go through this every night? I told you last night that I wish only to sleep. Nothing has changed since then."

"Then why did you remove the breechcloth you usually wear? You didn't take it off last night."

"No," he agreed. "The snake's venom left me weak and I wanted only to sleep." He studied her intently. "Do you always sleep in your garments?"

"Not when I am home, but here . . ."

He snorted with contempt. "Remove your garments then."

"No!" She was obviously horrified at the thought.

Suddenly angry with her, he reached for the buttons that fastened the neck of her shirt.

"Don't!" she cried, trying desperately to tear his fingers away from the fabric.

Her resistance added fuel to his anger. He was too tired to spend hours trying to make her remove the garment so she could get a good night's rest.

He gripped the neck of her shirt tightly, refusing to relinquish his hold while she struggled to free herself. The strain on the buttons was too much. They popped off and the shirt opened to expose the pale skin of her neck and the creamy swell of her breast.

"Dammit!" she exclaimed, her blue eyes glittering with anger. "Now look what you've done! You tore my shirt! Ripped the buttons right off. What do you expect me to wear now?"

"I care not what you wear, woman!" Spotted Wolf's lower body reacted swiftly to the sight of her swelling bosom, and he fought to bring it under control. He would not allow passion to sway him, dare not give way to such feelings. He must teach her to obey without question. He spun her around, jerked her shirt down until her arms were free, then tossed it aside.

She reacted instantly, curling her fingers into talons and raking them down the side of his face.

Ignoring her struggles, he pushed her onto the sleeping mat and held her there with his knee while he stripped away her breeches, leaving her bare except for her underclothing.

Staring up at him with wide, shocked eyes, she rolled away from him, snatched up her torn clothing, then ran from the lodge. She skidded to a halt immediately, staring at the crowd that had gathered around, drawn there, probably, by the sound of their struggles.

Apparently considering him the lesser of two evils, she ducked back inside the lodge. Her expression had changed in those few moments. The anger that had glittered in her eyes was gone. It had been replaced by fear. She tried to conceal it though, jutting out her chin and meeting his eyes.

Nevertheless it was there.

Jennifer's voice trembled when she spoke. "It seems I have no choice. It's either you or them. Very well, then. I cannot stop you. But I will never stop hating you for what you've done."

Her courage filled Spotted Wolf with admiration. Frightened though she was, she still found enough to defy him. He told himself that he should reassure her, that he should set her mind at ease, but somehow, the words he spoke were quite different from those he had intended.

"Never is a long time, *Mah-tao-yo.*" He felt his lips curling into a wry smile. "Are you sure you can hold out that long?"

She shuddered, still clutching her garments. "Have you decided not to return me then?" she asked, her voice wavering shakily. "To give up the reward my uncle is sure to offer?"

"Such a decision is not mine alone to make," he said. "The council of elders must be consulted."

"Why?"

"There are reasons," he replied. "We will speak of them later." He held his hand out to her. "Come, *Mah-tao-yo.* You are tired." When she hesitated, he said, "You need not worry about me. I spoke the truth. I wish only to sleep this night."

Hesitantly, she came toward him. "Do you mean it? You won't touch me?"

"My flesh may touch yours while we sleep, but nothing else will happen."

"You promise?"

"I have said nothing will happen. And my tongue does not speak falsely."

As he stretched out on the pallet, she approached slowly, hesitantly, still holding her torn garments against her breasts.

"Do not make me angry again," he said stiffly. "Lay your garments aside. Your body holds no interest for me."

She frowned at him and he wondered if his words had caused her displeasure. She was much like the women of his own tribe, he realized. Even if they had no desire for loving, they wanted to believe they were irresistible.

Patting the fur pallet, he said, "Come, woman. I am tired and before we know it, a new day will be dawning." He yawned widely to show her he meant no harm.

She moved nearer. "My name is not woman," she said. "It is Jennifer Carlisle. I would appreciate it if you would remember that."

"Jennifer." He liked the sound of her name. "Come, Jennifer. Stretch out beside me here. Allow me one night of unbroken sleep, for there is much to do tomorrow."

Reluctantly, yet knowing she had little choice, Jennifer stretched out beside the warrior. The moment she did so, his long arms reached out and pulled her trembling body into his arms.

She froze instantly.

"You s-said you w-wouldn't . . ."

"And I will not," he said quickly. "I wish only to sleep, but this is the only way I can assure myself that you will not take the moment to escape." His arms tightened around her and he rested his chin against her head. "Now close your eyes, Jennifer, and go to sleep."

Jennifer lay beside him, deeply aware of his naked flesh hard against her own. Somehow, she found his embrace comforting and was surprised at that. She'd only lain there a moment, though, before she became aware of other feelings, different feelings that she'd never before experienced. She felt a tingling sensation begin in her lower body, a heat that spread through her. There was a sense of fullness in her breasts that lay against his naked chest. She was aware of his flat male nipples, pressed hard against the round firmness that rose above her chemise, and the feeling gave way to a sense of excitement.

Oh God, how would she ever sleep when she was so thoroughly aware of his body? And what about him? Didn't he feel it too? Was he so unaware of the strangeness of their situation? It must be so, she decided, because his even breathing told her he'd already fallen asleep.

Feeling piqued that he'd so easily dismissed her femininity when his maleness was so disturbing to her senses, Jennifer forced her tense body to relax until she finally drifted off to sleep.

The arrival of the patrol brought Major Carlisle out of post headquarters. Several people gathered to watch them ride through the open gates. Carlisle scanned the troopers slumped in their saddles, hoping they might have found his niece. But, even though some of the cavalry horses carried double, none of the riders were female. He watched the last horse come through the gate and his gaze narrowed on it. A body wrapped in a blanket was tied across the saddle.

The detail halted on the parade ground and the

weary troopers waited for the order that would dismiss them.

Major Carlisle didn't wait for the order to be given. Instead he approached the sergeant who rode behind the form encased in the blanket. "Who is it, Sergeant Jefferson?" he asked harshly.

"Not her, Major," Jefferson said gruffly. "It's the driver from the supply wagon."

"The supply wagon? Not the rifle shipment?"

"Yes, Sir," Jefferson replied. "It damn sure was. That shipment had six troopers ridin' guard. And they was attacked by more'n twenty Comancheros. Wasn't no way they coulda fought 'em off, Major. They did good losin' only one man."

"Did you talk to the troopers?"

"Yeah. They said them Comancheros knowed they was comin' and was waitin' for 'em. Layin' amongst the rocks at Dobbs Pass. Somebody musta told 'em when the rifles was expected." He met the major's eyes with a long look. "We got us a traitor somewheres. An' I wouldn't be surprised to learn he's here, Major."

"You could be right, Sergeant. Not many people knew about that shipment. Too many have been lost lately."

"Yeah. And that means the Injuns got new rifles while we gotta make do with the old ones. Somethin' has to be done, Major. We gotta find out who the double-dealing turncoat is. And we gotta do it afore another shipment comes our way."

"I know, Jefferson." He heaved a weary sigh and ran a hand through his silver hair. "I'm afraid this thing with my niece has got me so worn out that I can hardly think straight anymore."

The sergeant nodded abruptly. "It's a bad business, Major. She was a pretty little thing too."

Major Carlisle squared his shoulders abruptly. "Not *was*, Sergeant. My niece is not dead. I don't know what happened to her, but I do know that she's still alive. And I won't rest until I find her."

"I hope you do find her, Major," the sergeant said. "I surely hope you do."

He sat there waiting quietly until Major Carlisle realized he had not been dismissed. "That's all, Sergeant," he said.

Major Carlisle watched the sergeant ride across the parade ground, heading for the fort hospital where he would leave the dead driver. Then he looked toward the houses that were lined up on Officer's Row, stopping at the Boseley house at the very moment Clara stepped outside. He knew the exact moment she saw him, because she stiffened and hurried back inside.

Why? he wondered. Why did his presence bother her?

Perhaps Clara knew something about Jennifer's disappearance, something that she refused to divulge.

He decided to have a talk with her father. Maybe there was something to be learned from her yet.

Twelve

It was dawn when Spotted Wolf woke with Jennifer snuggled close in his arms. His nostrils quivered as he inhaled the fresh, clean scent of her and his lower body reacted in a way that, were she to waken, would set her shivering with alarm.

Releasing her, he moved slowly until they were disentangled, then rolled off the sleeping pallet and reached for his breechcloth to cover his desire. When it was fastened securely, he allowed himself a long look at the sleeping woman. Her bosom swelled gently above the chemise and the fabric of her pantaloons were thin, clearly defining the soft shape of her hips, and the concave area between her thighs.

The memory of his former love Laughing Water and her tanned face and smiling eyes surfaced in his mind, reminding him of what was lost to him and he cursed himself for feeling desire for one of the hated White Eyes.

He spun on his heels, then pushed aside the hide flap and crossed the distance between his lodge and the one belonging to Star Woman.

"You are hungry, my son?" she asked in the Comanche language. Her dark eyes glittered and a small smile stretched her lips as she filled a bowl without waiting for his reply.

He seated himself across from her and scooped the warm mush into his mouth with his fingers. When the bowl was empty, she filled it again, holding her silence until he finished eating. Only then did she speak again. "Do you wish me to punish the woman for sleeping late?"

"No. Jennifer must be allowed time to become used to our ways." He looked ruefully at her. "Until then I will take my morning meal with you."

She smiled at him again. "It is a pleasure to have you eat with me. You have done more for this old woman than she could ever repay."

"If a debt is owed, then it is mine, Star Woman," he said. "I had no one to call family after the massacre at Pease River. I would have been with them had my father Buffalo Hump not sent me on an errand that day." His lips tightened as he remembered that day as though it were yesterday. A few of his People had survived, but the ones he called father and mother, Buffalo Hump and Many Rivers, were not among them.

"The events of that day tore many Comanche lives apart," Star Woman admitted. "It was there Naduah, she who the White Eyes call Cynthia Ann, and her daughter, Prairie Flower, were captured by the soldiers. Peta Nocona never got over the loss of his wife and daughter. He tried his best to find them, but they seemed to have been gobbled up by the White Eyes' world. Poor man. He never stopped hoping. He continued to search for them until the day he died.

"*Aiiieee!*" she said softly. "Many of our People suffered great losses that day. But at least most of us knew our loved ones passed on to the Great Beyond.

Peta Nocona and Quanah found no such comfort. They knew that wherever Cynthia Ann was, she was grieving for them."

"She grieved long, Little Mother," Spotted Wolf said. "Quanah learned of his mother's death only four summers ago. He was told that she had tried to return to us many times but was always returned to her white family. They took her East hoping that distance would lessen her desire to leave. It only lessened her desire to live."

"Aiiieee!" the old woman said again, expressing her horror. "I had no idea, was only told that she had passed on to a better world. How great her grief must have been." She covered his large hand with her smaller one.

"I, too, suffered from grief, my son. I lost my husband and the only child born to me that day. I was resigned to death until you pulled me away from my dead husband. Do you remember the words you said to me?"

He shook his head. His own grief had been almost unbearable that day.

"You took me in your arms for the whole world to see and whispered that you had just lost your mother." Her eyes became moist at the memory. "You said you needed me. Nothing else would have made me stay in a world that had become so cruel. So painful. But you knew just what to say, Spotted Wolf. I needed to be needed."

"I needed you as much as you needed me," he replied.

The two of them fell silent then. It was a moment to be cherished, since neither of them usually spoke of their feelings for each other. It was she who finally broke the silence.

"It was later that I learned you were not really alone in this world."

He looked at her sharply.

"You have a sister," she reminded solemnly. "A sister whose blood is the same as yours. Those who knew her speak of her courage and her love for the brother who refuses to accept her existence."

His expression darkened. "She is a White Eyes."

"Your blood is the same."

"My memories are of the People. I have no others. I do not belong in the White Eyes' world. My life is with the People. I would have no other."

Her lips thinned and her eyes glittered. "You are stubborn, Spotted Wolf. Sad though it may be, we, as a People, must change. The day is over when the Comanche could roam this great land unchecked. We must bend or break. There are no other choices."

"I know. The White Eyes' numbers are too many, and ours too few. It does no good to kill one of them when a hundred more are ready to take their place."

"Then why do you not leave us, go to your sister and . . ."

"Are you trying to rid yourself of me?"

"You know me better," she replied. "I think only of your welfare."

"Then stop it." He took her hand in his. "I never told you, Star Woman, but I swore on the life of my beloved to always hate the White Eyes."

"And was your beloved a vengeful woman?"

"Of course not! She was the kindest, sweetest, most loving . . ." He broke off, realizing he had fallen into Star Woman's trap.

"Such a woman would rejoice in life," she said softly.

He swallowed hard.

"She would feel great sadness for you, my son, if she knew how you cling to your hatred, how you embrace it so desperately and push every chance of happiness aside."

"You have been my mother for eleven summers, Star Woman. And, never, in all those years, have you ever spoken to me this way. Why now? What has loosened your tongue so much that you use it to chastise your son?"

"These old eyes are not blind. They saw the way you looked at *Ma-be-quo-si-tu-ma,* when you brought her here. Your desire is obvious." When he opened his mouth to protest, she quickly silenced him. "No. Do not worry. It is obvious only to me and this old woman's tongue is silent."

"Silent?" he asked wryly.

"My tongue knows how to remain silent when it suits my purpose. None except myself knows what I have seen. I speak as a mother to a son. You desire the paleface woman. And, it is possible that, if you lived in the world of the White Eyes, you could find happiness with her."

"No. That is impossible. Even if you were right about my feelings for the paleface, I would never live among the White Eyes."

"Your revenge is like a hot flame burning within your soul. But, surely you realize that if the flames of revenge are not carefully tended, they could spread unchecked until you are destroyed."

"Your words are wise," he said roughly.

"Yet they go unheeded," she said, her lips twisting into a rueful smile.

"Yes," he admitted. "They *do* go unheeded. As they must." He uncurled his long legs and straightened himself to his full height. "I have lingered here too long. The other hunters will be waiting for me."

"There will be no hunt this day."

He raised a dark brow. "No hunt? Why not?"

"Our *shaman,* Red Dog, returned in the night."

Red Dog. So he had returned. Now the council was complete. "Does the council meet today?"

She nodded, meeting his eyes with a long look. "You must make a decision quickly, my son. *Ma-be-quo-si-tu-ma's* life is in your hands."

"Her life will not be forfeited," he said sharply. "She will be used for exchange."

"For Cloud Dancer."

"Yes."

"And if the White Eyes do not agree to the exchange? Will her life be forfeited then?"

"Her life will not be forfeited," he growled. "The soldiers will agree to our terms."

She remained silent, but her eyes spoke volumes.

Spotted Wolf was on the verge of leaving the lodge when he suddenly remembered Jennifer's torn shirt. "The woman needs clothing."

"I imagined she would," Star Woman said. "I have a doeskin dress stored in my chest that I made long ago. It was meant to be a gift for your wife. But since you have not found a bride . . ." Her voice trailed away and she sighed deeply, as though despairing of him ever finding a wife.

And she was probably right. Since the death of his beloved, Spotted Wolf had wanted no other woman.

Until now.

But Jennifer was not for the likes of him. Instead, her destiny lay in another direction. She would find a husband among her people who would love her. A man who would prize her above all things.

Somehow, that thought caused a curious longing in Spotted Wolf who refused to acknowledge the feeling. To do so might weaken his resolve to remain uninvolved.

Spotted Wolf's emotions were under tight control when he joined the others in the council lodge.

When Major Carlisle heard the knock announcing Clara Boseley's arrival at post headquarters, he pushed aside the papers he had been studying. "Enter," he said.

The young woman entered slowly, urged forward by her father, Sergeant Major Samuel Boseley. "Go on, Clara," he urged. "No need to be shy with the Major." He closed the door behind them and wrapped his arm around her shoulders to give her courage.

Major Carlisle smiled at her. "There's nothing to be afraid of, Clara. I just have a few more questions about the night Jennifer disappeared."

"Go on, Clara," her father urged. "Tell the Major everything you know about that night."

"All right," Clara looked across at the post commander, her eyes bright with unshed tears. "I should've told you everything before, Major Carlisle. But I was afraid of what would happen to me."

Carlisle frowned and leaned forward to study her intently. "You deliberately held something back, Clara? Why would you do that?"

"I was afraid," she said again. "Afraid of what would happen to me."

"But you're willing to tell me now?"

She nodded her head. "I don't know much, though. Not really."

"Tell me anyway, Clara. Tell me everything you

remember, no matter how unimportant it may seem, about that night."

"Well," Clara began. "Jennifer had overheard One Eye and Lieutenant Carter arrange a meeting at Leaning Rock after taps. She thought it sounded suspicious and decided to investigate. She was gone more than two hours, and when she came back I went straight home."

Major Carlisle frowned at her. "Did she say anything about what took place at the meeting?"

"Just that her suspicions were correct."

"Nothing else?"

"No," she muttered, lowering her eyes. "I guess it was because I was so angry with her."

"Angry? Because she went out?"

"Because I had to cover for her when you knocked on the door. I was terrified you would open the door and discover she was missing." She brushed the tears from her eyes. "I should've told you she wasn't there. I should have. But I didn't do it. And now something's happened to her. Something bad."

"There, there, my dear," Sergeant Major Boseley said, patting his daughter's shoulder. "You couldn't have known. Jennifer was stubborn. We all knew that." He looked across the desk at his commanding officer. "You don't blame Clara for what happened, do you Major? It's not her fault that Jennifer insisted on going out alone."

"No, it's not her fault," Major Carlisle said sharply. "Dry your tears now and go on home."

He waved the two of them out of his room and crossed to the window, staring out across the parade ground, his thoughts on his niece.

Major Carlisle had been aware of Jennifer's dislike for Lieutenant Carter for some time. Yet he had refused to listen to anything she had said concerning the man. He should have heard her out.

What could they have been up to? The lieutenant and One Eye. Why did they feel the need to meet in secret, away from the fort? What possible reason could they have had for the rendezvous?

He couldn't ask those questions of Jennifer. His niece had disappeared. He couldn't ask them of Lieutenant Carter. He had been killed that very same night. That left only One Eye.

One Eye, the Kiowa scout, who had left the fort three days ago, bound for Fort Clark with a message of grave importance to that fort's very existence.

Had they received that message? Or had One Eye simply destroyed it, knowing the fort that had been established on the banks of the Las Moras Creek would be at risk from the Comancheros who were, even now, gathering on the west side of the Rio Grande?

But why would One Eye destroy the message? How could he profit from such an act? Was he working with the Comancheros?

Suddenly everything made sense to the major. If One Eye *was* working with the Comancheros, which was very likely, then he was the one who'd been passing information about the rifle shipments to them.

Major Carlisle smiled grimly.

Yes. It all made sense now. It was Carter and One Eye who were the traitors. There must have been a disagreement between them, probably a distribution of money, and Carter had come out the loser.

Thirteen

Jennifer was trying to find a way to mend her torn garments when Star Woman entered the lodge carrying a soft doeskin dress decorated with blue beadwork. "I have brought you something to wear," the old woman said.

"How thoughtful," Jennifer exclaimed. "But how did you know . . ." She broke off, feeling a flush wash over her cheeks. It was obvious how the old woman knew her garments were in need of repair.

"You need feel no shame," Star Woman said gently. "The walls of our dwellings leave no room for privacy, but there are none who will speak to you of what they overheard."

Jennifer chose to ignore the old woman's words. "I appreciate the loan of the dress and will return it when my own clothing has been mended."

"The dress is a gift, Jennifer."

It was the first time the old woman had used her given name. And Jennifer was so pleased that she couldn't have stopped her smile even if she had tried. "I am grateful for the gift, Star Woman. It is a beautiful dress."

After donning the dress, Jennifer joined the women beneath the brush arbor. She took her seat beside Helen and picked up the grinding stone she considered hers, reaching for the dried fruit that was always kept close by.

Noticing the women were unusually quiet, she spoke in a lowered voice to Helen. "I suppose everyone is curious about what happened last night."

Helen looked confused for a moment, then said, "Last night? What happened last night?"

"I was talking about the fight that Spotted Wolf and . . ." She broke off and looked curiously at Helen. "I guess that's not the reason everyone is so quiet. What *is* happening anyway?"

"Nothing. Not yet anyway. But naturally we're all wondering what the council will decide about you."

"About me? What do you mean?"

"Didn't you know? Red Dog returned last night."

"I don't understand. Who is Red Dog?"

"Red Dog is the *shaman,* the medicine man. He is the tribe seer, and ventures off alone occasionally, so that his visions remain undisturbed. Everyone has been waiting for him to return to make the council complete. They'll decide what's to be done about you now. Nobody told you about it?"

"No." Jennifer looked at the council lodge, wondering what was going on inside.

When Spotted Wolf entered the council chamber, he took his usual place on Quanah's right, then settled back to await the last few arrivals.

Most of the council were comprised of older men. Except for Quanah, who was the war chief, and Spotted Wolf and Coyote Man, who were both lower chiefs.

Red Dog, who sat on Spotted Wolf's right, seemed inclined to engage in conversation after his long absence from the village. "I have heard about your journey to the fort," he said. "And how the snake spat its poison into your body. Your spirit guide must have been with you for you to recover so quickly."

"My spirit guide was most certainly helpful," Spotted Wolf replied. "As was the white captive, Jennifer Carlisle. It was she who cared for me when the venom set my body on fire." His words were deliberate; he was aware that he needed the *shaman's* vote for what must be done.

"Ummmm," Red Dog grunted noncommittally. "Is that the reason you gave orders that she remain untouched?"

"The care she gave me is only part of the reason, Red Dog. In a moment you will hear the whole of it."

Although the *shaman's* gaze was curious, he asked no more questions. Instead, he settled back to wait.

The pipe was lit, and after puffing twice on it, Quanah passed it on to Spotted Wolf, who puffed an equal number of times, then passed the pipe on to Red Dog. Soon the pipe had completed the circle. Then Quanah spoke.

"Spotted Wolf has only recently returned from Fort Davis where Cloud Dancer is being held prisoner. He will speak to you of what he learned there."

Rising to his feet, Spotted Wolf told them everything he'd seen while watching the fort. "The fort is well-defended. Guarded by two troops of Buffalo Soldiers and many troops of White Eyes. Their numbers are too many and ours too few. We could not hope to win such a battle. But there is no need to risk such an attack. We have something to bargain with. A white captive. She is related to the fort commander. If the council agrees, we will offer to exchange her for Cloud Dancer."

"Are you sure about the relationship between the white woman and the fort commander?" Quanah asked.

"She claimed the relationship herself. There would be no reason for her to lie."

"She might claim such a relationship to obtain better treatment for herself," one of the council members pointed out.

"That is true," Spotted Wolf agreed. "But the woman is intelligent enough to know we would discover the lie and punish her severely. No. She is not lying. Jennifer Carlisle . . ." He deliberately used her name, hoping they would see her as an individual, not just an object of exchange. ". . . told me her uncle, Major Walter Carlisle, will do everything in his power to see her safely returned to him."

"Then it should be easy to arrange for an exchange of prisoners," Quanah said abruptly.

"No!" Coyote Man cried out, leaping to his feet. "She cannot be allowed to leave here!"

Spotted Wolf glared at Coyote Man. Why was he trying to stop the exchange of prisoners? "An exchange is the only way," Spotted Wolf said coldly. "It is a way to get Cloud Dancer back without bloodshed."

"It is a way to reveal the whereabouts of our stronghold!" Coyote Man said grimly. "Surely every warrior here is aware of the danger of allowing her to leave. She has seen our village. Knows where it is located. She would lead the White Eyes here. How could we leave each day to hunt without fear that when we returned our families would be dead? Do none of you remember Pease River? Has everyone forgotten so soon?"

"Jennifer poses no threat to us," Spotted Wolf said harshly. "Even if she tried, she could not lead the soldiers to us. The plains are neverending, the land unchanging, and there are only a few landmarks to show the way. Certainly none a White Eyes would remember."

"I agree with Coyote Man," Three Fingers said. "The woman should not be allowed to leave here."

Spotted Wolf's gaze narrowed on the man. Now why was he siding with Coyote Man? Could it be because he still hoped to obtain Jennifer for himself? It wouldn't happen, Spotted Wolf silently vowed. "An exchange of prisoners makes more sense than an attack on the fort," he said heatedly.

But Coyote Man would not relent in his decision. "I say the woman should not be allowed to go free. Each of you have suffered in some way or another at the White Eyes' hands. What better revenge than to treat their woman in the same manner?"

"Your thirst for revenge could cost Cloud Dancer his life," Spotted Wolf said, glaring at the friend who opposed him.

The arguments continued, the words growing more heated with each passing moment. Finally Quanah rose to make his thoughts known.

"It is my belief that an exchange would be in the best interests of everyone concerned. Perhaps the White Eyes will be so grateful to have the woman back, unharmed, that they will leave us alone." When Coyote Man started to protest, Quanah raised a silencing hand.

"I know it does not sit well with some of you. But Spotted Wolf is right. There is no sense risking the lives of our warriors when another means is at hand. Our numbers are becoming fewer and fewer with each passing moon. I wish only to live in freedom, to hunt our land and live without fear. Returning the woman should prove our peaceful intentions, should make them aware that we will fight if we must, but would rather live in peace."

"We cannot trust the White Eyes to abide by an agreement!" Coyote Man said. "They speak of treaties, hoping to bind us to their reservation. Since there is game for us to hunt, they say they will allot each of us a portion of meat and vegetables. But the meat is rotten and the vegetables are spoiled. Every warrior here knows of their promises, of their lies. Their treaties are false, fashioned to serve themselves and not the People."

"All of us here have heard the lies of the white man," Quanah agreed. "But at the moment we are not concerned with them. At this time the council is only concerned with freeing Cloud Dancer while he still lives. And I believe, as Spotted Wolf does, that we must exchange the woman for him."

Everyone was silent, each man occupied with his own thoughts. But Spotted Wolf knew he had won. Quanah had made his decision and most would vote with him. Before the day was gone, a messenger would ride out, bound for the fort, carrying word of their proposal. The exchange would then be made. Cloud Dancer would return and Jennifer would be with her people again.

That thought caused a heaviness centered in Spotted Wolf's chest, a curious, inexplicable feeling of emptiness that could not be explained. He tried to ignore the feeling, but it lingered.

When he left the council, Spotted Wolf looked for Jennifer. She was working beneath the brush arbor with the other captive women. He studied her for a moment, noticing the way the sunlight glinted in her bright hair. She wore a beaded doeskin dress and, with her flesh tanned from long hours in the sun, could have passed for one of the People if not for the fiery hair that curled around her shoulders.

Suddenly, she looked up and their eyes met and held. Even from the distance that separated them, he imagined he could see a strange, faintly eager look flash in her eyes.

Did she know then? Had she been aware the council had gathered to decide her fate?

As he watched, she rose and came to him.

"Has the council made its decision?" she asked.

"Yes."

"Will my uncle be allowed to ransom me?"

"You will be used for exchange."

"Exchange?" She looked bewildered, even a little wary. "What do you mean?"

He tried to keep his voice free of emotion. "An offer to exchange prisoners will be made. We have you. They have Cloud Dancer."

"When?" she asked. "How soon will I be going home?"

"That decision has not yet been made. A messenger is leaving today, bound for Fort Davis. He will relay the message and wait for an answer to our proposal."

Her gaze was suddenly accusing. "But what happens if they don't agree to the exchange?"

"I am sure they will agree," he said with a certainty that he didn't really feel. "Unless there is something you are not telling me."

"No. It's just that my uncle lives by strict rules. And even if I am his niece, he may not agree to release your friend. But he would pay you gold. I am sure of that. He would pay a lot to get me back." Her gaze pleaded with him. "What will happen to me if they refuse to release Cloud Dancer?"

"Better not to think of such things," he said stiffly.

He left her quickly, unable to bear the expression of utter horror written on her face, brought about by his words.

Fourteen

As Jennifer returned to her place beneath the brush arbor, Spotted Wolf's meaning lingered. She reached for her grinding stone and dropped a few pecans into the rounded out space used for pulverizing the nuts.

"What did they decide?" Helen's voice was a whisper. "Are they gonna let your uncle ransom you?"

Jennifer leaned toward Helen, intent on making her aware of the council's decision, when suddenly the hair on her nape prickled and she looked up to see Three Fingers's wife, Carries A Stick, glaring furiously at her.

Although disturbed by the woman's obvious hatred, Jennifer turned her attention to Helen again. "They plan on using me for exchange, Helen. I just hope my uncle will agree to their proposal."

She suddenly became aware that all the women had fallen silent. Every eye was on her now, even Star Woman's, and none of them seemed the least bit friendly.

"What are they angry about, Helen?" she whispered.

Helen shrugged. "I heard Carries A Stick was madder than an old wet hen about Three Fingers makin' an offer for you. He *did* buy Sarah. But that shouldn't matter to nobody but his wife." Her fingers moved faster. "Be careful, Jenny. Don't give her any excuse to beat you."

Beat me? Jennifer looked at the stout stick laying beside Three Fingers's wife and controlled a shudder. She had almost forgotten how savage these people could be. But she shouldn't have. Not with Sarah's bruised flesh a constant reminder. Surely though, the woman wouldn't dare lay a finger on her. After all, if she belonged to anyone, wouldn't her owner be Spotted Wolf?

Even so, her fingers trembled as she worked. She flicked a quick look at Star Woman, but the woman's face was expressionless. It was obvious Jennifer could expect no help from her.

She looked at Sarah. The woman had drawn into herself again as she so often did. Jennifer wondered if Three Fingers would treat Sarah any better than Cruel One had treated her. She certainly hoped so.

Her thoughts flew to the fort, to her uncle. Would he agree to the Indians' proposal?

"I need to talk to you in secret." The voice was little more than a whisper and yet the words were clear enough.

Jennifer glanced quickly at Helen, believing her to be the speaker, but she seemed totally absorbed in her work.

Perhaps she'd only imagined the voice.

Jennifer turned to her work again, scooping up the mashed pecans and placing them in a large clay bowl that was already half-filled with ground fruit and meat.

"Meet me at the spring just before dark. Please, Jenny."

Realizing the voice belonged to Sarah, Jennifer

looked her way. But Sarah's face was lowered, her eyes on the dried meat she was pulverizing.

"Don't look this way, for God's sake!" Sarah whispered, her lips barely showing movement. "Don't let them know we're carryin' on this conversation."

Deciding Sarah was overly fearful, Jennifer looked up and found the Indian women watching the three captives, their eyes bright with suspicion.

A quick glance at Sarah's white, strained features sent a surge of pity washing over Jennifer. It was plain to see that she was in abject fear of the Comanche women.

Realizing she must distract their attention before Sarah's clumsy fingers got her in trouble, Jennifer nudged Helen. "Help me distract them," she whispered. "Sarah's scared out of her wits."

"And well she should be," Helen muttered. "Carries A Stick wields a heavy hand when she's angry." She raised her voice slightly. "If you're here long enough, Jenny, I'll show you how to make a comb out of porcupine quills."

"That would be nice," Jennifer said, using the grinding stone faster, careful to give every appearance of being hard at work. "I've seen Star Woman's and it is beautiful." She flicked a quick glance at Spotted Wolf's mother, hoping to see some hint of softening on the old woman's face. There was none.

The Indian women began to mutter among themselves, but Jennifer ignored them and continued with her plans to distract their attention from Sarah. "I can hardly wait to sleep in my own bed again, Helen. I won't ever complain about a cornshuck mattress again."

"Shush!" Helen's voice was a frantic whisper. "Don't say anything else, Jennifer! For the Lord's sake, be quiet."

"No talk!" Carries A Stick snapped. "Work faster, lazy woman!"

Realizing the woman was speaking to her, Jennifer looked up with a frown. "I am not lazy!" she snapped indignantly. "And I am already working just as fast as I can! Anyway, it is not up to you to chastise me!"

Jennifer looked at Star Woman for support, but to her utter astonishment, the old woman's face became mottled with rage.

"Be silent!" Star Woman snapped. "A slave is not allowed to insult her keepers."

Her keepers? Jennifer stared at her in confusion. What did Star Woman mean?

In Jennifer's confusion, she was caught off guard when Carries A Stick attacked her. Although she tried to defend herself, raising her arms to shield her face and head, the woman continued to club her viciously, shouting words that meant nothing to the defenseless woman she seemed intent on beating to death.

Oh, God, would she never stop?

Jennifer jerked aside and tried to dodge through the women, but they formed a tight circle and would not allow her through.

Although she tried to stay on her feet, Jennifer felt herself losing her balance, falling beneath the blows that continued to rain down on her until she could do nothing but lay on the ground, a cowering mass of pain.

Then suddenly the vicious blows stopped. Harsh voices sounded, but she couldn't separate the words, couldn't make any sense of them. She could only lay there, her ears ringing, the darkness hovering around her, ready to receive her into its welcoming arms.

She became aware of the silence first. Then she felt hands moving over her flesh. "Are you hurt badly, Jennifer?" a soft voice asked.

Opening dazed eyes, she stared up at Spotted Wolf. He couldn't have been the one who'd spoken though, because there was nothing soft about his expression. It was angry, absolutely thunderous.

"Are you hurt?" His lips moved with each word; he *had* spoken before.

When she didn't answer, but continued to stare at him, he turned to look at Carries A Stick and spoke again, harsh angry words that caused her to turn fearful. She backed away from him as Spotted Wolf scooped Jennifer into his arms.

"Put me down," she whispered shakily. "I can walk."

"No." His arms tightened, his hard muscles pressing against her bruised flesh, and she caught her bottom lip between her teeth to keep from crying out with pain.

Jennifer could feel the animosity directed at her by the other women and took comfort in his presence as his long strides carried her away from them.

As Spotted Wolf stooped to enter his lodge, Jennifer heard a shrill cry that was quickly muffled by a loud, angry voice. She twisted around, trying to see past Spotted Wolf's shoulder, but he was already pulling the hide flap down, shutting them off from the outside world.

Gently then, Spotted Wolf laid her on the sleeping mat and bent to examine her. "Your injuries are not serious," he said. "There are a few places where the skin has been scraped off. A poultice will help ease the pain. There is nothing I can do about the bruises, but they will heal in time." He moved away from her and opened one of the hide bags that contained dried herbs, took out a small amount and mixed it with water. Moments later he smeared it on her scraped arms and legs.

"Why did they attack me, Spotted Wolf?" she asked.

He frowned at her. "They do not approve of the council's decision."

"Then why didn't they beat them instead of me?"

"Because they could not. They took their frustration out on you. They are afraid, Jennifer. You must understand and forgive them."

"Even Star Woman was angry. I could see it in her eyes. And when they attacked me, she just stood back and let it happen."

He finished with her legs and began applying the ointment to the scratches on her face. "She is afraid too."

"Afraid of what?"

"Of allowing you to go free. They are all afraid you will remember how to find our stronghold and lead the soldiers back to us."

She looked away from him, unable to hold his gaze. "I couldn't find my way back here. You know that, Spotted Wolf. There were no landmarks to guide me across the plains. I know, because I . . ." She broke off, afraid that she'd revealed too much.

"You know because you were watching for them. For some landmark to use in your journey home. I was aware of that."

Confusion swept over her. "And it didn't worry you?"

"Why should it? If I thought you recognized enough of the landscape to guide you back home, you would not be allowed to roam freely. You cannot escape here, Jennifer. You would die on the plains if you tried."

"Maybe I'd prefer death to captivity," she muttered.

"Do not say that! You have not been mistreated here, Jennifer. I have seen to that."

"How can you say that to me now?" she cried. "I've just been beaten within an inch of my life. And you say I haven't been mistreated."

He scowled down at her. "The beating was nothing compared to what usually happens to captives. Consider the other white captives' circumstances before you whine about being mistreated."

Jennifer felt ashamed of herself. He was right. "At least Sarah didn't get in trouble again," she muttered. "Carries A Stick is always looking for an excuse to beat her. Spotted Wolf?" She curled her fingers around his forearm. "Would you consider buying Sarah from Three Fingers?"

"He offered her to me, Jennifer, but I refused the offer."

"Would you please reconsider then? I could see that you are reimbursed for any monies when my uncle ransoms me."

"His price was not gold, Jennifer."

"Then what was it? Horses? Rifles? Horses could be bought with gold, but I don't think my uncle would agree to rifles." Her look was pleading. "But surely you understand and would . . ."

"Not rifles or horses, Jennifer. You!"

Her body stiffened in shock. "Me?" she squeaked.

"You," he repeated, his green eyes glittering. "But you should not be surprised. He has made several offers for you since we arrived in the village. I thought you were aware of that."

"Yes, but . . . I guess I thought he had finally given up."

"No." He was silent for a long moment. "Three

Fingers voted against your release, Jennifer. He will
bear watching. Make sure you are never left alone
with him."

"How much longer must I stay here, Spotted
Wolf?"

"There is no way to answer that question. Everything depends on your uncle now. If he agrees to
our proposal, you could be home before another
week has passed."

"Another week," she murmured. "Just another
week to hold out."

"You are anxious to return." He touched her
cheek in a wistful gesture, then looked away, his pro-
file rugged and somber. There had been something
in his voice that caught her attention, a hint of sadness perhaps.

Did he harbor any regrets about her leaving? She
realized that she would miss him. That admission
was dredged from a place beyond logic and reason,
yet she knew it was so, and wondered how it could
be. What was there about him that attracted her
when none of the soldiers at the fort had appealed
to her?

Realizing the direction her thoughts had traveled,
she mentally shook herself and lowered her lashes
to hide herself from his mesmerizing gaze. "W-would
you like me to make you something to eat?" she
asked.

"No. I am not hungry." His voice was grim as he
turned away from her, muttering in a low voice.

"What did you say?" she asked, her voice showing
her confusion.

"Nothing."

Why was he lying to her? she wondered. He *had*
spoken. His words had been uttered in a low voice,

as though he hadn't intended her to hear him. But they made no sense. Not one bit.

She considered them carefully, turning them over and over in her mind. *Not for food anyway,* he'd said. Now what did he mean by that?

Fifteen

The beating Jennifer had received left her exhausted. She lay on the sleeping mat, her knees drawn up like a babe in its mother's womb and allowed her mind to flee from reality. Moments later she was fast asleep.

It was late when she woke; the interior of the lodge was dense with shadows. She felt an immediate sense of urgency, of something important left undone. It nagged at the corners of her mind as she uncurled the length of her body and pushed herself to her elbows.

What had she forgotten to do? What was this nagging urgency she felt?

She searched the dwelling for some clue, but none was forthcoming. But as her gaze swept over the blackened smoke hole and she saw the clouds painted crimson from the setting sun, the feeling became stronger, even more urgent. Its cause remained elusive, unknown to her.

Her gaze swept the lodge again as she fought the cobwebs of confusion. Nothing was out of order. The chest was over there. And the hide bags were stacked beside it. Next came the basket of root vegetables that she'd dug yesterday and then . . . *Wait!* her mind screamed as her gaze returned to the bas-

ket of vegetables. That was it! The evening meal
must be prepared.

Even as the confusion lifted, she realized the urgency was still with her. The sense of something important left undone.

Not the meal then. But what? She didn't know.

Still, the meal must be prepared.

With that in mind, Jennifer pushed herself to her
feet, then stood there, swaying dizzily, unable to
move, afraid the threatening darkness would descend around her.

Slowly the world righted itself and she was able
to move again, slowly though, because any attempt
at quick movement brought on the dizziness again
and caused her head to pound, to throb.

Jennifer reached for the vegetables, noticing the
water jug was empty. She would have to fetch water
from the spring before she prepared the vegetables.

The spring? Oh, God! The spring! She had to
meet Sarah at dusk. Why? What was so important
that would cause Sarah to risk a beating . . . the
beating that Jennifer had received?

She winced in memory and the pain returned
with a vengeance. The scratches on her arms and
face stung, and the bruises on her flesh seemed even
more tender than just a moment ago.

Ignoring the aches, Jennifer scooped the water
jug into her arms and left the dwelling. She was
unprepared for the harsh light that seemed so
bright even though the sun was setting in the west.

She blinked several times, then noticed that several of the women who occupied nearby lodges had
stopped preparations for their evening meals to
watch her.

Ignoring them, Jennifer crossed the compound
and took the trail through the woods that led to the

spring. She had only gone a short way when she saw Helen approach with a water jug in her arms.

Helen's strides quickened suddenly. "Jennifer!" she exclaimed, her expression anxious. "I'm so glad to see you! I was so afraid for you. I think Carries A Stick was trying to beat you to death. And the other women! I can't believe they turned on you like that!" Her gaze lingered on her friend's bruises. "Are you in much pain?"

"It could have been worse," Jennifer admitted. "At least my bones are still intact." She looked at Helen's water jug. It was full. "Is Sarah at the spring?"

Helen's expression clouded. "No." She shook her head. "She's not there. And she won't be for awhile, Jenny. Not for a few days anyways."

Jennifer frowned at her. "How do you know that?" she asked. "Has something happened to her?"

"I'm afraid so. Carries A Stick was so furious Spotted Wolf stopped her from beating you that she attacked Sarah, the minute the two of you disappeared into his lodge. She didn't stop until Sarah was unconscious."

"Oh my God!" Jennifer was so shocked that she dropped the water jug. It clattered to the ground and rolled down the path, unnoticed by either woman.

"It was awful, Jenny. There was nothing I could do to help her. If I had tried, they'd have turned on me and both of us would have been beaten senseless."

"Do you know how badly she was hurt?"

"Bad enough that she couldn't walk. She lay there for several hours in the sun, not moving at all, but nobody paid attention to her. Finally though, Three

Fingers came along and carried her off to his lodge. I haven't heard a sound out of any of his bunch since then."

"We must find a way to help her, Helen."

"How?" Helen asked. "We can't even help ourselves, Jennifer."

"But we're not as bad off as she is. She's been beaten so long that she's not strong enough to withstand it for much longer."

"Maybe he'd trade her."

"He offered her to Spotted Wolf."

"Maybe that's the way then. You could talk Spotted Wolf into trading for her. He ought to feel some compassion for her, him being who he is and all."

"What do you mean?"

Helen looked curiously at her. "You really don't know? Haven't you noticed his green eyes?"

"Of course I have. I know he must be a half-breed. But he was obviously raised with the Comanches."

"A half-breed?" Helen's brows lifted. "Jennifer, don't you know about Spotted Wolf? He has a sister that . . ." Suddenly she broke off, her eyes widening as she focused on something beyond Jennifer's left shoulder.

Turning quickly, Jennifer saw Spotted Wolf watching them with a peculiar intensity. "Did you lose something, Jennifer?" he asked quietly.

"Lose something?"

When he indicated the water jug that lay at his feet, she hastened to explain. "I'm afraid I tripped over a rock and dropped it." Her tongue stumbled over the lie, but instead of commenting, he bent over and retrieved the water container.

He strode forward, remaining silent, yet watchful, his presence almost overwhelming both women.

Helen began to back away from them, her gaze flickering from one to the other.

"Well, I guess I'd better go now. I'll see you tomorrow, Jennifer." The words were no sooner uttered before Helen hurried down the trail toward the village.

Jennifer turned her attention to Spotted Wolf. "You frightened Helen," she said.

"She told you about Sarah," he said quietly.

"Yes. She told me what happened. And she told me Sarah wouldn't survive many more beatings like that one." Tears moistened her eyes. "Isn't there something you can do, Spotted Wolf?"

"Three Fingers owns her, Jennifer."

"But she is only property to him. And he apparently doesn't consider her of much value or he wouldn't allow her to be treated so badly. Couldn't you offer him something for her?"

"I only have one thing he wants. You. And he knows he cannot have you."

"You could ask him. He might consider something else." When he didn't answer, she said, "Please, Spotted Wolf. Would you at least try? For me?"

"Does Sarah mean so much to you?"

"I wouldn't want to see a dog treated the way she is," she replied.

"No," he agreed. "You have a tender heart, Jennifer. If you are not careful, it will land you into dangerous waters."

"It already has," she said.

"So it has." He nodded his dark head. "I owe you for my life. And because of that, I will make an offer for your friend."

"Thank you, Spotted Wolf."

He curled his fingers around her forearm. "Come

with me now. I have something to show you." He
led her down a path that veered to the right.

They'd only gone a short distance when she heard
the sound of rushing water and moments later, they
emerged into a small clearing, a sunlight-dappled
glade, where a waterfall not more than six feet high
cascaded into a natural pool.

Her eyes widened with surprise. "Oh, how wonderful!" she exclaimed. "Why hasn't anyone mentioned there was such a pretty waterfall nearby? And
the pool! It's so clear I can see all the way to the
bottom."

Several children played in the water on the far
side of the pool, laughing and splashing each other.
But other than a few curious glances, they ignored
the man and woman who had come among them.

Spotted Wolf stepped past the fern growing in
such abundance and stopped. "Take off your dress,
Jennifer."

"My dress?"

"Unless you want to get it wet. We're going into
the pool."

"But I can't just . . . there are children here."

"And they are paying you no notice. If you are
too modest, then leave your undergarments on."
When she continued to hesitate, he sighed. "The
hide dress will take a long time to dry if you get it
wet, Jennifer."

Without waiting for her agreement, he stripped it
away and tossed it aside. "There now. That was not
so bad. And your modesty is still preserved. Now
take off your boots."

While she removed them, he discarded his moccasins, then they entered the water. It swirled
around Jennifer's knees and she sucked in a startled
breath. "It's deeper than it looks."

"Yes," he laughed, a deep, husky sound that made her feel warm all over.

He waded deeper into the water, pulling her along with him. She laughed as the cold water rose past her thighs, her hips, then swirled around her waist, continued rising with every step they took until it foamed beneath her breasts.

"It's getting colder."

"Because it is deeper," he replied.

"This is far enough," she protested. "It's getting too deep. I can't swim."

"Cannot swim?" His eyes glinted with humor as he gave a sharp tug on her hand and the bottom dropped out from under her.

"Spotted Wolf!" she cried out, throwing her arms around his neck and clinging tightly. "Take me back!" Her fear was tempered by the warmth spreading through her lower body as she felt the heat of him against her breasts.

A rumble beneath her ear startled her and she looked up to find him laughing at her, his green eyes twinkling in a way that she'd never seen before. Even his features looked softer.

She must have looked startled, because his laughter suddenly stilled and he looked at her questioningly.

"What is it?" he asked. "Why do you look at me in such a manner?"

"You seem different somehow," she said quietly.

"Different?" His arms tightened around her waist, pulling her lower body harder against him. "How do you mean?"

"I can't explain. But you seem almost human. Quite unlike . . ." Her voice trailed away. She'd almost said, *unlike a savage.* And she didn't think he'd like being referred to in that way.

"I am a man, Jennifer," he said. "And like most men, I enjoy the sight of a beautiful woman."

"And you find me . . . beautiful?"

"Yes. Very much so." His voice was a husky caress, and his palm moved slowly across her bare shoulder, sliding closer to her neck, gliding moistly over her creamy flesh, creating a delicious warmth that seeped through her.

Jennifer tilted her head slightly to allow him more access to skin that had been so fiery only a short time ago. "That feels good," she whispered.

"Does it?"

Jennifer was vaguely aware that the children's laughter had stilled. She looked across the pool to see a woman herding them toward the village. "It's getting late," she whispered.

"Yes," he agreed. "Late." His lips grazed her cheek, their eyes met and held for a long moment, and she saw something in his, a smoldering passion that caused her to lower her lashes.

What manner of man was this? she wondered. Why did he have such power over her? She had never experienced such yearning, such intense longing. She wanted desperately to know more about him.

Helen mentioned a sister. Perhaps if she could discover something about the sister, she would know more about the brother.

"You never speak of yourself, Spotted Wolf," she murmured, her eyes half-closed as she continued to enjoy the warmth of his touch. "Why is that? Is there some mystery about you?"

His movements stopped momentarily. "No mystery," he responded.

Although there was a sudden wariness about him that warned her not to proceed, she ignored that warning. "You never speak of your sister. Why is that? Where is she?"

His body tensed for a moment, then slowly relaxed again. He leaned over slightly and brushed her neck with his mouth. Her heart gave a sudden lurch and her eyes flew open.

"My sister need not concern you," he said hoarsely, his teeth grazing on her ear lobe.

She tried to ignore the shivers his lips were causing, tried hard to concentrate, but his mouth was so warm, so moist, and his eyes seemed glued to the swell of her breasts.

Looking down at herself, she realized what had claimed his attention. Her breasts were perfectly outlined by the wet fabric of her chemise. It showed everything, even her nipples which were taut, erect.

The heat of embarrassment stained her cheeks, and Jennifer knew she should release him and cover her breasts with her hands. But she couldn't. The water was too deep and she couldn't swim. If she released him, she would sink just as surely as a stone.

Never mind that his gaze caused a curious tingling inside her belly.

Never mind that his touch sent heat spreading through her.

Never mind that . . .

Her thoughts were abruptly interrupted when he lifted her slightly, nudged her wet chemise aside and closed his mouth over the taut bud of her right breast.

The shiver that was already deep inside her began to spread quickly as though it had become a wild fire, until it finally erupted in a deep groan.

Oh, God, she must stop him! She must stop him before he was out of control. But somehow, it was hard to organize her thoughts. They were so confused. How had this come about anyway? Why hadn't she tried to stop him before it went so far? They were talking and she had wanted to know something, but what?

His sister! Yes, that was it! She had wanted answers about his sister!

What had he said? The words were dim in her memory, hard to recapture. But eventually she had them within her grasp.

"W-Why d-don't you want to talk about her, Spotted Wolf?" she whispered shakily.

He released her nipple, lifted his head and looked at her with passion-glazed eyes. "What?" He seemed even more confused than she had been.

She repeated her question. "Why don't you want to talk about your sister? There seems to be some mystery surrounding both of you."

"My sister has nothing to do with me," he said, his eyes glittering like emeralds. "There are only a few of the *Quohadi* who know of her."

"Why?" Her voice held a note of exasperation. "Where is she?"

"She lives far away from here. In the world of the White Eyes."

"Alone?"

"No. With a man called Pecos Smith." His eyes changed suddenly, became the color of a stormy sea. "Why are you asking so many questions? My sister is of no concern to you."

"I just wondered about her," she said, lowering her eyes to avoid his gaze.

"She is not someone that I speak often about."

To Jennifer's disappointment, he put her down, then turned away from her, making his way toward the distant bank, making her wish that she hadn't persisted with her questions. She had destroyed his playful mood.

He slid his moccasins on his feet. "It is past time we returned," he said, reaching for the hide dress and tossing it toward her.

"Of course," she said. "I have the meal to prepare yet." She struggled to pull the hide dress over her wet undergarments.

"And the water to fetch," he reminded. Suddenly he seemed to realize that night was almost on them and that they were quite alone. "I suppose I must accompany you to the spring now."

She tried to find a hint of the softness that had been there only a short time ago. There was no sign of it now. He had reverted to a man who had not a whit of kindness in him. A man to be feared.

She recognized his impatience to be away from her. "There's no need for you to go with me," she said stiffly. "The path is beaten down enough so there's no way I could get lost."

He seemed to hesitate for a moment.

"Go on," she insisted, even while she hated herself for doing so. "You know I can't run away. There's no place to run to. And there's plenty of time to fetch the water and return to the village before dark."

"Very well," he grumbled, turning away from her. "There is a path on the other side of the pool leading to the spring. Just follow it and the distance will be shortened by half."

She nodded abruptly. "I won't be long."

Regretfully, Jennifer watched him walk away from her and disappear into the densely wooded thicket of cedar trees.

Her thoughts were troubled as she headed for the

spring Spotted Wolf had said was only a short distance away.

How could he so easily dismiss what had occurred between them when her own body was still flushed from the heat of desire?

For awhile, she had actually thought he might have been attracted to her.

What a fool she had been! Oh, God, what a fool!

Spotted Wolf was too cold to become emotionally involved with any woman. She didn't know how he'd come to be that way, only knew that it was so. But that didn't stop him from desiring her. And he had felt that way toward her. She knew he had. It was something that he couldn't keep hidden from her. But it had only been that. Desire. That knowledge caused a curious knot of pain to lodge beneath her breast.

Uncle Walter! she silently cried. *Come for me quickly, or it may be too late!*

Sixteen

A dark crimson color stained the western horizon as the column of soldiers rode through the gates of the fort. And Major Carlisle watched them arrive, knowing by the dejected slump of their shoulders and the haggard looks on their faces that the latest attempt to find his niece had come to naught.

A moment later, Captain Brady stood before him, saluting smartly. "I'm sorry, Major," he said. "There was no sign of her." He looked toward the stockade. "Did you talk to Cloud Dancer again?"

The Major nodded. "He maintains that he knows nothing about her."

"Maybe he doesn't. But he sure as hell knows where the Comanche stronghold is. If you make him talk, we might find Jennifer before it's too late."

Major Carlisle sighed heavily. "I've been trying to make the man talk since we took him captive, but he refuses to say a word."

"There's ways of making a man talk," the captain said grimly.

"I refuse to torture the man, Captain Brady. Anyway, I'm not so sure it would any good." He frowned heavily. "He was already locked up when Jennifer disappeared. I'm more inclined to believe

One Eye had something to do with her disappearance."

A shout caught their attention. "Major!" It was the guard posted at the gate. "Somebody's ridin' in hard! Looks like an Injun!"

"Alone?" Major Carlisle asked, striding quickly across the compound.

"Looks like it," the guard replied, tightening his grip on his rifle.

"Easy, Private," Major Carlisle cautioned, climbing the wooden steps leading to the guard rail. "It might be One Eye returning." That thought caused his heartbeat to quicken. If the man was the Kiowa scout, maybe he would have some answers to his questions.

"It ain't One Eye," the guard said. "He rode out on a paint. This Injun's ridin' a buckskin. Look! He's raisin' a white flag. Now I wonder what in hell he wants."

"Let him in, Private. But keep that rifle of yours ready in case he's up to something."

"Yes, Sir!"

Major Carlisle descended to the parade ground to await the arrival of the Indian.

The purple shadows had lengthened while Jennifer was at the spring. Night was only minutes away.

"I shouldn't have stayed to gather watercress," she muttered, scowling at the greens she clutched in her left hand.

At least the path was clearly defined, easy enough to follow, and she wasn't really alone either. There had been another woman at the spring when she'd left. Jennifer had thought about waiting for her, but had quickly dismissed the idea when she remembered the hostility directed at her only a few short hours ago.

Her thoughts were interrupted as the shadows ahead shifted slightly. Was something there? Her heart began a slow, rhythmic thudding and she searched the area ahead, detecting nothing unusual in the green forest.

Lifting her gaze, Jennifer studied the multicolored cliffs that surrounded the valley. Deep red, satiny white, lavender, yellow, salmon pink, orange, and pale green, the most intense earth colors she had ever seen before. They lay one above another in precise horizontal bands. It was a magnificent prison she found herself in, and yet, it was still a prison.

That fact was abruptly brought to her attention when suddenly a man whose footsteps had been muffled by a thick carpet of grass stepped into her path and confronted her.

Jennifer stared at him, alarm sweeping over her as she recognized Three Fingers. He strode toward her, his flat, black eyes expressionless, as was his countenance. His lank, stringy dark hair fell over his broad shoulders.

Oh, God, what was he doing here?

He kept to the path, making it obvious that Jennifer would have to leave it in order to pass him. She did so quickly, but he moved to block her way. "Please allow me to pass," she said quietly. Even if he didn't understand English, surely he would know her meaning.

A crackling sound caused Jennifer to spin around. She'd hoped to see Spotted Wolf standing behind her, and was disappionted to see it was only the young woman who'd been filling her jug at the spring.

Before Jennifer could react, Three Fingers grabbed

Jennifer's wrist. "No!" she cried, her voice tight with fear. "Let me go!" Her fear loosened her grip on the water container and the watercress. The jug clattered to the ground, spilling the water onto the greens now soaking in the grass at their feet.

Three Fingers spoke harshly in his own language and the young woman, intimidated, scuttled quickly down the path toward the village.

"Don't go!" Jennifer cried. But it was no use. Her words only sent the young woman fleeing quicker down the path toward safety.

Jennifer struggled to break free of his grip, but it was no use. He was too strong. "Turn me loose!" she snapped, trying to control her fear.

"Be silent!" he snarled, twisting her arm cruelly. His black eyes gleamed with malice, yet there was something possessive too.

"I will not be silent!" she screamed. "Leave me alone!" Her heart thumped wildly as she fought to free herself but his grip was too strong, his strength too great.

He pulled her farther from the path, steadily drawing her into the heavy growth of trees where the shadows of night were too dense to penetrate.

She fought against her rising panic. "What do you want from me?"

When he twisted her arm again, she screamed out with pain. He reacted instantly, covering her mouth with one hand while the other continued to drag her into the woods. Her fear was almost overwhelming now, and Jennifer knew she must find a way to stop him before it was too late.

She kicked out wildly, hitting his shinbone. Although he grunted with pain from the blow, his hold on her wrist remained just as strong and cruel. Even so, Jennifer wouldn't give up. She couldn't.

Not while there was a breath left in her body. She continued to kick out at him. When her foot connected with his shinbone again, he retaliated immediately, balling up his fist and clubbing her against the side of her head.

Although the blow set her ears ringing, Jennifer refused to stop fighting. She lashed out again with her foot, and this time her blow struck him squarely in the softness between his legs.

"Ugggg!" he grunted, releasing her so abruptly that she lost her balance and fell to the ground.

After one quick look at him, Jennifer leapt to her feet and raced away as fast as her legs would carry her. His expression had changed, had become a mask of hate. And she had no intention of waiting around to see what he'd do next.

Jennifer continued to run, blindly, desperately. Even though she knew it was useless, there was no where in this canyon she could possibly find refuge, she could not stop. She could not. She knew that if Three Fingers caught her, she would be ravished.

Oh, God, don't let it happen! she cried inwardly.

She could hear footsteps thundering behind her, could hear him crashing through the underbrush as he began to pursue her.

Please, please, please, the inner voice pleaded, keeping time with her thudding heart.

Then suddenly his cruel fingers twined through her hair and her flight came to an abrupt halt. She cried out, pain blurring her vision. "No, no!" she screamed wildly, lashing out with her fists, hoping against hope that she would connect with some part of him that was weak, that she could somehow free herself.

But it was not to be.

His grip tightened painfully, and Jennifer was almost certain some of her hair had been torn out of her head. She gritted her teeth, trying to endure the agony in silence.

Then suddenly she heard a roar behind them.

At first Jennifer thought a bear was attacking. Even that would be preferable to the treatment Three Fingers had in store for her.

Finding herself abruptly released, Jennifer sank to the ground, her legs too weak to support her weight. Her breath came in quick gasps as she tried to gather her strength about her again. It was a relief to be free from the intense pain in her scalp, yet her fear was so great that she found only a small measure of relief in that fact.

She lay quietly on the ground, aware that a battle was being waged only a few feet away, and that she must take flight before it came to an end. That knowledge brought her to her feet again.

As she looked toward the sounds of battle, Jennifer's eyes widened with surprise. It was no bear that fought with Three Fingers. It was another warrior.

Spotted Wolf!

Relief swelled through her, but it was short-lived when she saw Three Fingers reach for his knife and swing it in an upward arc, aiming it toward Spotted Wolf's stomach. Had the weapon struck its mark, Spotted Wolf would have been disemboweled. But he reacted swiftly, leaping aside, his movements as lithe as a panther. He spun around, and with a movement almost too swift for the eye to follow, sent his foot upward, striking his opponent beneath the wrist that held the knife.

With a yowl of pain, Three Fingers opened his hand and the knife dropped into the high grass. Spotted Wolf quickly took advantage, striking the

other warrior a hard blow on the nose, crunching
it beneath his fist.

Three Fingers's eyes watered from the pain. Spotted Wolf wound his hand through his opponent's
hair and struck him in the face again. It was a hard
blow that would have knocked Three Fingers to the
ground if Spotted Wolf hadn't been holding him
upright.

Quickly, Spotted Wolf lashed out again, striking
Three Fingers over and over again until Jennifer
was forced to look away from them. Then suddenly,
with a grunt of disdain, Spotted Wolf released the
other warrior, allowing him to slide to the ground.

Three Fingers lay there for a moment, huddled
in the dirt, while Spotted Wolf stared at him coldly.
Then Spotted Wolf turned to Jennifer.

"Look out!" Jennifer cried.

The words had barely left her mouth when Three
Fingers sprang toward Spotted Wolf, the knife blade
raised high in his hand. Jennifer saw Spotted Wolf
spin aside from the deadly blade, and with an almost
casual movement, kick out, connecting with his opponent's belly. Three Fingers pitched backward,
striking the ground heavily and lay there, unmoving,
either unconscious or too weak to move.

Spotted Wolf turned his back on the other man,
and reaching out a long arm, he snared Jennifer's
wrist between his hard fingers. She opened her
mouth to speak, but the look on his face silenced
her.

"Come with me!" he growled, pulling her toward
the trail that led toward the village.

She wondered at his rage as she scuttled along
behind him. He was obviously furious, but whether
his anger was directed toward her or the man he'd
just fought, she had no way of knowing.

His pace didn't slacken as he hurried toward the village. Not until they reached the edge of the encampment. Only then did his pace slow enough to allow her to catch her breath.

"Go now!" he said suddenly. "Do not leave the lodge until you have my permission."

"What about the water?" she asked hesitantly. "I dropped the jug and the watercress I gathered to go with our meal."

"I will go back for it."

"Why are you angry with me? I didn't have anything to do with what happened."

"I did not suppose you did," he said, his voice softening slightly. "My anger is not with you, Jennifer. If anyone is to blame, it is me. I should not have left you alone when it was so late."

She felt a warm glow spread through her. "You have no need to blame yourself. I insisted that you go ahead."

He looked away from her then, back the way they had come. "Take care not to be alone again," he said huskily. "Three Fingers will blame you for what happened. And he will not forget the humiliation he suffered from the beating. If Yellow Moon had not seen you struggling with him, the results could have been quite different."

"Yellow Moon?" Jennifer remembered the young woman who had passed them on the trail. "So that's how you knew. I was afraid she would keep silent about what she had seen."

"Yellow Moon knows better than anyone else how important it is for you to remain unharmed."

"I don't understand."

"She is Cloud Dancer's chosen bride."

His words were like a cold dash of ice water. Spotted Wolf was keeping her safe so that she could be used for an exchange.

She turned away from him and headed for the lodge that was her prison cell.

Watching Jennifer walk away, Spotted Wolf silently chastised himself for his words. If they could have been recalled, he would gladly have done so. But they could not be, and perhaps, he told himself, he had been wise to remind her that she would soon be exchanged for Cloud Dancer.

Despite his great efforts to control his feelings, Jennifer had found a way into his heart. And he could not allow that to happen. She was a paleface, the enemy. He must remember that always. He would never forgive the White Eyes for what they had done.

Never!

He thought about the past, forced himself to remember the smallest details so that he could feed on the rage the memories brought with them. But somehow, the rage seemed no more than mere anger, not nearly as strong as it once had been, when the pain had been so new.

And it *had* been a long time.

Twenty years.

But I vowed to remember forever! he silently cried. *I vowed to make the White Eyes pay for your life!*

As though she had only been waiting for his silent cry, Laughing Water's face appeared in his memory. Her long, dark hair framed her delicate features and her laughing ebony eyes smiled up at him the way they had so many times in the past.

But only for the merest moment.

The memory of her face changed abruptly, became again as it had appeared when he'd found her, drained of blood, almost of life itself. And her eyes, those laughing dark eyes were somber, filled with such pain, such sadness for what might have been.

He felt the pain anew as his memory recalled the way she'd been after the trapper had finished with her. Broken, pale, her life blood slowly draining away, leaving her limp, broken.

The fury he had sought only moments before surged forth. And it felt good to him. He reveled in that rage, fed on it.

Yes. It felt good.

It reminded him of his duty. He had softened toward the captive, actually took pleasure from her body. But that was over now. He would not forget again, neither would he forgive.

I will remember, he silently vowed, raising his mutilated hand before his face and staring at the place where his little finger had once been. It throbbed with each beat of his heart.

I will remember my promise, Laughing Water. The White Eyes will pay for what they did to you, my love. I will make sure of that!

Seventeen

It was late when Spotted Wolf returned to the lodge. Jennifer was almost asleep when she heard him enter. She sat up quickly, shoving her tousled hair back from her face. "Did you eat with Star Woman again tonight?" she asked.

"No." He hung the bow he carried on a lodge pole near the sleeping mat and dropped a quiver of arrows beneath it. Then he turned to look at her, his expression shadowed by darkness.

For some reason his look made her uneasy and she scrambled quickly off the bed of hides. "I made rabbit stew for the evening meal," she said. "I left it warming over the banked coals outside the lodge. Would you like some?"

He nodded abruptly.

His continued silence made her nervous. "I don't respond well to long silences," she said shortly, hiding her apprehension beneath the guise of anger. "And don't expect me to jump out of bed to serve you every time you choose to stay out late!"

Although she expected her words to provoke a reply, none was forthcoming. What was the matter with him anyway? Had something happened since she had left him? He was too quiet, too wary, and for some reason that bothered her.

After filling a bowl with thick rabbit stew, she entered the lodge again to find him seated, cross-legged, on the earthen floor. Moonlight filtered through the smoke hole above, making it easier to see his expression, yet that brought her little satisfaction. There was a stern, grim look about him. Cold, implacable, as though he had come to some kind of decision that might not be acceptable to those around him.

His expression caused her apprehension to deepen. Something was amiss to cause him to appear so grim. And she would not rest until she knew what it was.

Needing answers to her questions, she handed them to him with the bowl of stew. "Has something happened that you haven't told me about?"

He paused in the act of scooping a mouthful of meat into his mouth. "I am sure many things happen that you are unaware of. But they do not concern you in any way."

"Something does concern me!" she snapped. "I knew it the moment you entered the lodge. It has changed your attitude toward me." Her accusing voice stabbed the air.

"You imagine things." He turned his attention to his meal, brushing away her questions as though they were of no more consequence than a fly on the wall.

Jennifer shot him a cold look, wondering why he was evading her question, knowing that something *had* happened to change him. But what could it be? Whatever it was, he obviously had no intention of explaining himself. Instead, he finished eating, then set the bowl aside, completely ignoring her presence.

But Jennifer refused to be ignored. "Do you want another bowl of stew?"

"No."

A heavy silence fraught with tension settled around them, but Jennifer tried hard to ignore it. There was every possibility that her uncertainties, her fears, had made her imagine something that wasn't really there.

"I'm too tired to worry about it now anyway," she muttered.

She gathered up the used utensils and stacked them with the dirty bowls beside the water jug. Since it was so late, she would leave them overnight.

Sighing heavily, Jennifer stretched out on the sleeping mat and stifled a yawn. Through the dense shadows, Jennifer watched him leave the earthen floor and step into the moonlight streaming through the smoke hole at the top of the lodge. The sight of him caused her fear to rise anew. She hadn't been imagining things.

The change in his expression was drastic. It was hard, cold, and his eyes were dark, dazzling with rage. The man who'd taken her to the waterfall had completely disappeared. In his place was the fierce warrior, the man who had taken her captive only a short time ago.

She felt weak and vulnerable, in the face of his fury. Oh, God! What caused him to change that way? What could have happened?

He unfastened his breechcloth and dropped it to the ground, exposing the maleness of his body, and she turned quickly away, her cheeks flushed with color.

Jennifer waited quietly, trembling, very much aware of him. The rushes rustled beneath the sleeping mat as he stretched out beside her. When his bare thigh brushed against hers, she reacted as though she'd been stabbed, jerking away from the contact.

"Go to sleep," he snarled.

Squeezing her eyes shut, Jennifer tried to do exactly that. But sleep refused to come. Questions tormented her. Finally, the need to have answers outweighed her fear, and she could no longer keep silent. "Why won't you tell me what's happened, Spotted Wolf?"

"Why do you continue your questions when I have already answered them?" His curt, impatient voice lashed at her.

His tone aroused her anger. "Because you didn't answer them!" she snapped, rising up on one elbow to stare down at him. "You keep saying nothing has happened when I know damn well it has! You're different than you were at the waterfall and you . . ."

"Is that what this is all about?" he asked harshly, digging his fingers into her shoulders. "Is it your wish to continue where we left off?"

She stared at him wide-eyed, feeling as though she had unleashed a tiger. "N-No," she stuttered. "Of course not!"

"Then what do you want?"

"I just want to know why you're treating me this way. You seemed almost compassionate before. Sympathetic. You seemed to care about my feelings then." She paused momentarily, then asked, "Was I completely wrong?"

"I hold no sympathy for the White Eyes."

"Not even one who saved your life?"

"You need not remind me, Jennifer. I have been aware of the debt I owe you. But the events of today should void the debt."

"I never considered a debt to be something that is owed," Jennifer said stiffly.

"Yet you constantly remind me."

"I don't mean to. No. That's not true. But you must understand that you're the only hope I have of coming out of this alive." She expelled a heavy sigh. "Since you considered the debt repaid when you saved me from Three Fingers, does that mean you won't offer your protection anymore?"

"Three Fingers has nothing to do with this," Spotted Wolf replied. "There were many at the council who spoke against the exchange of prisoners. They preferred to attack the fort and force the bluecoats to release Cloud Dancer."

"But that would never work!" Jennifer protested. "There are too many troopers stationed at Fort Davis!" Fear for his safety loosened her tongue. "You don't have enough warriors here, even if every brave in this village rode against them, to force them to do anything. You know that, Spotted Wolf! Every man among you would die within hours of such an attempt.

"I know that." His voice held an odd, wondering tone. "That was my only reason for convincing the council to agree to the exchange of prisoners."

"Your *only* reason?"

"Yes!" His hands reached out, gripped her shoulders, and his fingers dug into her flesh. "It would serve my own needs better to keep you with me, Jennifer!" His voice was a harsh whisper. "Never forget that for one moment! If there was another way to gain Cloud Dancer's release, then I would never let you go!"

"Why?" she whispered huskily. "Why do you want to keep me here?" Her heart fluttered wildly beneath her rib cage, and she held her breath, waiting impatiently for his reply.

"Need I explain?" his breath whispered across her cheeks. "Do you not know of a man's needs, white woman! Are you such a child that you feel no desire in that pale body of yours?"

"Desire? Is that all you feel for me, Spotted Wolf? Is it only desire?"

A slender, delicate thread seemed to form between them. It broke when he released her abruptly, shoving her away from him. "What else could it be?" he asked coldly. "What else does a man need a woman for? I have Star Woman to make my meals and keep my lodge clean. She is happy to tend to those chores."

"Of course. How foolish of me to think otherwise."

Then, stretched out as far away from him as the sleeping mat would allow, Jennifer turned over and presented him with her back. Tears moistened her eyes and she blinked rapidly to dry them. She wouldn't allow such weakness, she told herself.

She was a fool. A simple-minded fool who should have known better than to think he might care about her.

Jennifer opened her eyes the next morning, expecting to find herself alone in the lodge.

"So you are finally awake."

Startled, Jennifer turned her head to see Spotted Wolf's large frame filling the entrance. The memory of the words they had exchanged the night before colored her voice when she spoke. "What are you doing here?"

"I live here." He took in her scowl as he entered the lodge. He placed a water sack on the ground.

"I know. But you're usually gone when I wake up," she grumbled, pushing her tumbled hair away from her face. "I suppose you want me to prepare your breakfast."

"Of course. Do you expect me to continue eating with Star Woman when there is a woman in my own lodge who is perfectly capable of preparing my meals?"

A guilty flush stained her cheeks. She felt like a child who'd been chastised and the feeling didn't set well with her. It was the reason for her sharp retort. "You told me last night that you didn't need me to make your meals!"

"I do not. But since you are here, there is no need to trouble Star Woman. She has enough to do without adding to her labor."

"I apologize for troubling your mother," Jennifer said stiffly. "Do you want me to prepare some corn-meal mush like she usually makes?"

"No." He frowned heavily at her, obviously taking umbrage from her tone of voice. "I prefer ash cakes and honey this morning. We are delaying our hunt for awhile in order to sharpen our arrows."

She was surprised he felt the need to explain. "You don't use your rifles to hunt?" she asked curiously while she poured water into a large clay bowl.

"No. Ammunition must be saved for other things."

She felt his eyes on her as she washed her face and hands in a large clay bowl, then used her fingers to comb her tangled hair.

"Have you nothing to comb your hair with?" he asked suddenly.

"No." She raised an eyebrow. "I have nothing.

No comb, no brush and no clothing since you tore them off me."

"You are not without clothing," he pointed out. "Star Woman replaced the torn garments."

Her lips tightened. "I know she did. But one dress doesn't constitute a wardrobe. I am not used to sleeping this way." She looked down at herself. "My garments are wrinkled. They need washing. And . . ."

"Then do not sleep in them!" he interrupted brusquely. "You need nothing to cover your body when you sleep."

"Are you suggesting I sleep naked?"

"It is the best way to sleep."

"No!" she snapped. "My body is not something to be placed on display!"

He laughed abruptly and, for some reason, the sound unleashed her temper. She strode forward, leaned over and slapped him across the face.

He reacted immediately, pulling her across him and turning her so that she found herself beneath him. She stared up at him wide-eyed, fear moistening her eyes, draining the color from her face.

For a long moment, as Spotted Wolf held her gaze, she noticed that there was something in his eyes that frightened her. Then, as abruptly as he had snatched her, he set her aside again. "Do not strike me again, Jennifer, or the results may not be to your liking."

"I'm sorry," she said, ashamed of herself. She had purposely antagonized him, yet could not say why.

She busied herself with the morning meal, taking the cornmeal from the stack of supplies and pouring some into the center of a clay bowl. After adding a pinch of salt and some hot water, she stirred the swollen cornmeal into two balls and buried them in the hot ashes.

While the ash cakes were cooking, she put water on to boil and added a handful of dried, roasted corn that had been finely ground. When the resulting liquid had boiled long enough, she poured some into two clay mugs.

"Do you take yours sweetened?" she asked.

His reply was a grunt which she took as yes. She reached for the honey-pot and put a dollop in each cup, then handed one across to him. He took it with another grunt, then looked at her across the rim.

"It seems Star Woman taught you well," he said. "Had I known, I would have decided sooner to take my meals in my own lodge."

"I admit Star Woman has taught me many things, but making ash cakes and corn coffee are not among them," she said. "I learned those things from my mother at an early age."

"I am surprised," he admitted, sipping the hot corn coffee. "I thought the bluecoats always kept a plentiful supply of food in stock. Hardly a day passes without supply wagons traveling the road to the fort." He didn't seem to notice that he'd revealed that the actions of the fort were being closely monitored by the Indians.

"I suppose supplies are plentiful enough at the fort, but I have only lived there for a short time," she said, bending to rake an ash cake from the coals to see if it had cooked long enough. She poked it with a sharp stick that came out with some raw dough clinging to the end, then shoved the cake into the coals again.

"Where did you live before you went to the fort?"

Jennifer threw a quick glance at him. He was watching her and appeared interested in her reply, but he might only have been making conversation.

"I lived for a time with my mother's family back East. But I didn't particularly like it there." She grimaced wryly. "Actually, I hated living there. So I appealed to my uncle for help and he sent me enough money to make the journey West."

"So you were raised in the East," he mused. "And they made ash cakes there, where you were raised?"

She laughed at him. "Ash cakes at my grandmother's! Heaven forbid! She wouldn't allow an ash cake in the house. No. I learned about ash cakes in Texas." She raised an eyebrow. "We *are* still in Texas, aren't we?" He didn't answer, but she hadn't really expected him to. "I was raised near the coast. Not too far from Washington on the Brazos. My parents owned a farm there."

"A big farm?"

"Not very big. Papa owned sixty acres. But it was good bottom land and there was plenty of water because our land bordered the Brazos River. We lived a simple life. But it was a good life. We were happy there."

"Yet you left and went East."

"Not by choice. Another man wanted our farm. He had my parents killed. He missed me," she said grimly. "When my mother's father came for the funeral, he took me home with him. I should have stayed on the farm, should have fought for what was mine, but I was too stunned by their deaths. I felt so completely alone that I didn't hesitate to go with him."

Aware of the heavy scent of baking bread, Jennifer realized the ash cakes must be done and bent to rake them out of the coals. She brushed them, performing the chore automatically as her thoughts returned to that time when the world she had known and loved had been swept away so completely.

She had felt lost in that world of richly furnished houses, of expensive clothing and glittering chandeliers. It was a house without love, a cold, formal place where Jennifer was constantly reprimanded for her lack of knowledge about things that were of prime importance to her grandmother.

"You look sad when you speak of your parents," Spotted Wolf said softly.

"I feel sad," she admitted. "It was a bad time for me. It was a deliberate act. They were shot down by hired guns a year ago. Sent there by Tom Harris, who owns the Circle H ranch. Pa's farm was the only thing that stood between him and the Brazos River. My father refused his offer to buy our ranch so Harris had him killed."

"So now your father is dead and the farm is part of the Circle H ranch."

"No," she said grimly. "My father *is* dead. But Harris doesn't own the farm. And he never will. That farm belongs to me now. And nothing he does can ever change that."

"He could kill you too. The farm would revert to your next of kin then. Not your grandparents though. You said they were your mother's parents. Which means the farm would go to your uncle and, as a military man, he would have no use for it. He would probably sell out to the highest bidder."

"Which would be Tom Harris! But that doesn't matter because I'm still alive . . . and I intend to stay that way."

"Meanwhile he uses the farm for his own purposes."

"Yes. That's about the size of it." She handed an ash cake to Spotted Wolf, then seated herself across from him. They finished their meal in silence, each of them busy with their own thoughts, and when they were done and he had joined the other hunters, Jennifer remembered their conversation and wondered how an Indian warrior came to know so much about the white man's laws.

Eighteen

After Jennifer tidied up the lodge, she scooped the blanket off the sleeping mat and carried it outside, intent on hanging it over a bush so that the fresh air would take away the musty smell.

Suddenly a scream shattered the silence. Her gaze skittered over the compound, searching for the source of the disturbance, stopping at the sight of women gathered at the base of the cliff a short distance away.

The scream came again, shrill, piercing, containing so much fear and rage that Jennifer was forced to react. She tossed the blanket over the nearest bush and hurried toward the group of women.

"Stay back!" a woman screamed in English. "Don't anybody come closer!"

"Oh, God," Jennifer muttered. "It's Sarah!"

Jennifer raced forward, afraid of what she would find when she arrived, feeling certain that Carries A Stick was somehow involved.

But the wife of Three Fingers was not among the women gathered around Sarah. Nevertheless, the scene was horrifying.

With the stone face of the cliff at her back, Sarah faced the crowd. A sobbing child, a little girl not more than two years old, was clutched against

Sarah's breast. The woman's knife was pressed firmly against the little girl's throat.

"Get back!" Sarah screamed, pressing the knife harder against tender flesh. "I mean it! Get back or I'm gonna kill her!"

"No, Sarah!" Jennifer cried. "Don't hurt her!"

Sarah's gaze flickered to Jennifer, then returned to the crowd of women edging closer. "Get back!" she screamed again. "I'm not gonna let them hurt me any more, Jennifer!" she cried in a shrill voice. "I've taken all I'm gonna take. I'm leavin' here now! I'm gettin' away from here and this kid is gonna help me do it!"

"Where would you go?" Jennifer asked, trying to reason with the woman. "You couldn't survive by yourself out there."

"I don't care. Anything that comes my way out there would be better than what I got waiting here."

"Turn her loose," Jennifer said gently. "Don't hurt the child. She's done nothing to you. Please let her go."

"Not on your life, Jenny. These heathens are just waiting for me to do that. They'd tear me apart if they could." Her voice became pleading. "Help me, Jenny. Come with me. We could make it together. I know we could."

"I'm trying to help you," Jennifer said softly. "I've already talked to Spotted Wolf about you. He's going to make an offer for you that Three Fingers won't refuse. You'd be safe with him, Sarah."

"There's no way in hell Three Fingers would let him have me. Not now. Don't you know what happened, Jennifer? I killed Carries A Stick. Stabbed her with this knife here. And when Three Fingers finds out, he's gonna be awful mad about it. I reckon he'll prob'ly kill me if I'm still around."

"Oh, God, Sarah!"

"Yeah. I know. I shouldn't've done it. But I couldn't take no more. You see now what this is all about. I don't really want to hurt the kid, but I will if I have to."

"Give her to me, Sarah. Please give her to me."

"No." The words were a sigh. "I can't do that."

"Then I'll come with you," Jennifer said suddenly. "Just put the little girl down, Sarah. And we'll leave here together. I give you my word, Sarah. We'll leave here together."

"No. You're right, Jenny. We'd die out there. Looks like I ain't gonna win no matter what I do. I'm a dead woman sure as I'm standing here. But I'm not gonna die alone." She pressed the knife harder and the terrified child's wails rose as blood beaded on the soft flesh.

"No, Sarah! She's only a baby!"

"She's an Injun!"

Jennifer realized she had to do something; she was the only one who could. The women were afraid to move, fearing that Sarah would slice through the little girl's throat.

Sarah's eyes were focused on the crowd, unaware that Jennifer was creeping closer. Jennifer made her move, leaping forward so fast that she knocked Sarah's knife out of her hand before the woman realized what was happening.

Then, jerking the screaming child out of Sarah's arm, Jennifer shoved her toward the nearest woman and turned back to face Sarah again. But it was too late. Sarah, obviously fearing the results of her actions, had already buried the knife in her own chest.

"Oh, God, Sarah," Jennifer cried, kneeling beside her friend. "I didn't mean for this to happen. I was only trying to help you."

"Don't need anybody's help anymore," Sarah said, blood bubbling from the corner of her mouth. "Gonna see my Sammy again now." Her eyes were already glazing over.

Jennifer stayed beside Sarah until she shuddered with her last breath. Then she rose and made her silent way toward the lodge she shared with Spotted Wolf. She felt chilled to the bone. It was her fault that Sarah was dead. She and nobody else carried the blame. If she had not interfered, then Sarah would be alive now.

But an innocent child would be dead.

That realization released the pain within her chest. Jennifer threw herself across the sleeping mat and allowed the tears she'd been holding at bay to fall.

She didn't know how long she cried, had no sense of time, but finally her tears began to dry. She rolled over and stared up at the patch of blue sky that showed through the smoke hole. It seemed impossible that Sarah was gone. And so quickly too. A life was over and yet the sun continued to shine as though nothing of consequence had occurred.

She was wiping her eyes when Star Woman arrived, requesting permission to enter. Her shoulders were turned in as though she carried a heavy burden.

"This old woman has come to beg forgiveness, *Ma-be-quo-si-tu-ma.*" Her dark eyes were sad and her lips quivered slightly. "I should have stopped Three Fingers's wife from beating you, but I was angry that you would be going back to your safe world while the rest of us must continue to live in fear. My tongue refused to speak out in your defense."

Surprised at the old woman's humility, Jennifer

hugged her. "You could have done nothing to stop her."

"I could have reminded them of why you were here," the old woman said.

"Forget about it," Jennifer said. "It's over and done with now."

"No. Not over." The old woman held Jennifer's gaze. "I was at the spring when Sarah took the child. When I returned to the village, I heard what happened. I am sorry your friend is dead. You are a brave woman to act as you did when everyone else could do nothing. Because of you a child's life has been saved."

"Sarah wouldn't have hurt me," Jennifer said. "She only took the child because she was frightened. She didn't know what else to do."

"You blame yourself for her death."

"Yes."

"You must not. You did not take her life."

"Please. I can't talk about it now."

"I understand. You need something to keep your thoughts occupied and this old woman knows what to do. Come with me, Jennifer. And bring your fruit baskets with you. Both of them. I know where there is a plum bush loaded with fruit. It is past time we harvested it."

"Star Woman," Jennifer said hesitantly. "What about Sarah's body. Has it been . . ."

"Do not trouble yourself. Others have taken care of it. Your friend Helen helped them." Her voice became brusque. "Come now. Do not drag behind, child. There is much work to be accomplished before the day is gone."

Curling her fingers around the handles of her fruit baskets, Jennifer followed the old woman from the lodge. Her gaze scanned the village, stopping near the edge of the woods. The hair on her neck rose in fear.

Three Fingers stood watching her.

An icy chill crept up her spine and she almost turned and went back inside the lodge. But she stopped midstride. With the women gone and the men off hunting, there would be nobody around to hear her screams if Three Fingers came after her.

Realizing there was safety in numbers, Jennifer hurried to join the women gathered beneath the brush arbor.

Star Woman had been right about the plum bush. It was laden with plums so ripe that Jennifer couldn't help popping one in her mouth every now and then. They had been picking fruit for more than an hour when she stopped to wipe her brow. She stooped to set her basket on the ground, then straightened again, arching her tired back muscles while she allowed her gaze to roam the unfamiliar landscape.

They were at the far end of the canyon, several miles from the village where the men were hunting. She hadn't expected it to be so far away, and that made her uneasy. But she quickly dismissed the feeling, knowing that Three Fingers wouldn't dare try anything when there were so many people around.

As time passed, she was able to put him completely out of her mind. The women, although not inclined to include her in their conversations, seemed friendlier than before. Jennifer wouldn't allow herself to wonder why; she was afraid she knew already.

The sun overhead was hot, but Jennifer had become used to the heat, even found it curiously pleasant. She continued to gather plums while she listened to the women around her chatter away. Although she couldn't understand their language, the tone appeared friendly.

As the plumper plums became scarcer, Jennifer began to wander away from the women, searching for another bush that had riper plums. If she could fill her baskets completely, then she could take one into the lodge and prepare the plums for supper. She might even attempt a pie, since she had plenty of honey on hand to sweeten the fruit.

Could acorn flour and animal fat be blended together to make a pie crust? Maybe she shouldn't make a pie. Maybe a pudding would taste better. Yes. That would be best.

Imagining the taste of pudding, Jennifer hurried to find another plum bush. She was unaware that she'd moved out of sight of the other women until she heard a rustle nearby. Even then she didn't know what had occurred. Not until she saw Three Fingers.

She opened her mouth to scream, but he was too fast. One hand covered her mouth while the other bound her arms against her sides, squeezing so tightly that she dropped her fruit basket.

Jennifer didn't see the fruit spill out and scatter on the ground beneath the bush. She couldn't see anything but Three Fingers, looming over her, his face a mask of hate as his hand covered her mouth, stopping her breath so effectively that her lungs burned from lack of air.

Oh, God, please help me! It was a silent cry, a desperate plea that came just before the shadowy darkness enveloped her.

Nineteen

The setting sun spread a red haze over the canyon as Spotted Wolf reached for an arrow and strung it in his bow. For some reason game had been scarce today; this was the first time he'd seen anything that even faintly resembled meat since they'd left the village.

He watched the fat turkey scratch the ground more than a hundred yards away. Then, drawing back his bow string, Spotted Wolf rose from his hiding place and released his arrow.

He knew the exact moment the arrow penetrated the turkey's breast; it squawked loudly, fluttering its wings as it danced around. Then, it finally dropped to the ground, kicking and thrashing in its death throes.

Sprinting forward, Spotted Wolf picked up the turkey and lifted it to judge its weight. It was a large one, fat enough to provide meat for several pots, yet not enough to go around.

After attaching a leather thong to the legs of the turkey, making it ready for quick transport, the warrior returned to his hiding place, hoping another bird might seek food where the first one had been.

A movement nearby caught his attention and he swung around quickly, eagerly stringing another arrow in his bow. He snorted with disgust as Coyote Man emerged from a thicket of trees.

"I hoped you were a turkey," Spotted Wolf said.

"A turkey!" Coyote Man's eyes glinted with humor. "A deer would fill more bellies." He eyed the turkey laying on the ground. "It is a good thing the woman in your lodge is a paleface captive."

Spotted Wolf was suspicious of the humor in the other warrior's eyes, but nevertheless, he rose to the bait. "Why do you say that?"

"Because my woman would not accept such a puny offering for her cooking pot. She would expect me to provide something better."

"And have you done so?" Spotted Wolf was not inclined to accept the teasing with good humor. Normally, he did better on a hunt.

"Of course. My arrow killed a deer. It was a large buck that is, even now, being carried to the village." The corners of his lips twitched as he continued to tease. "My deer and the buck and doe that Red Cloud and Kicking Dog Man killed."

Spotted Wolf scowled at him. "It appears I would have fared better by joining your group." The hunting party had split into three groups, each taking different directions. It was bad luck that Spotted Wolf had chosen the wrong direction. "Even though I have only slain one turkey, I am glad that you and the others had more luck."

"Do not concern yourself, brother. Your cooking pot will also contain venison this night," Coyote Man assured him.

He need not have made the assurance, because it was the way of the People. Game was shared among those who had need of it. It had been so since they could remember, something that was always done.

At least as long as the Comanche continued to roam the earth.

That thought had a sobering effect upon Spotted Wolf. If the White Eyes had their way, the Comanche would cease to exist.

"Your thoughts are not on the hunt, Spotted Wolf."

"No. My thoughts are on the White Eyes and the trouble they constantly visit on us. Most of our People are already confined to reservations, but the bluecoats will never rest until every Comanche among us has been sent there."

"Your words are true, Spotted Wolf. But our stronghold is safe. Cloud Dancer will never reveal its location. He would die first." He was thoughtful for a long moment, then, "Do you think there will be a problem about the exchange you proposed?"

"No. The White Eyes are sure to agree. They value their women as much as do we. I feel certain the bluecoats will be at the meeting place we have chosen even before we arrive there."

"Then perhaps we should go early to make sure there are not more soldiers than we bargained for."

"My thoughts exactly."

Coyote Man grunted. "It is good we brought the woman with us. I would have killed her on the mountain if you had not stopped me. Sometimes my anger overcomes my good sense."

"It is the same with me."

A silence fell between them as Spotted Wolf thought about the woman who waited in his lodge. Would she be glad to see him when he returned? It was quite possible, he knew, because there had been a change in her attitude the last few days. His lips curved in a smile. And suddenly, he was eager for the day to end.

* * *

A hard thump brought Jennifer back to a state of awareness. Her eyelids flickered open and she was surprised to see a streak of scarlet sky.

"So you are awake," a voice growled above her.

She jerked upright and stared at the man who'd taken her captive. Three Fingers. Oh, God, where had he brought her?

Her frightened gaze skittered around her surroundings. She was in a round, rocky enclosure of some kind. Probably a cave in the face of the cliff, hollowed out over the centuries by wind and rain until it formed a circular room about twelve feet in circumference.

Jennifer's heart pounded with dread. She was alone with Three Fingers, his to torment at will. She had been foolish to wander away from the others. And that foolishness would cost her dearly.

"You won't get away with this."

"There is nobody to stop me," he snarled. "Spotted Wolf cannot help you now. He is away from the village."

"When he returns and discovers me gone, he will kill you!"

His laugh was a harsh sound. "You are wrong, paleface. No one saw me take you. They will believe you ran away."

"No!"

His grin widened. "You will never be found."

Her dread deepened. "Where is this place?"

"We are where the eagle dwells." He bent closer. "Spotted Wolf will never look for you here. I could keep you alive for many seasons and none would know. If I choose to throw you over the cliff, they could not stop me."

Needing to know more about her prison, she pretended to be cowed. "Surely there is no place in the valley that is so secret."

"Not secret," he growled. "A place of spirits. Below is where we bury our dead."

The graveyard! Realizing it was at the far end of the canyon from the village, Jennifer was finally convinced there would be no help for her. She had only herself to rely on.

Suddenly, he reached for her and she rolled quickly away. But it was only a momentary thing. He threw himself on her, pinning her beneath him.

Jennifer screamed, gripped by a claustrophobia so intense that she could hardly stand it. Curling her fingers, she clawed at him, trying to push him away from her. He ignored her feeble efforts to dislodge him. She felt numb with horror as he groped her and she whimpered, turning her head from side to side.

He appeared pleased by her distress and ground his hips against her, pressing his engorged manhood firmly into her thighs.

"It is big," he said with a grin. "Swelled to a thickness that will fill your body in a way that you never knew before now." His eyes narrowed on her face and he licked his lips. "But then perhaps you have never felt a man's thickness inside you." He read the truth in her eyes, the abject fear she displayed and laughed.

"I see I am right," he chortled. "I will be the first. And you will feel my seed flood your body many times before I am through with you."

Jennifer's stomach churned with fear as she struggled against the leather thongs that bound her wrists so tightly. She could do nothing but stare at him pleadingly. But she needn't have bothered. He would not be swayed from his goal, that of taking her innocence for himself.

Suddenly, her loathing overcame her terror. She knew there was no way her strength could be used against him. Therefore she must use her wits. She sagged limply, closing her eyes as though she'd fainted. He bent lower, grunting with anger, and she felt his head hover just above her own.

She reacted swiftly, reaching up with her head to clamp her teeth against his throat.

With a yell, he gripped her head and yanked it aside, but she kicked frantically at him and he slid off her.

Pushing herself to her feet, she stumbled away from him as she stared in revulsion at the blood streaming from his throat.

He leapt for her, making a fist of his hand and slamming it against her head with tremendous force.

Jennifer's head reeled back and the salty taste of blood filled her mouth as she stumbled backward. Unable to retain her balance, she struck the floor hard. She was aware of immense pain at the base of her skull.

Jennifer felt the darkness closing around her again, and was afraid that, this time, there would be no waking from the netherworld into which she was rapidly descending.

Trying to keep the eagerness he felt from being so obvious, Spotted Wolf left the other hunters at the edge of the woods. There was a spring in his step and a smile on his lips as he hurried toward his lodge.

Although he had eaten nothing since early morning and his stomach growled at the prospect of supper, he was in good humor. Enough so, that even the camp dog that followed close at his heels went unnoticed.

His thoughts were on Jennifer, the copper haired woman with sky colored eyes who waited for him to return. He didn't wonder at the eagerness he felt to see her again, had decided earlier that he would allow himself to enjoy her, to take pleasure from her company without judging himself.

When he reached the tepee, he pushed aside the hide flap and entered his home. Carefully controlling his expression, he turned to greet Jennifer, but she was not there. There was nobody in the lodge except himself.

His dark brows pulled into a frown. A quick glance at the fire pit told him that no attempt had been made to start a fire for the evening meal. Nor had there been a fire beneath the tripod outside. He scanned the interior of the lodge, narrowing his eyes on the water jug. She hadn't gone to the spring.

Pushing open the hide flap, he checked the wood supply, judging its height. There was more than enough to cook several meals, so it wasn't likely she was gathering wood.

A faint twinge of alarm washed over him as he left the tepee and scanned the village. There was no one beneath the brush arbor. The women were all busy preparing the evening meals.

Perhaps she was with Star Woman.

He strode quickly to the older woman's lodge.

"No!" she replied to his question. "I have not seen her since we went down the canyon to gather plums."

"And you found nothing unusual in that?" he inquired sharply, a cold knot of fear forming suddenly inside his stomach.

"No," she admitted. "I might have another time.

But not today. When I noticed she was missing, I thought that she needed to be alone because of what happened to her friend, the paleface captive."

"Something happened to Helen?" he asked sharply.

"No. The other one. The one called Sarah. Did you not know, my son? Sarah is dead."

"No," he said, expelling a heavy sigh. "No, I had no way of knowing. I suppose Jennifer blames herself for being unable to stop the beating. She should not, though. It was none of her doing. Carries A Stick enjoys dealing out punishments."

"No more though." At Spotted Wolf's curious look, the old woman said, "Carries A Stick is dead. And it was Sarah who killed her."

A sudden thought occurred to Spotted Wolf. "Where was Three Fingers when this was taking place?"

"I have no idea," Star Woman replied. "But he would not dare to attack Jennifer again. I am sure she felt the need of solitude to mourn her friend. You must be patient. Give her time to work out her grief."

"She is not grieving over Sarah," he said. "Jennifer felt sorry for the woman, but would not mourn her so much that she would seek solitude and risk her own well-being. Something has happened to her and I am afraid Three Fingers is responsible."

"I hope you are wrong."

"As do I," Spotted Wolf replied.

He hurried away from her, feeling an urgent need to find Jennifer as quickly as possible.

Three Fingers stared down at the unconscious woman with disgust. He could not have her now.

Not when his member refused to rise at his bidding. The blow she had dealt had been a wounding one, and he would need time to recover from it.

Glancing skyward, he realized for the first time how late it had become. The sun had already disappeared below the horizon and soon shadows would cover the land.

He looked down at Jennifer again, his disgust almost overwhelming. He had no intention of releasing her, had planned and schemed too much to let her go.

No. The cave would offer shelter from bad weather, and its location would insure the privacy he needed for many days of pleasure with the white captive.

Another glance at the darkening sky told him to hurry. The hunting party would probably be returning to the village soon. If he were to remain free of suspicion, he must be there when they returned and discovered the woman was missing.

He smiled at the thought of Spotted Wolf returning to an empty lodge. He would look for the paleface but would find nothing. Three Fingers had been careful to erase both the woman's footprints and his own. The woman would not be found.

It was too bad about Cloud Dancer though. Without the woman to exchange, he would remain a prisoner of the White Eyes. Three Fingers felt little concern for him; he would not reveal the location of the stronghold. He would die first. But then, no man could escape death.

Suddenly realizing that he was wasting time, Three Fingers bent over and checked Jennifer's bonds. Then he gagged her with his headband so that none would hear her cries if they ventured this far up the canyon. He left the cave and descended the cliff, wiping away all trace of his passing as he went.

Returning to the river, he retrieved the stringer of fish that he had staked out earlier in the day. Then with his excuse properly in hand, he hurried up the canyon. A short distance from the village, he veered off the path and circled around the encampment so that he could enter the village from the opposite direction.

Three Fingers had known the woman would already be missed, but he was nonetheless surprised to find the village in a state of agitation. People were rushing about, men, women, and children, searching every lodge.

He reached his dwelling without mishap. And as he cleaned his catch, the entrance flap was flung aside and Spotted Wolf entered with Coyote Man only a few paces behind him.

"Where is she?" Spotted Wolf demanded, his face a mask of rage. His whole body was tense, his hands curled into angry fists, and every muscle in his body was taut.

"Where is who?" Three Fingers asked, trying to sound unconcerned. He had never seen Spotted Wolf so angry before, not even when they had fought. And to find that hatred directed toward himself was reason enough to make him feel afraid.

"The woman!" Spotted Wolf snarled. "Jennifer! What have you done with her?"

"I have seen no woman," Three Fingers replied, keeping his eyes on the fish he was scraping.

"You lie!" Spotted Wolf growled. "You know where she is!" He wrapped iron fingers around Three Fingers's forearm and jerked him upright. "Tell me where she is!"

"If the woman is missing, then she must have run

away." Three Fingers tried to hide his fear. "Why do you come here and accuse me? I have spent my time fishing!" He jerked his arm, his anger at Spotted Wolf's rough treatment overcoming his good sense.

"You lie!" Spotted Wolf snarled, his green eyes glittering with rage.

"If you had given her what she needed, then perhaps she would not have fled," Three Fingers taunted.

Spotted Wolf's fury could no longer be contained. He doubled up his fist and struck Three Fingers a hard blow, knocking him clear across the fire pit.

"Stop, Spotted Wolf!" Coyote Man cried, digging his fingers into his friend's shoulder. "Think a moment. Three Fingers may be speaking the truth. Jennifer may have run away. If she has, then we must find her quickly. Without her, there will be no exchange of prisoners."

Spotted Wolf threw a hard look at the man who was sprawled on the earthen floor. "If she fled, then she left a trail behind her," he said harshly. "Hear me good, Three Fingers. If there is no trail to be found, then she did not leave on her own. And you can be certain I will return to finish what I started."

Spinning on his heels, Spotted Wolf strode out of the lodge to join the other warriors who waited outside. Three Fingers picked himself up from the ground and made his way out of the tent. Among the warriors was the war chief, Quanah, whose all-seeing gaze was pinned on Three Fingers.

A chill washed over Three Fingers and he quickly diverted his gaze. Perhaps, he considered, it was time to move on to another village. It would not be the first time he had done so. The villages were becoming fewer with each passing moon. Even so, he could find another one, could make himself a new life among new people.

But first there was the paleface woman to dispose of.

He looked toward the mountain, unable to contain the excitement he felt when he remembered her womanly curves. Too bad he had to leave her behind. He could have had many moons of pleasure from her. He expelled a disgruntled sigh. There was nothing he could do about it. He had learned long ago that a man could travel faster alone.

At least he would have no trouble disposing of her body when he was finished with her. The earth in the place of the dead was soft, the soil easy to turn. Nobody would ever think of looking for her there. And if they did, he would not be around to accuse.

Humming softly beneath his breath, Three Fingers returned to his lodge and turned his attention to his fish once again.

Twenty

It was happening all over again. Oh, Great Creator, I cannot go through this yet another time!

Spotted Wolf tried hard to convince himself that he was wrong, that Jennifer was safe. But it was impossible. There had been something in Three Fingers's eyes that told Spotted Wolf his enemy knew something about Jennifer's disappearance.

It was too much like before. Too much like that other time when Laughing Water had disappeared.

A heavy pain settled in Spotted Wolf's chest as he remembered that other time. He had left early that morning to hunt with the other warriors. And while he was searching for game, the women had gone out to gather berries. They never saw the white man take Laughing Water.

It had been late when Spotted Wolf returned to the village. He had wasted no time searching for Laughing Water to brag about the game he had brought. He could not find her, and had questioned the women she worked with. No one remembered having seen her since they left the berry thicket.

He had felt the first stirrings of alarm then. His heart had raced with dread as he hurried to the berry thicket and found her basket, overturned on the grass. The marks of the White Eyes' boots told their own story.

It was the next day before he found the cabin where she had been taken. The White Eye's horse waited outside, its head drooping wearily. He had felt an intense hatred for the White Eyes. Only a cruel man would treat his mount in such a manner. And that man had Laughing Water inside his cabin.

He had almost reached the door when he felt a stab of pain so intense that he stopped in his tracks. For a moment he thought he had been attacked, then realized the pain was not his own but Laughing Water's, his beloved.

He had leapt forward, crossing the distance to the cabin, heedless of the noise he made. Pushing the door open, he stared into the shadowy interior. When his eyes adjusted to the darkness, he saw a man, sprawled on the floor, dead. And across the room was his beloved, her eyes open, staring at him in shock.

"Thank you, Great Spirit!" he had cried, leaping across the room and stooping to gather her into his arms.

But he had given thanks too soon, he realized. Something was wrong. Her voice seemed to have no strength when she spoke to him.

"Spotted Wolf. I knew you would come. But it is too late." She closed her eyes for a moment, then her lashes fluttered weakly and she looked at him again. "I am sorry. I wanted so to be your wife."

"And you will be," he had said harshly. "Nothing can stop our marriage." But even as he spoke, a coppery scent assailed his nostrils and he felt a thick wetness against his bare chest. Blood. It flowed from a small wound near her heart, spreading in a wide stain across the front of her dress.

She had died moments later, without ever speaking another word. But he had known without having been told that Laughing Water had killed the white man who had abused her, then taken her own life, rather than face the horror of what had been done to her.

That night, Spotted Wolf had gone high into the mountains and sliced off his little finger, as was the custom of the People when they lost a dear one.

But it would not happen again. He would not allow Jennifer to be taken from him. There was no way he could endure such pain again. He could not bear to lose another woman who meant so much to . . .

He rejected his thoughts. Jennifer was important to the People as a whole. She would be traded for Cloud Dancer.

He cursed Three Fingers, knowing he was responsible for Jennifer's disappearance. And when it was proven, the man would pay for what he had done. He would pay with his life.

Hearing footsteps approach, Spotted Wolf turned to see Quanah. "Three Fingers cannot be trusted," Spotted Wolf said grimly. "I feel sure he knows what happened to the woman."

Quanah raised a questioning brow. "And your reason for believing that?"

"Once before he tried to force himself on her. He has lusted after her since she came to the village. He offered to trade for her. I should have watched him, should have known he would steal her away from me."

"From you?" Quanah's gray eyes glittered. "Surely you mean from the People. She was brought here to use for exchange. To free Cloud Dancer. Is it not so?"

"Yes, of course."

"It is best you remember that. If the woman is found, she must be returned to her people."

"I have not forgotten."

"Good." Quanah eyed Three Fingers's lodge. "It is hard to believe Three Fingers would betray his people for a woman. His actions affect every one of us. The messenger we sent to the fort will soon return. The White Eyes are sure to agree to our proposal. But if we cannot produce the woman, then Cloud Dancer will be returned to the fort. The bluecoats may punish *him* for Three Fingers's treachery."

"Do not give Jennifer up so easily. She is braver than most, and will not be easily defeated."

"If she is alive, Three Fingers will try to leave the village. He knows we suspect him and would not dare to leave her alive lest she reveal his treachery."

Spotted Wolf's fingernails dug into his palms and he welcomed the resulting pain. "He must not be allowed to leave the village."

"Have no fear."

Dread settled over Spotted Wolf's shoulders. In time, Jennifer's body would be found, broken and lifeless. He knew. He had seen it all before. That thought caused a heavy pain to settle deep inside.

He cared too much for her, Spotted Wolf silently admitted. He had been fighting a useless battle since the day they met. Jennifer had found a way around his defenses and taken possession of his heart.

He remembered the way she had sung to him when he was weak from venom and fever. Her voice had been sweeter than the trill of a meadowlark and it had pierced his delirium, soothed his turbulent mind.

Was that beautiful voice stilled forever now?

"No," he muttered.

Quanah looked at him curiously, then said, "Walks With Eagles will go with us to the plum thicket. If the ground has been disturbed, he will know."

A short time later, Spotted Wolf hurried down the valley, remaining behind Walks With Eagles but ahead of the other warriors who were taking part in the search. All of them realized they needed to find Jennifer as quickly as possible.

A smile played around Three Fingers's lips as he watched the other warriors leave the village. They would find nothing at the plum thicket. He had gathered broomweeds and swept away all sign of her struggle. But they would not give up easily, so he must hurry and take his pleasure from her. Later, he would slay her and bury her in the sand.

His smile widened as he slid his blade into its sheathe, then fastened it around his waist. He left the lodge and found himself confronted by the barrel chested strength of Crawling Turtle.

Slowly, Jennifer regained consciousness. She opened her eyes to a shadowy darkness that was impossible to see through and, for a moment, felt completely disoriented. Then reality slammed into her.

Oh, God, she moaned, but only a muffled sound escaped her lips, as she'd been gagged with a dirty rag.

Squeezing her eyes shut, she tried to will her fearful thoughts away, unable to face her enemy again. She remained quiet, her body frozen, muscles tense, her ears straining for sound. Then suddenly, she became aware of the silence around her. It was extreme, absolute, almost as though she were alone. She opened her eyes to a narrow slit, her gaze darting quickly around the cavern, searching for her captor. But he was no longer there. She was alone in her rocky prison.

A small measure of relief washed over her until she heard a sound that caused the hair at the nape of her neck to rise. A wolf howled in the distance. Its cry was echoed by another, and then another and another. Then finally the canine voices were silent and again, silence prevailed.

Jennifer tried to reach for the rag tied across her lower jaw and realized that her hands were bound to her feet by a short length of rawhide.

Damn Three Fingers's cowardly hide! He'd trussed her up like a Thanksgiving turkey! Tears welled into Jennifer's eyes. Since there was no one to see her weakness, she allowed herself to cry, allowed the tears to slide down her cheeks freely.

What was to become of her? Was she fated to die here alone in this cave? Even such a fate was preferable to what Three Fingers planned to do to her. He had obviously found it prudent to leave for the moment, but she had no doubt that, in time, he would return.

And will you be lying here waiting for him, Jennifer? an inner voice asked.

What else can I do?

Coward! the voice cried. *If you're so spineless that you accept your fate without even trying to escape, then you deserve whatever you get!*

Anger began to burn within and Jennifer pushed herself to a sitting position. She'd be damned if she'd wait passively for her enemy to return. She was born of fighting stock. Her father, before becoming a farmer, had fought in the Civil War. And his father had died at the Alamo. And his grandfather, Colonel Brigham Carlisle, had fought the British at the Battle of New Orleans. Every one of them would be ashamed of Jennifer if she allowed a cowardly Indian warrior to defeat her.

There must be some way to get this damn rag off of her mouth, and if there was, then she was going to find it!

Jennifer hunched over, holding her hands around her knees. That released the tension on the leather strips enough so that she could stand on her feet. Then, bent at the waist and with her shoulders turned inward, she hopped toward the narrow opening. If she could reach it, she might be able to scrape the rag off her mouth using the edge of the rock for leverage. And if she managed that, she intended to scream her head off. Somebody was bound to hear her.

She hopped awkwardly, managing only a foot or two at a time, yet covered enough distance to give her hope. She was only a few feet from the entrance when her head suddenly collided with stone. The blow was so hard that she was knocked to the ground. She lay there, momentarily stunned, unable to reclaim her breath, unable to see the shadow of the wolf that stopped at the entrance to the cave.

Even though torches were lit at the scene, Walks With Eagles could find no trace of the boots Jennifer had worn. "There is nothing to show the paleface was ever here," he remarked. "But we know that she was." He looked up at Spotted Wolf.

"It appears someone has taken great pains to erase every trace of her." He pointed to a spot on the ground. "See how evenly the dirt has been distributed? The ground has been swept clean there."

"Then we were right," Quanah said. "Three Fingers is responsible for this. But he will never reveal his treachery. To do so would be to condemn himself. As long as there is no proof of what he has done, he will continue to proclaim his innocence. To say that she ran away."

"She is in grave danger," Spotted Wolf said. "We must find her quickly . . . before it is too late." He looked skyward, his gaze skimming the cliff tops.

Suddenly, a sound split the night. Yip, yip, aroooo! Yip, yip, aroooo!

Spotted Wolf looked toward the sound. It had come from down the canyon, somewhere above the floor of the valley, and yet, not atop the cliffs. It was as though the wolf was somewhere on the face of the cliff.

He narrowed his gaze, searching the portion of the cliff that was visible in the pale light of the moon.

There was something puzzling about the wolf's location on the cliff, something that screamed out to be remembered. Yet it remained elusive, somewhere just beyond his grasp. What was it?

Then suddenly he knew. The dead lay buried at the base of that cliff. And Three Fingers had attacked Jennifer only a short distance away. But how could that knowledge help them now? Could it? Had Three Fingers deliberately chosen that particular spot? Or was it only chance that made him attack her there?

Spotted Wolf scanned the valley with his searching gaze, but the shadows were too dense, too thick to penetrate. His gaze lifted again, and in the moonlight, he saw a darker spot on the face of the cliff.

Yip, yip, aroooooo!

Spotted Wolf tried to locate the wolf by the sound of his cry. Yip, yip, aroooo! Yip, yip, arooooo! The wolf appeared to be somewhere in the vicinity of the cave located halfway up the face of the cliff.

The cave!

It would be the perfect place to hide her. Dammit! Three Fingers must have carried her up there. "The cave!" he shouted. "She is there! We must hurry."

Twenty-one

Jennifer's moan was muffled by the dirty rag Three Fingers had tied around her mouth. The hard blow to her head had been sufficient to cloud her vision. Even if she could free herself, she needed her eyes to make the descent from the cave. Without her sight, she was doomed to fail.

Blinking rapidly, she narrowed her eyes onto a bright patch of moonlight. Although it was obviously the entrance to the cave, it seemed to be marred by a darker spot at its center . . . a strange silhouette. She narrowed her gaze even more to sharpen her vision and the strange silhouette became a solid form.

Oh, God! It was a wolf!

Icy fear slithered through her, starting in the pit of her stomach and spreading outward, leaving her numb, frozen to the spot.

Spotted Wolf, help me! she silently cried. *Oh, God, please come and help me!*

Even as she uttered the silent cry, Jennifer knew it was useless. There was no way Spotted Wolf could help her; he was miles away and probably unaware that she was in trouble. There was no one to rely on except herself.

Although the wolf appeared not to have moved a

muscle, its yellow gaze was unwavering, never leaving her. Perhaps, she thought, if she remained absolutely motionless, the animal would believe her dead and depart as quietly as it had appeared.

Jennifer closed her eyes to shut out the frightful image and concentrated on keeping her breathing to a minimum. She could feel cold sweat lining her forehead and beading her upper lip, but tried hard to ignore it. Everything she had, every ounce of energy she possessed, must be used to make the wolf believe she was dead if she were to survive.

Suddenly the animal shifted positions, dislodging a stone and disturbing Jennifer's forced calm. Her eyes flew open. The wolf had moved to the edge of the cliff and was staring down into the canyon. It was then she heard the first, unmistakable sound of sliding shale.

Oh, God! Someone was coming. Three Fingers!

Jennifer knew in that instant that she would prefer to be torn apart by the wolf than be left at the mercy of Three Fingers. At least death beneath the wolf's fangs would be swift. Three Fingers would not be so merciful.

But the choice had been taken from her, it seemed. The wolf rose from its haunches and darted away, the silhouette of a man taking its place. Jennifer cringed, moaning with dread over what was to come.

"Jennifer?" The husky voice was easily recognizable and held something undefinable.

Spotted Wolf? Oh, God, was it really him?

"Jennifer?" he said again. Then, with a muffled exclamation, he bounded forward and jerked the gag away from her mouth. It settled somewhere at the base of her throat, leaving her free to speak.

"Spotted Wolf." The name trembled on her lips.

"Oh, thank God you came! I didn't think you would! I thought—Oh, God, I thought—But I was wrong," she babbled. "You're here! You came after me. You . . ."

"Shush!" He sliced through her bonds and pulled her against him. "I am here now, little one. My Spirit Guide, Wolf, showed me where you were. You are safe now."

With a shuddering sigh, she slid her arms around his neck and gripped him tightly, resting her cheek against his chest, reveling in the warmth of his sheltering embrace.

Sliding an arm beneath her knees, he lifted her in his arms and cuddled her close. "All is well, little one," he muttered hoarsely, his warm breath whispering against her ear. Then, with Jennifer clutched tightly against his chest, he strode out of the cave and paused near the edge of the cliff to look down into the valley below.

"Do you think you can you climb down the cliff?" he asked. "I could carry you across my shoulder, but . . ."

"I can manage. If you promise not to leave me."

"I will be close beside if you need me."

He appeared reluctant to release her, and when he did so, he helped her descend the rocky slope. Then, scooping her into his arms again, he carried her to the village, sweeping past the rescue group who had gathered to watch their approach. Jennifer saw Three Fingers standing beside a burly warrior and turned her face against Spotted Wolf's chest to shut out the sight of her captor. His strides never faltered until they were inside his lodge.

He lowered her gently onto the sleeping pallet. "You can rest without fear now. Nobody would dare harm you now."

"Don't leave me alone!" She tightened her arms around his neck. "Three Fingers took me there. He was going to . . ."

"He will not harm you. I make you a promise, Jennifer. My word of honor. He will never bother you again."

"I am sorry to be such a coward," she whispered. "Poppa would be ashamed if he could see me now."

"You are wrong. He would be proud of your courage. You are a brave woman who has been badly abused, but you will be avenged." He smoothed his hand across her tangled hair. "Do not worry, my love. I will not be away long."

My love. Did he mean that or was it just his way of comforting her? Did he know how much he meant to her? she wondered. Could he possibly know how much she cared?

A noise at the entrance caught her attention and her heart surged with fear as she stared, wide-eyed, at the newcomer. But it was only Star Woman.

"Stay with her until I return," Spotted Wolf said, using English for Jennifer's benefit. "See that nobody enters the lodge while I am gone."

Nodding her head, Star Woman seated herself beside the pallet, crossed her legs and began to hum softly. It was a strange melody she hummed, quite unlike anything Jennifer had ever heard before. But it was soothing to her shattered nerves. She lay on the sleeping mat, listening to the old woman until her mind finally sought the solitude of oblivion.

Moments later Spotted Wolf confronted Three Fingers in his lodge. The other warrior was seated cross-legged on the earthen floor beside his fire pit.

"You know why I have come," Spotted Wolf said grimly.

"Yes." Three Fingers's dark eyes glittered with hate. "Is it your intention to meet me in combat? Or are you too cowardly to allow me to defend myself?"

"You deserve no more chance than you gave my woman."

Three Fingers's lips curled contemptuously. "Your woman! You are no better than me, Spotted Wolf, but you will put the good of the People before your own needs. Such a man of high principles!" His voice was mocking, his lips stretched thin. "You are stupid! A stupid man who has betrayed his own people! Why should you care what happens to the Comanche? They are not your people. Comanche blood does not run through your veins."

His words struck Spotted Wolf to the core, and he clenched his hands to keep from striking the man. "You are wrong, Three Fingers. I am Comanche. There are none among us who would deny that. Except scum like you. But your tongue will be silenced soon enough. Take your blade in hand and meet me in the battle circle if you wish to die like a man. If not, you may die here. The choice is yours."

Three Fingers licked his lips nervously. "You speak brave words, yet only a coward would force a man with only three fingers to fight him."

Spotted Wolf snorted with contempt. "You will not escape your fate by claiming to be at a disadvantage. Your three missing fingers are all on your left hand, which does not interfere with your ability to handle a knife." He turned to go, then paused.

"You have until the drum ceases to beat. If you have not joined me by then, I will return and you

will die slowly." He left, knowing his enemy would
consider his choices carefully.

As he walked toward the center of the compound
where a crowd had gathered, he heard the first beat
of the drum. Thrum . . . thrum . . . thrum . . . At
first the sounds came slowly as was the custom, then
the drummer picked up speed.

Spotted Wolf's heartbeat kept time with the drummer as he stepped into the wide circle that had been
drawn in the dirt. Coyote Man joined him there.

"He has agreed to fight?" Coyote Man asked.

"No. But he will soon realize there is no choice."

"Have a care," Coyote Man said. "Do not count
yourself winner until the battle is over. Three Fingers is a good fighter. He might defeat you."

"Yes. There is that chance," Spotted Wolf agreed.
"And if he does defeat me, you must look after Jennifer. Make certain she is returned safely to her people. Even if the bluecoats do not agree to make the
exchange."

"You have my promise."

A stirring among the crowd caught their attention. Spotted Wolf watched the warriors part to allow Three Fingers into their midst.

"He has accepted your challenge," Coyote Man
muttered.

"So he has." Spotted Wolf heard the anticipation
in his own voice.

He watched Three Fingers approach, watched
him enter the battle circle with his blade already in
hand. It was obvious he was prepared to defeat his
opponent, apparent from the way his eyes narrowed,
from the smile that spread slowly across his face.

"I have been waiting a long time for this," Three
Fingers said, bending slightly and spreading his legs

in a fighting stance. "Soon everyone will know which of us is stronger."

No sooner were the words spoken than he leapt forward, jabbing at Spotted Wolf with the sharp blade of his knife. Had the blow entered his flesh, it would have entered his heart and been the end of the battle. But Spotted Wolf had anticipated the move and countered it with a backward leap that carried him beyond the reach of the deadly weapon.

Striking before Three Fingers could recover, Spotted Wolf brought his blade down against the side of his opponent's head, slicing through his ear as cleanly as he would have sliced through a haunch of venison.

Uttering a howl of pain, Three Fingers retaliated, striking out quickly, but again, his opponent was prepared. Spotted Wolf laughed and leapt backward, then with a forward motion, laid open his enemy's upper right arm.

Another howl of pain erupted from Three Fingers and he struck out again, but he had lost most of his confidence and it proved to be his undoing. Spotted Wolf continued to play with him, his rage for what the other warrior had done to Jennifer overcoming his need to end the battle as quickly as possible. He continued to jab his knife into his opponent's flesh, finding satisfaction in his screams of pain. Finally though, when the other warrior turned to flee the battle circle, Spotted Wolf decided it was time to end the deadly game . . . and the other warrior's life.

When the battle was over and Three Fingers lay dead at his feet, Spotted Wolf took his scalp and returned to his lodge. Star Woman lifted her black eyes to him and found the answer to her question in his. Silently, she left his lodge, left him alone with the girl who lay fast asleep on his sleeping mat.

Jennifer was lost in a nightmare of a thickly wooded forest filled with so much evil that it pulsed around her, the shadows coalescing, converging until they became one huge entity. Her heart thudded heavily, each beat punctuated with fear as she stumbled backward on wooden legs, trying desperately to escape from the dark, shapeless mass that continued to draw nearer and nearer. Finally the pulsing mass converged, forming the shape of a man she suddenly realized was Three Fingers.

She awoke, jerking upright on the sleeping mat and stared into the darkness of the lodge. She gasped, her heart hammering so hard it seemed capable of shattering her ribs with its furious blows. Her mouth was dry, her hands curled into fists. Her terror was so great that it left her breathless, shaking as though with palsy.

"God help me," she whispered shakily. "Please help me."

"Hush, hush," a soothing voice said, moving closer to her. "There is nothing here to harm you, little one. It was only a nightmare and it is over now. You are safe here with me."

"Spotted Wolf?" She strained her eyes to see through the shadowy darkness. "Is that you?"

"Yes, it is me." The sound of his voice enveloped her like a silken web and she felt his strong arms grip her. She was thankful for his touch, grateful for his strength, for the tenderness in his gruff voice.

Jennifer burrowed her head against his chest and wrapped her arms around his neck. He stroked her hair, speaking soothing words to her as he slid down onto the sleeping mat, laying her down again tucked against him. "Did you have a bad dream?"

"Yes. It was horrible."

Pushing the tangled hair away from her face, he placed it behind her ear. "It is over now, little one. There is nothing here to harm you. We are alone. Just the two of us. And I will keep you safe. Remember that, dear one."

Just the two of us. Jennifer liked the way that sounded. She could close her eyes and pretend there was nobody in the world except the two of them.

Heaving a shuddering sigh, Jennifer snuggled closer against his strength and felt an almost overwhelming gratitude that he was beside her, that he had promised to keep her safe. Needing desperately to express that gratitude, she tilted her head and placed a soft kiss against his lips.

"Thank you, Spotted Wolf," she whispered shakily.

His reaction was immediate. His arms tightened around her and his body became taut. She drew back slightly, intrigued by his reaction. "Have you never been kissed before, Spotted Wolf?"

"Not often," he muttered. "And not for a long time."

His expression was incredibly gentle and his eyes glowed like the embers of a slow-banked fire. A peculiar warmth spread through her, making her feel weak as a kitten.

Jennifer wondered if her feelings showed in her face but the thought held no real concern for her. His gentle strength had calmed her, completely dispelling her fears until they scattered like leaves in the wind. "The kiss was my way of thanking you for saving me from Three Fingers."

His head lowered until his lips hovered mere inches above hers. "You do not place enough value on yourself, little one. Surely your life is worth more than one kiss."

His mouth covered hers in a kiss so sweet that it stole her breath away. And when he lifted his head, she uttered a moan of protest, but she needn't have done so. He seemed perfectly willing to continue.

Twenty-two

Jennifer sucked in a sharp breath as Spotted Wolf drove his tongue into her mouth, tasting, exploring. A hot flame speared through her, making breathing suddenly difficult and she uttered a low, throaty moan. She needed him so badly, needed to feel his flesh against hers, but her clothing was in the way.

She pulled away from him with great difficulty. "M-My clothes," she whispered, fumbling with the lacings on her doeskin dress.

Pushing away her fingers, he unfastened the dress and stripped it over her head. Moments later her undergarments joined the dress which lay in a crumpled heap on the earthen floor.

Although she craved him, she felt a sense of embarrassment, but it was only momentary, gone almost as quickly as it had come. The way he looked at her made her skin feel blazing hot, but it also made her proud too. She could tell by the shine of his green eyes that he found her body pleasing.

Bending slightly, his mouth covered hers in a kiss so tender, so filled with yearning that its sweetness brought tears to her eyes. His callused palm slid smoothly down her rib cage to her hips and over her thighs, a caressing, teasing movement that caused heat to spread through her lower body.

His fingers were deft and sure as he taught her the ways of love and his mouth moved continually, pressing kisses on her lips, her eyes and nose, then paused to nibble on her earlobe.

Jennifer quivered at the moist contact and stirred restlessly until he moved lower, blazing a fiery trail down her neck, her shoulders and finally reaching the swell of her right breast. He played with her then, teasing, taunting, bringing the nipples to straining hardness with his tongue and teeth. And when she quivered with desire, he lifted his head and looked at her, watching her reactions closely as his feathered caresses over her flat belly moved lower, stopping only when he reached her womanly place. His fingers delved into the moistness and Jennifer jerked with pleasure.

His lips covered hers again, his tongue probing and she opened her mouth and felt the warmth of his sweetness. His fingers continued their tender probing, moving against her moistness in slow circles until her body reacted senselessly, arching and pulsating, aching for more, for something that would satisfy the intense longing she was feeling, the exquisite torment that he was responsible for.

"Please," she whispered with desire. "Please, Spotted Wolf. My body aches with wanting."

As though he'd only been waiting for that moment, his fingers moved farther into her and began to move with a slow, torturously sweet rhythm. Her body trembled and burned, throbbed, aching with unfulfilled desire. Little cries poured from her mouth, words that were indistinguishable to her ears, their content unmistakable. As he continued to stroke her, the flames of desire rose higher and higher. She pulled at him, her nails digging into his back as the pleasure built beyond anything she'd ever dreamed possible.

His lips curled and his expression took on a fierce pleasure as he watched her. Oh, God, how much more could she stand? Even now her heart was racing wildly, thudding in her eardrums like a thousand hooves thundering across the hardpacked earth.

Jennifer moaned again. She must have relief soon. She could hardly stand the exquisite pleasure that his movements were producing.

Spotted Wolf knew the time had come. Her body was ready. It was the moment he had been waiting for.

Nudging her shivering legs apart, he fitted his long body over her and prepared to thrust down with one fierce, smooth movement that would cause her as little pain as possible.

"Spotted Wolf!"

The voice washed over him, turning his body cold as though he'd been drenched with ice water. It came from just outside the tepee, jerking Spotted Wolf into awareness of what he had almost done,

He felt the color drain away from his face as he looked down at the woman beneath him. Her wide-eyed gaze flickered from him to the entrance flap, then returned to him again and he saw the hunger in her eyes.

"Don't answer him," she whispered frantically. "Maybe he'll go away!"

Despising himself for what he'd almost allowed to happen, he rolled off her and reached for his hide breechcloth.

"Spotted Wolf!" The voice came again. "Wake up!

"I am awake," Spotted Wolf called loudly. Securing his breechcloth on his hips, he pulled the bedcover over Jennifer's naked body, hurried across the lodge and pushed the hide flap aside to see Coyote Man hovering near the entrance.

"You come late to visit," Spotted Wolf said, noticing that his voice held a harsh note.

"It is on a matter of grave importance," Coyote Man said grimly. "A messenger has just arrived with grim news. The bluecoats have been spotted near Blind Horse Mesa. They are headed this way. Quanah is gathering the warriors together to stop them. He waits in the council lodge now."

Although Spotted Wolf knew it was twenty miles to Blind Horse Mesa, he also knew the bluecoats must be turned back before they ventured closer. But the feat must also be accomplished without arousing their suspicions.

Ducking into his lodge again, he gathered up his weapons and his canteen, then added a pouch filled with pemmican as he was uncertain how long it would be before he returned.

"What are you doing?" Jennifer asked frantically. "Why are you taking your rifle?"

"I must go away for awhile," he said gruffly.

"Away?" She sat up, startled. "Why? Where are you going? How long will you be away? Need you go now?" she whispered.

"I have no answers for you. But you need not concern yourself. You will be safe here in the village."

"Don't go," she whispered, tears suddenly moistening her eyes. "Stay with me. Forget whatever you are planning. I can't bear to think of you in danger."

"Hush." He bent lower and kissed her forehead.

"Go back to sleep, little one. I will return before you know I have gone."

"Please, don't leave me."

Ignoring her plea, he left her alone in the lodge and hurried toward Coyote Man who waited for him. The two of them strode quickly across the compound and entered the council lodge to join the warriors already gathered there.

Quanah waited until the newcomers took their places, then spoke. "It is on a matter of great urgency that we are gathered together. The bluecoat colonel, Ranald MacKenzie, rides this way. And with him are more men than ten times all my fingers. We cannot allow them to continue their journey or they will surely discover our stronghold. A means must be found to divert them."

He continued to speak, telling them of his plan, and before an hour had passed the warriors had mounted their ponies and were riding out of the village.

Tears rolled down Jennifer's cheeks as she lay on the pallet and listened to the warriors ride away from the village. How many times had countless other women listened to their men ride out while they silently wondered if they would ever see them again?

How could they live with such fear without going insane? Jennifer knew she could not. But how could she do otherwise? It was all part of Spotted Wolf's life.

"Please come back," she whispered. "Don't leave me when I've only just found you." Feeling as though her heart would break, Jennifer turned over and laid her head within the circle of her arms. She stayed that way long into the night, and finally, as dawn began to break over the horizon, she fell into a deep, exhausted sleep.

The war party rode hard, and dawn had not yet chased away the shadows of night when they arrived at the cavalry camp of Colonel Ranald MacKenzie. Quanah led the charge through the camp, yelling and dragging buffalo hides along the ground, stirring up dust that helped to hide them from their enemies who emerged from their tents, their eyes so dazed with sleep they could barely see the targets, much less shoot them.

"Stampede the horses!" Quanah yelled, swerving his mount toward the corral. "Drive them off and the enemy cannot follow!" He swung his rifle up and shot the hapless fellow who crossed his path, then uttered a bloodcurdling war cry that chilled even Spotted Wolf's blood.

Spotted Wolf's lips curled in a grin. Quanah might only have seen twenty-six summers, but his courage was that of a man twice his years. He was a fiercely aggressive Comanche warrior, his courage equaled by few.

Following Quanah's lead, Spotted Wolf uttered his own war cry and fired his rifle, scattering the frightened horses to the four winds. With no mounts, the soldiers would be afoot, unable to continue their journey.

Out of the corner of his eye, Spotted Wolf saw Black Crow and Coyote Man climb on the supply wagons. Coyote Man ripped open sacks of flour and sugar and tossed them off the wagon while Black Crow shot holes in the water barrels and sent arrows through the tinned goods, making certain they would be spoiled.

A movement near the outer circle of tents jerked Spotted Wolf around, but it was only Black Thunder carrying a flaming torch. Within the space of a few moments he had set fire to several tents. Even as the soldiers turned on him, he raced away to join the other warriors already leaving the camp.

The soldiers had recovered enough so that now their shots were more careful. Taking note of that fact, Quanah ordered a retreat. Spotted Wolf urged his mount away, knowing it would take time for the bluecoats to round up their scattered mounts. Some of them would probably never be recovered. The bluecoats could do nothing except return to the fort for more supplies.

Having effectively accomplished their mission, the warriors urged their mounts toward their village again, satisfied that they had accomplished what they had come for. Bad Hand Ranald MacKenzie would not bother them again for awhile. At least long enough to determine their best move, whether it be to move their stronghold or use some other means to divert him.

It was late when Jennifer woke. She poured water in a bowl and splashed it across her face, then reached for the drying rag. She dried her face then returned the rag to its original position. Her hand brushed across something hairy that hadn't been there before. It was only then that she saw the grisly scalp that had been tossed carelessly beside the water jug.

Her stomach recoiled in shock. It was fresh, she knew, because the blood had barely dried on it. She turned away quickly as her stomach threatened to dislodge its contents, wondering who the scalp had belonged to.

Unable to eat so soon after the grisly discovery, Jennifer hurried out of the lodge to join the other women beneath the brush arbor who were already hard at work on their daily chores.

As she approached, Helen threw a curious look in her direction. "You slept late," she said. "I was beginning to wonder if you were all right."

"I had a restless night," Jennifer explained, casting an apologetic look toward Star Woman. "I overslept without meaning to."

"I'm not the least bit surprised," Helen said. "If Three Fingers had abducted me, I would probably be a raving maniac by now. I'm glad he's dead."

"He's dead?" she whispered. "How?"

Helen shrugged. "I heard Spotted Wolf killed him. Didn't you know?"

"No." She swallowed hard, knowing now whose bloody scalp she had seen in her lodge. "But I did see his scalp."

Helen's lips curled into a smile. "Good. He deserved to go without it in his journey through the land of the dead. Going without his hair will insure that he finds no happiness there. And he deserves none. Not after what he did to Sarah."

"You heard about Sarah?"

"Yes. I heard. I was at the river doing my laundry when it happened. It was late when I was finished and I didn't know you were missing until this morning. I'm sorry about what happened, Jennifer, but you mustn't blame yourself."

"I do though. She was so afraid and I could do nothing at all to help her. I should have done something."

"There was nothing you could do." The voice

came from the group of women seated across from them. Noticing Jennifer's puzzled look, the young woman spoke again. "It is my little daughter that you saved and I must thank you for your kindness. Your friend was frightened. She had been badly used by Three Fingers for so long that she could take no more. But there was nothing you could do for her. You could not set her free and she could not endure the punishment any longer. Do not blame yourself for what occurred."

Several women muttered, casting favorable looks toward Jennifer as though they too approved of what she had done. Then they turned their attentions to their work again, leaving the two captives to continue their conversation.

"I never expected that of them," Helen said, her lips twitching in a smile. "Did you?"

"No." She was silent for a long moment, her thoughts on Spotted Wolf. "Do you know why the warriors left the village, Helen?"

"I heard it was because of Colonel MacKenzie," Helen replied. "He was getting too close to the canyon. The Indians are always careful to keep the soldiers away from here."

"I'm surprised that doesn't make them suspicious," Jennifer commented.

"It's done in such a way as to keep from arousing suspicion," Helen replied.

Jennifer nodded her head. "I suppose there is a good chance some of them won't come back."

"There's always that chance. Last time they went on a raid, three of the warriors were killed and another one was wounded. He died a few days later."

The news did nothing to quiet Jennifer's fears. But she tried her best to keep them hidden. It wouldn't do to allow others to know how much she had come to care for Spotted Wolf. It was a weakness that might eventually be used against her.

Instead, she worried in silence, keeping her fingers busy, hoping that might give her less occasion to worry about Spotted Wolf. But God, she wished he would come back soon! Before worry drove her completely out of her mind.

Twenty-three

As Jennifer sat beneath the brush arbor mending a pair of Spotted Wolf's moccasins, she heard the sound of hooves pounding along the canyon floor. Her fingers stilled as alarm swept through her. Her heartbeat slowed, began to thud with dread and she looked across at Star Woman who continued to work steadily, her head bent over her sewing. Only the slight tremble in her fingers gave away her emotion. She, too, was alarmed.

Was it the warriors returning or the enemy approaching?

Her gaze touched on each of the Indian women. Although they appeared calm enough, she could tell they were hiding their fears. They faced life's uncertainties every day, knew each time their husbands left the stronghold that they might not return.

As though reading her thoughts, Helen spoke softly. "There's only one horse, Jenny. Nothing to worry about. It's prob'ly the lookout coming in with a message."

The rider appeared in the distance and Jennifer realized Helen had been right. As he drew closer, the braves who had been left behind gathered at the edge of the village. The messenger reined up his mount and spoke rapidly to those around him, then he rode out again, retracing his path down the canyon. An old man broke away from the others and began to chant as he circled the village.

Although Jennifer had learned some of the language, the old man spoke too swiftly for her to understand him. "What is he saying?"

"The old man is the village crier," Helen replied. "The warriors are returning, are descending into the canyon now. The messenger said the raid was successful."

"The raid!" Jennifer heard the alarm in her own voice. "Is that where they went? Was anyone hurt?"

"He did not say," Helen replied. "He only knows they have returned. Now the People will celebrate."

"They wouldn't celebrate if anyone was hurt. Would they?" Jennifer asked.

Helen's gaze was compassionate. "Jenny, you are too involved with him. You must not allow your feelings to overcome good sense."

"I don't know what you mean."

"You'll be leaving here soon. Alone."

"My uncle may not agree to the exchange."

"I cannot believe that. He would not abandon you. No man worth his salt would leave his kin with the Indians if he had a chance to save them." Her gaze was sympathetic. "Even if Spotted Wolf wasn't born an Indian, Jenny, he's still one of them."

"What do you mean?"

"Don't you know? They stole him when he was a baby."

Jennifer's eyes widened. "He's not one of them? No. You must be wrong. He looks like the others. His skin is just as brown."

"He was born white, believe me. But it don't matter. He's as much a Comanche as any of them. And he puts their welfare first."

Jennifer wanted more information, but Helen's owner was eying them. She stifled her questions and turned her attention to the basket she was weaving out of slender reeds.

Moments later, Star Woman set aside her sewing and rose to her feet. "The time for rejoicing is at hand." As though she had given a signal, the other women followed suit. "Our warriors have once again defeated Bad Hand MacKenzie. *Ma-be-quo-si-tu-ma,* fetch our root baskets and digging sticks and come with me. We must gather mescal before nightfall."

"But we have plenty of roots," Jennifer said.

"Not enough for a feast," the old woman said. "Now be quick. Go fetch our digging tools lest we be gone when the warriors arrive."

Jennifer hurried to obey. She joined Star Woman and the other women who were going to search for mescal.

The two captive women worked together, slicing away the sharp points of the mescal spears, then digging the root from the ground and adding them to the growing pile in their baskets. The sweet, fleshy base of the plant, roasted in pits, was a favorite food for the Indians and Jennifer found the taste quite pleasant.

Although the women hurried with their root gathering, the warriors had already arrived by the time the women returned to the village.

Jennifer searched the throng of warriors gathered beside the communal fire, looking for the tall warrior who had come to mean so much to her, but there was no sign of him. "I don't see Spotted Wolf," she said.

Star Woman eyed Jennifer appraisingly. Then there was a slight softening to her expression. "If my son were not among those who returned, then I would already have been told."

Thank you, God! Jennifer silently cried.

"There will be time enough to greet my son later, child," Star Woman said. "We must work quickly now. The roots must be taken to the river and scrubbed." She bent over to pick up one of the baskets, then uttered a sharp moan that was quickly stifled.

"Are you all right?" Jennifer asked anxiously.

"This body has seen too many years."

"You do too much, Star Woman," Jennifer said. "Stay here and rest while I wash the vegetables."

"You are a good child," Star Woman said. "I will be sorry to see you go." She patted Jennifer's arm. "Go along with the others now. Spotted Wolf will be here when you return."

Was she so transparent? Jennifer wondered. Did everyone know how she felt about Spotted Wolf? How could she care so much when she had known him only a few weeks?

After scrubbing the root vegetables, Jennifer returned to the village and left the baskets beside the fire pit. Then she hurried to the lodge she shared with Spotted Wolf. Disappointment settled over her when she found the dwelling empty. That feeling quickly changed to fear.

Had Spotted Wolf been injured? Perhaps killed? Oh, God, no! Star Woman would have been told if he had not returned. Unable to dispel her fears, she rushed out of the lodge and hurried to Star Woman's dwelling. The old woman was digging through her reed trunk, but when Jennifer entered she straightened slightly and turned to look at her. "What troubles you, child?"

"Spotted Wolf. I can't find him. I'm afraid he didn't come back. That he's been hurt or . . ."

"Hush, foolish child. He returned safe and sound."

"Are you sure?" Jennifer whispered.

"Yes. I have spoken with him. My son is well enough." She bent over the trunk again and pulled out a doeskin dress, decorated with blue and white beads. "Look what I have for you!"

"How beautiful," Jennifer murmured. "Did you make it?"

"Yes. Many seasons past. It was meant to be a gift for Spotted Wolf's bride. But it is yours now. A gift from me."

"Spotted Wolf's bride," Jennifer repeated softly, holding the dress up so that she could study the intricate beadwork. "It is beautiful. But you were saving it for his bride. Surely you don't mean for me to keep it?"

"It is yours to do with as you wish," the old woman said. "I am without hope that my son will ever take a bride."

A bride. Jennifer hated the though of Spotted Wolf becoming another woman's husband. She fingered one of the blue beads that adorned the soft doeskin dress. "Do the Comanche have weddings, Star Woman?"

"Yes we have those. But, unlike your people, the ceremony is simple. A warrior takes a gift to the lodge of the woman of his choice and if she accepts the gift, then she is obliged to accept the man as her husband."

"Has Spotted Wolf ever taken a wife?"

"No. There was a time when he meant to do so. But his beloved died."

"What was her name?"

"I cannot speak aloud the name of the dead."

"Oh, of course not! I forgot that custom. But you could answer questions if I asked them?"

"Perhaps."

"Then . . . was she beautiful?" Her voice sounded wistful and Jennifer hated that fact.

"Yes. She was very beautiful. To look upon her was like looking upon the sunshine after many days of rain. When he lost her, he lost himself for a time. But that was many seasons ago, child. More than two times all my fingers in summers have passed since then, but he continues to suffer for that loss, refuses to allow anything to quench the fires of rage." She became silent as though her thoughts had turned inward.

"It was my hope that he would put aside such thoughts and allow himself to enjoy what he has found, but I fear it is hopeless. He will never forget . . . or forgive . . . the way she died."

"How did she die?"

"She took her own life after being abused by a white man."

"Oh, God!" Jennifer clapped a hand across her mouth. "No wonder he has so much hatred for my kind."

"Not for you, *Ma-be-quo-si-tu-ma.* He does not hate you." Although her face remained expressionless, her voice was sad. "It will be hard for him when you leave us, in more ways than one."

Jennifer felt a sudden affection for the old woman. "Leaving doesn't hold the same appeal for me as it did before," she said.

"You wish to stay with us?" Star Woman's dark brows rose in surprise.

Jennifer thought carefully about her words. "Nobody likes being a slave, Star Woman. But to live free among you with Spotted Wolf . . . well, I think I might like that." She thought about what Helen had told her. "Star Woman, are you really Spotted Wolf's mother?"

The woman's body stiffened. Her eyes became hard. "I am his mother in every way that counts."

"I'm sorry. I didn't mean to . . ."

"Enough talk!" the old woman snapped. "Go now and make yourself ready for the celebration. There will be much feasting and dancing, and memories to make." Her voice softened slightly. "Forget what you have heard, child. Some people talk to exercise their jaws. Go and make your memories this night. They will keep you warm when you grow old."

Memories to make. Yes. Jennifer would make memories tonight. At least she would have those to take with her when she left. There would be memories of their time together. She would hold them in her heart, knowing they were all she would be allowed.

Jennifer suddenly hurried to the lodge she shared with Spotted Wolf and gathered up several items that she considered necessary. She added the dress and a pair of moccasins, then took the path leading to the secluded waterfall. She had to see him.

Twenty-four

Spotted Wolf took advantage of the excitement in the village to bathe in seclusion. The pool was deserted and he wasted no time wading into its cooling depths. The water was soothing to muscles wearied by long hours of hard riding. He soaked awhile, then swam the length of the pool several times before settling down beside the waterfall with a yucca root to scrub away dirt accumulated on his journey.

He had only just finished rinsing the lather from his hair when he heard the sound of humming.

His lips curled into a smile. The newcomer could only be Jennifer. She was humming the tune she'd sung to him when he was sick with fever.

Intent on surprising her, Spotted Wolf slid quickly into the narrow space behind the waterfall and watched her approach through the thin sheet of water.

Jennifer glanced around the pool, then stripped away her dress and flung it aside, leaving only her lacy undergarments. Spotted Wolf's smile deepened. He would wait until she was actually in the water before leaping out to surprise her.

Although he'd expected her to bathe in her undergarments to protect her modesty, she surprised him by stripping them away and entering the water naked. He knew he should announce his presence then, but somehow could not bring himself to break the silence.

The water lapped sinuously around her hips and waist, beading on her breasts, making him want to lick the moisture from the rounded mounds. He felt a tightening in his lower body, a twisting in his loins that signaled his need for a woman. But not just any woman. He needed Jennifer. But he had to resist that need. He *must* resist it.

He closed his eyes against the sight of her nakedness, but the memory could not be ignored. Her naked breasts beaded with moisture lingered in his mind, causing his body to react in a way that was almost painful.

Spotted Wolf opened his eyes again and allowed himself the pleasure of watching her rub yucca root across her breasts and upper body, then work it into lather for her hair.

Unable to watch her bathe any longer, he left his hiding place and swam through the water until he reached her. She stood with her back to him, unaware of his presence until he reached around her for the root, accidently brushing the swell of her breasts as he did.

Uttering a fearful scream, she spun around, both hands raised to strike. Her eyes widened, her tightened mouth relaxed, curving in a welcoming smile. The hands that had been clenched into fists uncurled and slid around his neck.

"So there you are," she whispered, lifting herself on tiptoe so her mouth hovered mere inches below his. "I have been looking for . . ."

Spotted Wolf didn't allow her to finish. He could not. With her breasts pressed so tightly against his chest and her thighs brushing against him, his desire was too intense to be ignored.

His lips covered hers and he buried his tongue in her warm mouth, tasting the sweetness he found there. Her hands gripped his shoulders tighter and her tongue battled with his. His breathing was labored but so was hers, and when he lifted his mouth to lick droplets of moisture from her neck, she moaned softly and dug her fingernails into his shoulders.

It was Spotted Wolf's undoing.

Lifting her into his arms, he carried her to the bank and lowered his mouth to hers again.

There was no trace of shyness in her actions as she pressed her naked body closer against his. This was what she wanted. Even though she would not be allowed to live with the man she loved, at least she would have the memory of their loving.

Every inhibition she had ever possessed had completely vanished, leaving only the pleasure of his palm against her flesh, the deft sureness of his fingers intent on teaching her the ways of love.

His tongue probed the moist darkness of her mouth while his fingers worked magic on her. Her body reacted senselessly and she began to shiver as though she had developed chills. But it wasn't cold that made her react that way. No. Her body was on fire with need. She arched against him, achingly, desperate to ease the fire that threatened to consume her.

"Oh, God, Spotted Wolf," she pleaded. "I need you so much."

But he ignored her pleading, continued to move

his fingers in that slow, sweet rhythm that caused her to go wild with need.

"No more," she begged. "Take me now."

Still he ignored her, taking great pleasure in having brought her to such a fevered pitch that she begged for his possession. She moaned and babbled while she dug her nails into his body, trying to force him to merge with her own, yet still he continued to resist.

She felt herself building to an explosion and tried to hold it back until he joined with her.

"Now," she whispered, opening her mouth and biting down on his earlobe. "Don't make me wait any longer!"

Oh, God, she must have relief. She could hardly stand it . . . the exquisite pain of such pleasure.

Spotted Wolf fitted his body over hers and plunged downward. Her eyes widened and she cried out as he took her.

But she didn't draw back.

Even at the faintly piercing pain that quickly diminished in the face of a slow, anguished pleasure that fed on itself and grew and grew with each sharp, downward movement of his body.

Somewhere along the way, his taut face became a blur, and she shuddered with untold passion and release just as she heard his hoarse cry and felt the deep dragging convulsions of his body.

Jennifer opened her eyes at last, feeling new, reborn. Her skin was damp and cool. So was his. He was lying over her, deadweight now that the passion had drained out of him and her arms enfolded him tenderly, holding him to her. She moved and felt him move with her, awed by the fusion of her body with his, with the devastating intimacy of their lovemaking.

* * *

Feeling replete from their loving, Spotted Wolf held Jennifer close against him. Although he realized he should not have taken her innocence, he could not regret having done so. She would be leaving soon, going beyond his reach and he would have nothing of her except the memory of their loving.

This night.

How could he stand losing her when he'd only just found her? It would be hard, and yet the pain of losing her must be endured.

Would his actions have repercussions? He had agreed to return her unharmed, yet he had taken her innocence, compromised the bargain they had made with the bluecoats.

Suddenly the enormity of what he had done struck him fiercely. Great Creator! He had endangered Cloud Dancer's life. And there was no way he could put things back the way they were. No way he could restore her innocence.

Did he even want to?

"Spotted Wolf?"

Her voice came to him, soft, tender, filled with so much love that Spotted Wolf cursed himself roundly. But it was too late to set things right.

"Spotted Wolf?" she whispered again. "Are you asleep?"

He could hear the smile in her voice.

"No."

"What are you thinking about?"

"You don't want to know."

"Yes. I do want to know." She laughed softly and snuggled closer in the circle of his embrace. "I had no idea you could make love like that. Oh, God, it was fantastic. *You* were fantastic. So magnificent."

Each word she spoke was like a knife thrusting deeper into his heart. Had she no idea of the consequences of their actions? Apparently not. Or else she didn't care.

"I should not have allowed that to happen," he said.

"Yes, you should have. It was destiny that brought us together and, no matter what happens, I will never regret loving you." She propped herself on her elbow and stared down at him. "Do you really regret it?" she asked, sure of his answer.

Yes. "No," he replied. What good would it do to say otherwise? The deed was done. And, if truth be known, he could recall the exact moment when he'd looked down at her, when she'd cried out with ecstasy. Cried out for him. For Spotted Wolf. "I don't regret it." Time enough later for regret. Time enough then to think of what he'd done.

And what exactly had he done besides take her innocence and compromise the bargain that had been struck? The answer was simple. He had fallen in love with her.

He couldn't say how it had happened or when. He only knew that it had.

But it was not in his destiny to love her. Nor in hers to love him. They were from two different worlds. Nothing could change that. He had found love again, only to lose it, as he had done once before.

But not now, his heart cried. Not yet. Allow me a short time with her. Just a few days . . . days that must last me the rest of my life.

Satisfied with his answer, Jennifer laughed softly. "I don't suppose we could miss the celebration, could we?"

"No," he replied. "But I wish we could."

"So do I." She rolled away from him. "If we must attend, then I need to wash my hair." She grinned down at him. "Would you like to help me?"

"Yes." His eyes caressed her. "Perhaps you need another bath too. I could lather your breasts and . . ."

"Then we'd never make the celebration," she said laughing. "I think I'd better wash myself."

When she had finished and wrung the excess water from her hair, she used the porcupine comb she'd brought to work out the tangles. Then, with unhurried movements, she donned the beaded dress that Star Woman had given her.

"Do you like it?" she asked, turning around slowly for his inspection.

"Very much," he said softly. "And I think I have something that will be perfect with it." He produced a necklace for her. It was an octagon shaped crystal hanging from a delicate gold chain.

"What an exquisite necklace," she said, taking it in her palm. "I love it, Spotted Wolf. Wherever did you get it?" She ran her fingers over the faceted edges of the clear crystal.

He smiled at her obvious delight. "I traded for it many years ago. It is a healing stone."

"A healing stone?"

"Yes. Many of the People believe those who wear it will live a long life."

"It's beautiful," she whispered.

"So are you. I especially admire what is beneath your dress."

She stood on tiptoe to press a quick kiss against his mouth. "I like what's beneath your loincloth too," she said, gazing pointedly at his maleness.

As though gratified by her admiration, his member swelled beneath the hide covering, making her smile widen even more.

He swatted her on the behind and muttered, "Stop your teasing before I throw you down on the ground again."

"Ummmm. That might be interesting."

He reached for her, then stopped as they heard the sound of drums. "It is too late," he said wryly. "The celebration is beginning. Come now." He took her hand. "Let us take our place among the watchers. The celebration dance will soon begin."

Soon they were seated beside Star Woman, watching the dancers circle the fire, their feet keeping time with the drums. The flames leaped and jumped, casting eerie shadows against the hide dwellings, coloring the dancers with an orange glow. The drums pounded steadily, beating in time to stomping feet and exultant voices that rose and fell.

The medicine man leaped forth, wearing a cloak made out of pelts, his headdress covered with brilliant plumes. His feet stomped the ground while he chanted loudly, his head tilting back, his arms raised skyward.

"He is giving thanks to the Supreme Being for allowing us to return safely," Spotted Wolf said.

Although the ceremony was completely alien to her, Jennifer felt it had a savage beauty unequaled by any other she had ever seen. She leaned against Spotted Wolf's shoulder, comforted by his presence, and watched the ritual of the dance played out.

"They are getting ready for the Love Dance, Jennifer. The Comanche Love Song."

"What are the women doing?" she asked, as they formed a circle.

"Readying themselves for the Love Dance," he

said. "Go on. Join them. Helen is there. She will
show you what to do."

"Oh, but I couldn't," she said. "I don't know how
to do it. I'm afraid I would feel foolish."

But he would not be refused. He stood and led
her toward the other women. Helen moved aside to
make a place for her. Jennifer listened to Helen's
instructions which seemed simple enough. She
stood in the circle with her back to the musicians
facing the audience.

The tom-toms began their rhythmic beat very
slowly and the singers began to chant the Love Song
in a weird low tone. Then the women began to hum
the song. Jennifer listened carefully and followed
along easily. The women knelt and rose from heel
to toe in time with the cadence of music and song.
Each time they rose on their toes, they glided to the
left and went around in a circle. Young and old
women alike held out their arms as if for an embrace. They turned back, moved to the circle of
seated warriors, and held out their hands.

Having been told it was considered an insult for
a warrior to refuse to dance with a woman, Jennifer
nudged aside a maiden and stood before Spotted
Wolf, her arms stretched out beckoning him.

He rose instantly to his feet and faced her, his
hands on her shoulders, hers on his. They glided
to her left at arms length. Round and round they
went, circling the women who beat the tom-toms
and the musicians who played the flutes.

Jennifer swayed and dipped with the others, her
eyes glittering with pleasure as she danced with
Spotted Wolf. And when the dance ended, she sat
beside him and wished the night would never end.

It was late when Jennifer rose and followed Spotted Wolf to their lodge. She threw a smile at him.

There was no hesitation in her movements when she slipped the doeskin dress over her head and discarded her undergarments, stretching out on the sleeping mat to watch Spotted Wolf. He avoided her gaze as he stripped his breechcloth away.

When he lay down beside her, she curled her arms around his neck and pressed herself tightly against him, eager for the moment when he would possess her again.

An errant sunbeam teased Jennifer's eyelids and she moved her head slightly to escape it. She felt a warm breath against her neck, smiled and opened her eyes.

"Spotted Wolf," she breathed softly, reaching up to encircle his neck with her arms.

He pressed a kiss against her neck, then quickly released her.

She pouted at him. "Do we have to get up now?"

He smiled down at her, but the smile didn't quite reach his eyes. Instead, she detected a curious longing, something she couldn't quite understand. "Yes," he said harshly. "We have to get up."

"Why?" she persisted.

"Because there's work to be done!" he said.

Disappointed, she watched him move across the lodge. His sinewy muscles rippled as he reached for the bow and quiver of arrows hanging from the pole near the entrance.

"You're leaving now?" she asked, pushing herself to her elbows. "Without eating breakfast?"

He looked at her and she saw a deep sadness in his eyes. "I have no hunger in my belly," he said. His lips curled slightly as though attempting a smile. "I will be back before you know I am gone."

She smiled up at him. "Good. I'll have something ready for you to eat then."

He nodded his dark head and left the tepee.

She watched him leave, puzzled over his behavior. What was wrong with him? She had expected a different reaction from him this morning. After their night of lovemaking, she'd hoped he would stay and talk awhile, tell her about himself, utter words he'd never spoken with anybody else.

She didn't know much about him, but she wanted to learn. She wanted nothing to remain hidden between them.

Although Jennifer took extra pains in cleaning the lodge, that chore took hardly any time at all. She went to join the women who worked beneath the brush arbor, keeping her eyes out for Spotted Wolf's return.

Helen was working on the reed basket again and Jennifer took her place beside her.

"I understand you will be leaving tomorrow," Helen said. "I imagine you're glad to be going. I'm going to miss you, Jennifer. It will be lonesome now that Sarah is gone and . . ." She broke off and her eyes widened. "What's wrong, Jenny?"

"How do you know I'm leaving tomorrow? Who told you that?"

"Why, everyone is talking about it. They're all excited about Cloud Dancer being released. There'll be another celebration and that will involve extra work."

Jennifer swallowed. "Spotted Wolf said four days."

"He was probably allowing for travel time."

"I will miss you, Helen."

"And I shall miss you too."

"Will you be all right?"

Helen nodded. "There's a good chance that I'll

be going home soon too. There's been some talk that the Mexican who rode in this morning offered gold for me. He said he would take me to the nearest fort. Wouldn't it be wonderful if it's Fort Davis? I feel funny about leaving here though. I don't know how they will accept me after everything that's happened, and I have a peaceful life here, despite everything."

Jennifer was still trying to absorb Helen's words. "Helen, who did you say rode in?"

"A Mexican. He came with a one-eyed Kiowa." She laughed abruptly. "The Mexican's name is Chavez. The Kiowa is called One Eye."

A cold chill shuddered over Jennifer. "Don't go with them, Helen. They can't be trusted. Did they say what they were doing here?"

"I don't know. I suppose they came to talk to Quanah. What do you mean they can't be trusted? Do you know them?"

Jennifer nodded her head. "I know One Eye. And I know they are stealing army rifles. And I think they would do anything for gold. They might even lead the soldiers here if they were offered enough money."

She noticed the silence suddenly and looked up to see the Indian women watching them. She looked at each of them in turn.

"Tell your husbands not to trust those men. They are evil. *Che.* Bad. *Noo-be-er!* They would kill all of you with no regret."

"We know that," Star Woman said. "But the Comancheros have traded with us a long time. Very rarely do they come to our villages." She nodded her head thoughtfully. "You must tell Spotted Wolf everything you know of them. He will know what to do."

Twenty-five

Jennifer was waiting for Spotted Wolf when he returned late that evening. "Why didn't you tell me we were leaving tomorrow?" she asked. "Why did I have to find out from others?"

"I knew you would be upset."

She gave him a withering stare. "Upset? Why should I be upset? We're just talking about the rest of my life here!" She stood with clenched fists, glaring at him, trying to sustain her anger, afraid if she let go of it that she would dissolve into tears. "Everyone knew except me." She pressed her lips together, trying to control herself.

"Do not weep, little one. Our love was never meant to be. I should never have allowed myself to take your innocence." He traced her cheekbone with his thumb, cupped her chin with a gentle palm. "It is my fault. I should be whipped for treating you so."

Please, God, give me strength, she silently cried. Don't let me break down. Despite her efforts at control, a tear crawled slowly down her cheek.

"Don't! Don't say things like that!" She flung herself into his arms. "Hold me, Spotted Wolf. Hold me tight. Don't let me go!"

His arms curled around her and he hugged her

fiercely against his chest. "You are making things difficult, little one."

"Why should I make it easy for you?" She pulled back and struck him on the shoulder. "It *is* your fault! You made me love you! Why did you do that if you didn't want me? How could you be so cruel?"

"Oh, my love, I tried so hard to leave you alone!" He pushed her head beneath his chin. "I tried so very hard, but it did no good. I was too weak to resist."

She broke down and released the flood of tears she'd been holding back. He held her tightly, rocking her back and forth while she cried. And when her sobs finally subsided, he kissed her cheek as though he were comforting a child.

A sad smile lifted one corner of his mouth and the anguish in his eyes mirrored the torment that twisted her heart.

Why? Oh, God, why had she found him when he could never be hers? She was filled with a terrible sadness, a hurt that went deeper than pain.

"I don't want to go, Spotted Wolf. Isn't there some way I can stay here with you? Isn't there something we can do? Anything at all?" She hated herself for pleading, but knew she had to try to make him see how miserable life would be without him.

"I would keep you beside me forever if I could, my love. Please understand why you must leave. If there was a way to keep you beside me, do you think I would ever send you away?"

"There *is* a way," she insisted. "Don't you see? We could just not go."

"And leave Cloud Dancer to his fate?" His voice was hard, his gaze boring into her. "Do you really expect me to abandon him? He suffers untold torment in that prison of his. And he could easily be free of it. All he has to do is tell what they want to know. How to find our village."

She felt a momentary shame for having suggested leaving Cloud Dancer to his fate. "All right." She swallowed hard and looked away from him. "I'll go back. I apologize for . . . for . . ."

"Oh, Jennifer." He sighed deeply. "I wish I could make you understand how important this is."

"I understand."

"We have several days left, Jennifer," he grumbled. "We could make the most of those days."

"No!" she said sharply, pinning him with hard eyes. "How could you even suggest such a thing?"

He ran his fingers through his dark hair and looked away from her. "You are right. It would serve no purpose, would only make the parting worse. We will leave at first light. It will take us three days to reach the rendezvous."

Rendezvous. The words struck a chord in her mind. She told him about the men who had arrived in the village and what she'd overheard at the leaning rock.

"Chavez offered to take Helen back to the fort, but he can't be trusted," she said fiercely. "I'm afraid she'll wind up in a bordello or as a permanent fixture with the Comancheros. They would betray anyone for a few pieces of gold."

"Do you want me to stop them from taking Helen?"

"I don't know. It might be her only chance to go back."

"No. I will see she is returned to her people."

"You would do that for me?"

"Yes."

"Those men might lead the soldiers back here."

"We have dealt with men like them in the past,"

he said hoarsely. "Precautions are being taken. Another location has been found for our stronghold."

"Where?"

"I cannot say, Jennifer. You know that."

"Yes. I'm sorry." If they were moving to some unknown location, there was no way she would ever find him again. "Are . . . are you hungry?" Her voice was barely a whisper, a quiver away from a sob.

"Yes," he groaned. "But not for food."

His husky voice was her undoing. It unleashed another flood of tears. He curled his arms around her again. "Do not weep, little one. I should not have spoken. It was very foolish of me!"

"I d-don't want to cry," she sobbed. "But I can't seem to help it. I don't want to leave you."

"I know." His arms tightened. "But you must."

"But it won't be over then." She looked pleadingly at him. "Say it won't be over between us. Promise me, Spotted Wolf. Say you will come for me later."

He looked away from her as though he couldn't bring himself to say the words she wanted so desperately to hear.

"Look at me, dammit!" she cried, digging her fingernails into his shoulders. "Just say it! Say the words. Just say this isn't all we'll ever have!" She shivered with the force of her emotion.

With a muttered exclamation, he turned back to her. "I cannot do this," he groaned. "I cannot allow you to go this way." A single tear rolled down her cheek and he wiped it away with a large, callused hand. "Do not weep, my love. I have no intention of leaving you there. But you must return to them. The exchange must be made."

She stared at him, wide-eyed. "You have something in mind? Some way to gain Cloud Dancer's release and bring me back?"

"Yes. But I was afraid to tell you."

"But why?"

"The bluecoats will stop at nothing to find us, Jennifer. Never forget that. And they will use any means available to them . . . even stoop to badgering you endlessly to make you reveal your knowledge of our location." He gripped her chin tightly. "Do you understand? If they believe you care for me, they will question you endlessly. You must not allow them to know how you feel."

"So you were trying to make me believe that you would leave me there." The knowledge did little to diminish her pain. "You should have trusted me. I wouldn't reveal anything that would cause any of you harm. You should have known that."

"I know you would not do so intentionally. But they have ways, Jennifer."

"My uncle wouldn't allow them to hurt me!"

"I hope you're right, my love. I despise myself for sending you back to them. But there is no other way. You do understand that?"

She nodded her head. "Yes. I understand." She realized he was worried and tried her best to reassure him. "They won't hurt me. Please believe that. My uncle is a good man."

They spent the night in each other's arms and at dawn, after many good-byes and expressions of goodwill from the women, Jennifer went to Helen and kissed her on the cheek.

"You won't be here much longer, Helen," she whispered. "Spotted Wolf told me last night that he'd make arrangements to send you home again."

"Is that true?"

"Of course. I trust him completely."

"So that's why Chavez wasn't allowed to buy me."

"Yes. I was afraid for you."

Helen smiled widely. "Then maybe this isn't good-bye after all. Maybe I'll see you at the fort soon enough."

Jennifer didn't bother to correct Helen. Everything depended on her ability to keep silent, and she might as well start now.

They mounted their ponies and rode away from the village. Jennifer turned in her saddle to wave goodbye to Helen who stood apart from the others. Then she turned and faced forward again.

That night, Spotted Wolf told her of his plan. "I will come for you in two weeks, Jennifer. When it is time to move the stronghold. Do you remember the place where you first met me?"

"Beside the big boulder?"

"Yes. It is a good place to wait. The small cave will provide shelter from prying eyes."

"You won't have to wait," she said fiercely. "Just tell me when to be there."

"At sunset," he replied. "I will be there at sunset, Jennifer. If you love me, then come to me there."

"If I love you?" she questioned huskily. "You know I do. Haven't I proved it over and over again? But you might change your mind about me." She looked away from him, focused on the flames that leaped and danced in the fire pit, waiting for him to deny her words.

"Never!" he whispered. "I love you. Please believe that."

"I do," she said tremulously. "But you might see things differently then . . . after we've been apart for awhile."

His body became rigid, tense. "You might change your mind, but not me."

"Are you sure? Sweet Willow wants you." She tried to hide her jealousy. "She could hardly keep her eyes off you during the Love Dance."

"Were you jealous?" he teased.

"A little. But only the tiniest bit."

"You need not be. Sweet Willow is a beautiful woman, but these eyes of mine see no one but you, my love."

Sweet Willow is a beautiful woman. Somehow, the words could not be dismissed so lightly. "Spotted Wolf. If you aren't there waiting for me I will understand."

"Do not be foolish. I will be there." His green eyes became darker as they gazed softly down to her mouth. Her lips went slowly to his. His lips parted and she could feel his breath mingling with her own.

His fingers eased into her hair and he gripped her head and tilted it back, exposing the smooth line of her neck. His green eyes glittered down at her; his nostrils flared. He watched her with an unblinking intensity that increased her hunger for him.

"Kiss me," she murmured.

As though that was all he had been waiting for, his mouth opened to taste her own. She felt his body harden against hers and it fired her hunger, making her flames of desire leap higher and higher. His tongue mingled with hers, caressing the moist cavern of her mouth, leaving her shaking, weak with desire.

When he pulled away she groaned, "No, Spotted Wolf! Kiss me again!" She tugged at him but he resisted her efforts to pull him close again. She opened her eyes and saw him fumbling with the ties of his breechcloth.

Hurriedly, she pulled her dress over her head and discarded it, then fumbled with the fastenings of her chemise.

Moments later they came together again. Their loving was swift, passionate, and when it was over they lay together, arms wrapped around each other and slept.

After breakfasting on hot corn meal, they continued on their way, the days spent riding, the nights loving. It ended too soon and they looked down into the valley where the exchange would be made. Jennifer turned to Spotted Wolf and swallowed hard. "I don't want to leave you. Even for two weeks."

"Nor do I want to leave you. If there was any other way, I would not."

"Will you hold me one last time?"

"As much as I want to, I dare not do so. Someone may be watching us this very moment. They must not know of our love for each other, lest they use it against us."

The wind blew a thick strand of hair across her eyes and she brushed it away with a trembling hand. Oh, God, how could she stand leaving him without knowing for certain he would come back for her?

In the valley directly below them she could see three mounted horsemen. Two were wearing blue uniforms while the other was wearing buckskin. It was easy to see why the valley had been chosen to make the exchange. There were very few trees there, only grass covered the ground. There would be no place for soldiers to hide from eyes that would be searching for some sign of a trap.

Squaring her shoulders, Jennifer raised her chin and followed the man she loved into the valley, feeling as though she were riding to her doom. As they drew closer, she recognized her uncle. He had taken up position on the left side of the buckskin clad man. He kneed his horse forward when he caught sight of her.

"Jennifer!" Major Carlisle's voice rang out. He reined his mount up beside her. "My dear, it is so good to see you again!" Leaning over, he gripped her by the shoulders. His eyes bored into hers as though they could see into her very soul. "Have you been harmed, Jenny?"

"No." She shook her head. "They didn't hurt me, Uncle Walter. I am quite all right." She looked at the Indian warrior that had kneed his horse toward Spotted Wolf. There was nothing unusual in his appearance. Nothing to show that he was worth so much more than herself. "And their medicine man, Uncle. Is he all right?"

"Of course." Major Carlisle's gaze met Spotted Wolf's. "The exchange is made now. And I came without weapons as you requested. But be warned, Indian. I will never rest until I see you suffer for the pain you caused my niece. Even now Colonel MacKenzie is gathering forces to hound you to the ends of the earth if necessary. He won't rest until he sees the lot of you on a reservation so you can't do decent folk any more harm than you already have."

"Come on, Uncle," Jennifer said. "Let's go home."

Spotted Wolf looked at Jennifer as though she were a stranger. Then, suddenly, he reined his horse around. Her breath caught in her throat. He was leaving her so easily. Without even a backward glance. He reined his horse around again and kneed it forward until he was beside Jennifer. His face was grim and his eyes wild as they held hers.

Her heart gave a sudden lurch. Had he changed his mind? Would he take her with him now?

"Watch out for Captain Brady." His voice was low enough so that the others could not hear. "He cannot be trusted."

Before she could ask what he meant, he dug his heels into his mount and raced away, leaving her staring after him yearningly.

"What in hell was that all about?" Major Carlisle asked. "What did he say to you, Jennifer? Could you understand him?"

"Yes. I learned some of the language. Just enough to know he warned me against Captain Brady."

"Warned you against him? What do you mean?"

"Spotted Wolf said he couldn't be trusted."

"Balderdash!" Major Carlisle exclaimed. "Brady's a good man. Salt of the earth!"

Jennifer met her uncle's look with one of her own. "Is he? I wouldn't bet on it."

"That Indian is just trying to stir up trouble. It's their way, Jennifer. Divide and conquer. Well, it won't work with me." Even though his words were said with certainty, his expression suddenly became thoughtful.

Jennifer knew that her uncle wouldn't completely dismiss Spotted Wolf's warning. He was a stubborn man, but also an intelligent one as well. He would think about the warrior's warning, would consider his words carefully and if Captain Brady made one misstep, if he did anything out of place, her uncle would find out.

Twenty-six

By the time they reached the fort the sun had already dropped below the western horizon. As the gates loomed before them, tension stiffened Jennifer's spine and squared her shoulders. She was suddenly conscious of the way she looked riding astride the Comanche pony with her bare legs showing beneath the hem of her doeskin dress.

They rode across the parade ground and she lifted her chin slightly, tilting it at a defiant angle. She refused to apologize for what had happened to her.

A door was suddenly pushed open and a woman stepped from the Suttler's store to watch their progress. Jennifer reined her mount toward the long row of houses, stopping beside the one assigned to her uncle.

He dismounted and reached to help her down. "There are some people here who'll be waiting to talk to you, my dear," he said flatly. "But I should be able to hold them off until you've bathed and changed." He looked at the doeskin dress with distaste.

"Who's here to speak with me?"

"An officer sent here by Colonel MacKenzie who heard about your abduction and our plans to exchange you for their medicine man. He's hoping you'll be able to give them some information about the Comanche stronghold."

His words sent a chill through her. Spotted Wolf had been right. "How long will this questioning last, Uncle Walter?" she asked in a deliberately cool voice.

"I don't really know, my dear. I imagine it won't take very long though. You must not hold anything back though. Major Holt will need to know everything."

"Exactly what do you mean by that?" Her voice dripped icicles.

His face colored slightly. "Just that they'll need to know the direction you were traveling. You should know that, unless you were blindfolded." He coughed slightly. "You weren't blindfolded, were you?"

"No. I wasn't blindfolded. But I'm afraid I can't help very much. There was nothing to see out there. No landmarks to speak of."

"Even that tells us something. If there were no trees about, then we need not look in the cedar brakes." He cleared his throat. "You go on now, honey." He avoided her gaze as he used the endearment, something that he never had done before, increasing her suspicion that the interview was likely to become unpleasant. "Take your bath and change your clothes and take time to eat something before you come to my office. We'll wait for you there."

With her mouth tightened into a grim line, Jennifer climbed the porch steps and entered the parlor. She had barely closed the door behind her when it was flung open again.

Jennifer spun around to face Clara.

"Oh, God, Jennifer!" Clara cried. "I didn't think I would ever see you again!"

"Hello Clara."

"Hello Clara?" The girl's eyes widened. "Is that all you have to say to me after all this time? Just 'Hello Clara?' "

Jennifer controlled the urge to laugh at her friend. "What did you expect me to say?"

"For God's sake, Jennifer! Tell me what happened while you were gone!" She gripped Jennifer's upper arms tightly. "Just look at you! Look at the clothes you're wearing. What did those savages do to you?"

"I'm tired, Clara. I need to sit down."

"Of course you are. Poor dear."

Jennifer pushed a cushioned chair toward her friend. "Sit down and try to control yourself."

"Control myself?" Clara squeaked. "Jennifer! You disappeared! You act like nothing happened at all!"

"Exactly what have you been told, Clara?"

Clara settled herself on the chair. "We were told that a messenger had come." Her eyes widened dramatically. "I saw him, Jennifer. He was a savage! He gave your uncle a message saying the Indians were willing to exchange you for the medicine man they were holding in the stockade." She squirmed on the cushioned seat, obviously too excited to sit still.

"We didn't know where you were until then. Whether you were alive or dead. My God, why did you go out again that night? Do you know how much I suffered? All this time I've been blaming myself for leaving you alone! Why did you do it?"

Jennifer sighed. "I can't talk about this right now, Clara. My uncle is expecting me as soon as I've bathed and changed clothes." She looked down at herself. "He doesn't like my dress either."

"Are you supposed to talk to that Major Holt that rode in this morning?"

"Yes. I think so." She rose to her feet and gave Clara a gentle push toward the door. "I don't mean to be rude, but I must hurry. We'll have a long talk tomorrow."

"Tomorrow?" Clara's eyes narrowed. "Why not tonight?"

"Because I have a sneaking suspicion the officer Colonel MacKenzie sent to interview me will be keeping me up late tonight."

"I hope not. You look dog-tired."

Clara's reluctance to leave was evident in every step she took toward the door. When the door was firmly closed behind her, Jennifer drew water for her bath and laid out fresh clothing. She intended to have a long soak before she faced the man who'd been sent to question her.

Spotted Wolf's heart was heavy as the distance lengthened between himself and the woman he loved. But he had other things to occupy his mind, especially since Cloud Dancer was in bad shape from his long confinement. He was an old man, already weakened from several months behind bars, and the long ride was taking its toll on him. They had to stop more often than they would normally have done to allow the old man to rest.

It was on the third day, when they were no more than ten miles from the canyon, that Spotted Wolf realized they were being followed. Suspecting the tracker was from the fort, he deliberately made camp early that night as the sun dipped below the horizon.

"We are being followed," he told the old man.

"We dare not ride closer to the stronghold with the enemy on our trail."

"No," Cloud Dancer said. "We are too close. If we eluded our enemies at this point, they would search until they found the canyon. You must kill them, Spotted Wolf."

"I know."

"I am an old man, too slow to react when there is need. But I will bait the trap that will bring them into the open."

Leaving the old man beside the campfire, Spotted Wolf took up his bow and arrows, as though he were intent on hunting meat for their evening meal, and walked away from the camp.

Night descended, covering the plains with purple shadows, but the old man kept a fire burning to keep away the cold night air and to make himself more visible to the enemy.

Under cover of night, Spotted Wolf scouted the area. He found the tracks of two shod horses, confirming his suspicions. They *had* been followed.

Hidden by the darkness, he circled back to the campsite and waited in the shadows, alert for the slightest movement that would expose his enemy.

Jennifer sat stiffly on the straight backed chair in her uncle's office and eyed the man who continued to hammer her with endless questions. "I have already told you everything I know," she said calmly.

"I don't think so." He was a big man with a face that looked as though it had been stomped on. If she wasn't mistaken, his nose had been broken at least once. Perhaps more. But it was his eyes that bothered her the most. They were steel gray and just as hard. He was a man who wouldn't give up easily.

"Are you calling me a liar, Major Holt?"

"Of course not," he said smoothly. "I'm merely saying that you might not be aware of the knowledge you possess. But it is there, locked in your mind."

"You can't know that."

"It is highly unlikely that, given the weeks you spent with the Comanche, you would come away with no knowledge at all. For instance, what did the terrain you traveled over look like?"

They had been at this for over four hours now and Jennifer felt completely exhausted. But she refused to speak without first considering each word carefully.

"It almost seems as though you're trying to protect someone," Major Holt said, eying her suspiciously.

"Major Holt!" Jennifer's uncle snapped. "You go too far, to suggest that my niece would do anything of the sort. She's trying her best to cooperate with you. But you must understand the stress she has been under. She hasn't had any rest at all, and there's no telling how far she's been made to travel in the last few days."

"That's exactly what I'm trying to determine here. The distance this young lady has traveled." Major Holt's gaze bored into her as though he would delve into her innermost thoughts. "Were you under stress, Miss Carlisle? Or were you, perhaps, enjoying moments of your captivity?"

"Dammit, Major! That's enough!" roared Major Carlisle. "I will not have you insulting my niece in that manner! Apologize, sir! At once, before I stuff your words down your throat!"

"I apologize if I was out of line, Miss Carlisle," Major Holt said gruffly.

Jennifer knew from his tone that he wasn't the least bit apologetic, that he was only voicing the words for her uncle's benefit. She smiled widely at him, showing a lot of teeth so he would know he hadn't fazed her in the least and was instantly rewarded by his purpling face.

"Your apology is accepted, Major Holt," she said sweetly.

"There," Major Carlisle said. "My niece understands your concern, sir, but, in the future, please refrain from shouting at her. It does no good and only serves to confuse the issue."

"And we certainly wouldn't want to do that, would we?" Major Holt said smoothly. "We certainly wouldn't want to confuse her any more than she is already."

"I am not confused, Major Holt. But I have told you everything I can. And, if you're finished with this inquisition, I would like to go home. I've been a long time without sleep."

"Exactly how long, Miss Carlisle? How long did it take you to get to the rendezvous point?"

"I've already told you!" Jennifer snapped furiously. "It took us five days to get there. Spotted Wolf rode in circles to deliberately confuse me."

"And where did you sleep when you stopped?"

"What?"

"Where did you sleep, Miss Carlisle?"

"Why, on the ground."

"Alone?" he whispered, pushing his face closer to hers. "Did you sleep alone or in his arms?"

"Damn you!" Major Carlisle roared. "How can you even suggest such a thing?"

"Because it happens." Major Holt strode to the

window and stared toward the mountains, then turned back to her again. "If you are trying to protect someone, you'd better tell me now, young lady."

Jennifer rose to her feet. "I've had enough of your insinuations. I'm going home."

Major Holt grabbed her arm and dug his fingers viciously into her flesh. "You'll go nowhere until I finish questioning you, young lady."

She glared at him fiercely. "I will not say another word! You may keep me here until hell freezes over, Major, but I will say no more."

"Turn her loose, Holt," Major Carlisle said wearily. "Go home, Jennifer. We'll talk again tomorrow."

"I will *not* discuss the matter further," Jennifer said. "Not tomorrow or any other day! You have no right to treat me this way. I am not a criminal. And, as far as I'm concerned, the matter is closed."

"Go home, Jennifer," her uncle repeated, his voice hoarse with frustration.

She left them, her body weary with tension. She would soon make them understand she meant what she said. She refused to say another word about the time she had spent with the Indians. And if she repeated that often enough, they surely would learn she meant what she said . . . in time.

When the attack came, it took Spotted Wolf by surprise. A slight sound was all he heard, but it was enough to make him spin on his heels to face the man wearing the blue uniform.

Moonlight glinted off steel, catching the warrior's eye, and he leapt aside, taking the blow that would have killed him had it struck its target just beneath his right shoulder blade.

The blade went deep. Spotted Wolf could feel blood bubbling from the wound as he yanked it out and turned it on the bluecoat who had attacked him, stabbing it deep into his body.

A strangled cry came from behind him and he turned to see Cloud Dancer crumpled on the ground. Spotted Wolf had no way of knowing if the old man was dead or alive, and no time to find out. The bluecoat who had struck the old man down launched himself at the younger warrior now, knife hand upraised, ready to strike.

Enraged, knowing that he must make his strength last, Spotted Wolf kicked upward, missed, then moved away from his opponent's knife thrust. Not far enough. The blade sliced through the warrior's side, leaving him with a white-hot pain.

Weakening fast, Spotted Wolf knew he must defeat his enemy quickly if he was to defeat him at all. He struck out again and his blade sliced across the other man's throat. His jaw slackened as blood spurted forth.

Satisfied that he'd dealt a killing blow to his enemy, Spotted Wolf slumped to the ground, unconscious.

Twenty-seven

The day Major Holt left the fort, Jennifer was baking cookies. She knew of his intentions, having been informed by her uncle, and had invited Clara to spend the afternoon with her. It had been a wise decision, she discovered, when the major turned up on her doorstep unannounced.

Jennifer was sliding a tray of cookies out of the oven when a knock at the door caught her attention. "Oh, darn!" she said. "Clara, would you get the door? If I don't scoop the cookies out, they'll burn on the bottom."

"Don't worry," Clara assured her. "I'll get it. It may be Marybelle. I mentioned that we were baking today and she begged to be allowed to come."

The knock sounded again and Clara hurried toward the door. A moment later Jennifer heard the sound of voices approaching. But it definitely wasn't Marybelle who accompanied Clara.

The voice was distinctly masculine and Jennifer was almost certain of the caller's identity. She continued scooping the brown sugar cookies onto a platter until his voice demanded her attention.

"Good afternoon, Miss Carlisle."

Jennifer's gaze flickered briefly to Major Holt and

returned to the cookies she was carefully scooping from the baking sheet onto the platter.

"What brings you here, Major Holt?"

"I am leaving today, Miss Carlisle, and felt I had to speak to you once more before going, to impress upon you the importance of my mission so that . . ."

"You should have told my uncle," she interrupted shortly. "I believe that is the correct procedure. Does he know you are here?"

He cleared his throat. "Well, no. Not exactly. But I'm sure . . ."

"If you have something to say to me, then my uncle should be present." She glared at him. "Please leave my home immediately."

"Look here, Miss . . ." He broke off and cleared his throat. "I'm afraid we might have gotten off on the wrong foot."

"Indeed?" She arched her brow questioningly.

"Well, yes. And I wanted to try to put things right before leaving."

"Hogwash!" she snapped.

"Now see here, young lady. I'm trying hard to be nice to you!"

"You have no knowledge of the word," she said icily. "Now I've asked you to leave, sir, and if you don't oblige me, and quickly, I'm going to the front door and scream my head off. Do you know how many troopers that will bring? Do you have any idea of the consequences to your burgeoning career?"

He moved quickly and blocked her way. "You will go nowhere until I have some answers."

"You have already been given all the answers you will receive from me," she said, facing him with rage.

"What about your clothes!" he snapped. "You were wearing a deerskin dress when you came back.

That very fact indicates something happened to your other clothing, yet you refuse to admit to rape!"

Jennifer heard Clara's outraged gasp and snapped. "Clara! Open the front door please. And scream as loudly as you can."

"Stay where you are, young woman!"

Major Holt glared at Clara, obviously hoping to intimidate her and Jennifer quickly took advantage of moment to slip around him. Before he could stop her, she crossed the parlor and yanked the front door wide open. A big, burly sergeant was headed toward the mess hall.

"Sergeant Willis," she called out. "Would you come here a moment please?"

He changed course immediately. "What could I do for you, Miss Carlisle?"

"I have an uninvited guest," she said, "and I would appreciate it if you would escort him from my home."

His brows drew together in a heavy frown. "Of course, Miss," he said. "Just show me where he is." He entered the house and was brought up abruptly by the sight of the major. But one glance at Jennifer was all it took to identify the unwanted caller.

His voice was brusque when he said, "I imagine you must be looking for Major Carlisle, but as you can see, he's not here at the moment. I would guess, judging by the time of day, you might find him in his office."

"I know where he is," Major Holt snarled. "And if you don't want to be busted to a private, then you'd better get the hell out of here."

"Wouldn't be right to do that, Sir!" Sergeant Willis said sharply. "Not when Miss Carlisle invited me over 'specially for some of them cookies she's been baking." He sniffed the air. "Smells mighty good too. Been a long while since I've had some of your cookies, Jenny."

"Sit down, Sergeant," Jennifer said with a smile. "The coffee's already hot and the cookies are still warm." She looked at Major Holt again. "I am so sorry you have to leave us, Major. Do come again when you can stay longer."

Muttering curses beneath his breath, the major left the house, mounted his horse and rode on his way while the burly sergeant sat at the table stuffing himself with cookies. When he had finished a good dozen of them, he pushed back his chair and patted his stomach.

"Best dang cookies I ever had," he said. "Holler at me next time you're baking and I'll come on the run."

She smiled at him. "Thank you, Sergeant Willis . . . for everything."

When they were alone, Clara looked at her with admiration. "I'd have been scared out of my wits, but you handled Major Holt as though you'd been doing things like that all your life." She picked up a cookie and nibbled on it. "I'm glad he's gone, Jennifer."

"Good riddance."

"Jenny . . . why *were* you wearing that Indian dress? Is Major Holt right about what happened to you?" She blushed. "I know it's none of my business, but we've always told each other everything and . . ."

"No, Clara. I was not raped." Her gaze turned inward as her lips tilted in a smile. "I was not raped. Spotted Wolf's mother gave me that dress. It was meant to be his wife's, but he never married."

"I believe you're in love with him, Jenny!" Clara's tone was shocked.

"Yes. I am."

"Oh, my God! You can't mean it!"

Jennifer looked at her. "Believe it, Clara. I do mean it."

"But Jenny. How can you be so happy when he's there and you're here?"

"He's going to come for me," Jenny admitted.

Clara's expression became resigned. "Tell me about him."

So Jennifer did.

When the day of her rendezvous with Spotted Wolf finally arrived, Jennifer could hardly contain her excitement. She wanted so desperately to shout her joy for the whole world to hear but could not. Nobody, not even Clara, knew she would be leaving tonight. Although she'd spoken to her best friend of the love she had for Spotted Wolf, she would not tell her when she expected him, or where, only that he would come one day. It was better that way, because Clara could not divulge what she didn't know. But when Jennifer was found missing tomorrow, Clara would be able to reassure Jennifer's uncle that she had gone voluntarily this time.

It was near sunset when Jennifer finally slipped away from the fort and made her way up the mountain toward the rendezvous destination. She was certain nobody had seen her leave, and she'd covered herself by telling her uncle she was spending the night with Clara.

As she neared the cave, her pace increased. But she knew the moment she arrived that the place was deserted. It felt that way . . . empty, lonely.

Having no doubt that Spotted Wolf would arrive

soon, she settled down to wait. Time passed slowly. Each second seemed an hour, each minute an eon.

She watched the sun drop below the horizon, was aware of night descending, casting shadows across the land as she waited for him to come. She waited.

And waited.

Overhead, the clouds that had threatened were breaking. A thin moon was revealed, bathing the landscape in shades of silver and gray. It was a good moon for traveling, she knew. Enough light to insure safe passage, yet not enough to alert those who would want to stop them.

A scraping sound jerked her head around, a smile on her face. It died when she saw a rabbit hopping toward a low bush.

She settled down again, forcing her tense muscles to relax. He would be here soon. She had no doubt of that. He had promised her.

Hadn't he?

She tried to remember the exact words he had spoken before they rode into the valley. He'd said he would come for her in two weeks, when it was time to move the stronghold. Two weeks had passed. This was the day.

Maybe he had forgotten.

No. He would not. No more than she would.

She looked at the big boulder. This was the right place. He'd told her to come here. In two weeks. Today was two weeks. At sunset. It was past sunset, way past.

She tried to ignore the pain that had become lodged in her chest. He would come. She was positive. He was just late. She remembered how he'd been the last night they'd spent together, so loving, so tender. And he'd even teased her.

What had he teased her about anyway?

Oh, yes. He had teased her about Sweet Willow. The woman who'd watched him so avidly at the Love Dance.

Jennifer remembered his words as though he'd only just spoken them. *Sweet Willow is a beautiful woman, but these eyes of mine can see no other but you, my love.*

A beautiful woman. Yes, Sweet Willow was that. But it was Jennifer he loved. He'd said so. And she was positive he meant it too. She leaned back against the boulder. He would come soon. He was bound to come.

Suddenly she heard the bugler sounding taps.

Ten o'clock!

She could no longer ignore the lateness of the hour.

Why hadn't he come? It had been three long hours since sunset. Had something gone wrong? No. He would be alert for trouble. He would come. She was certain of it. He would not leave here, knowing how she felt about him.

Her grip tightened on the bundle of supplies that she'd brought with her, then relaxed again. They were near to hand, easy to reach when he arrived.

As he would.

Soon.

Jennifer remained in place, huddled throughout the long, lonely night. It was near dawn when she finally admitted the truth to herself.

He wasn't coming.

Feeling as though her heart would break, Jennifer picked up her bundle of supplies, straightened her stiff body and made her way back to the fort.

Twenty-eight

Spotted Wolf opened his eyes and stared up at the hide ceiling. His mouth felt as though it were filled with cotton and he licked his dry lips.

"So you are finally awake, my son."

Turning his head, Spotted Wolf saw Star Woman watching him with teary eyes. She unhooked the gourd dipper from the lodge pole above the water container, then brought it to him.

After he'd swallowed several times, she set it aside and felt his forehead. "The fire that burned so long in your body has cooled now," she said, smoothing his hair away from his forehead. "But it will be a long while before you regain your strength."

A long while? He thought of Jennifer. He was supposed to meet her on the mountain. But when? He had lost track of time.

"How long?" he rasped.

"How long have you been ill?"

"Yes."

"It has been a long time, my son. This old woman thought she had lost her son for sure."

"How long?" he asked again.

"Almost twice all my fingers in days have passed since Coyote Man brought you back to the village."

Almost twenty days? "Think hard, Star Woman.

Exactly how many days have passed?" He clutched her forearm. "I must know the exact number."

She thought for a moment. "It has been one less than twice all my fingers since you returned. A long time for your body to be with no nourishment save the liquids I could force down you. It has left you weak."

Nineteen days. Jennifer would already have gone to the meeting place and left again. He would have to go inside the fort to fetch her and that would be dangerous.

He tried to sit up and failed. "So weak," he muttered, sweating from the strain.

Star Woman nodded her head. "You are weak. Too weak to travel if that is what you had in mind."

"I must go after her."

"Jennifer will wait," she said. "You cannot do the impossible."

"Cloud Dancer," he said, belatedly remembering the medicine man. "Is he all right?"

"He has passed through this life to a better world."

He sighed heavily. "It is my fault."

"No. Not yours. He lived long enough to explain what happened. He had no regret about passing on. He was an old man, ready to go to a better world."

"The soldiers were close to the canyon."

"Yes. It has been decided that we will move tomorrow. The village is being dismantled even as we speak."

"I must help them."

"You cannot help yourself," she chided. "You will be carried on a litter to the new stronghold. Now lay back and rest."

"That is all I have been doing for more than three weeks."

"No. Illness does not allow rest." She studied him intently. "Would you try to eat something? I made a rabbit stew. The meat is cut into tiny pieces."

Spotted Wolf knew food would give him strength. "Yes," he said. "Bring me some of your stew. I feel no hunger but I will eat. I must recover soon so that I can go back for her."

And he *would* go back, he determined.

Nothing could keep him from going in that fort and bringing Jennifer out again. Even if he had to cut his hair and go in the guise of a white man.

Jennifer had felt numb for days, ever since the morning she'd returned from the mountain. A shawl covered her chilled flesh as she sat in a parlor chair darning a pair of her uncle's socks.

Although anyone watching would believe her attention was focused on her task, it was not. She worked automatically, but her thoughts were on the time she'd spent at the Indian village.

She had gone over that time in her mind, over and over again, trying to find some reason, something Spotted Wolf might have said that would explain the reason he'd failed to keep the rendezvous.

But she could not. Spotted Wolf had been sincere, she felt, when he'd said he would come for her.

That left only one alternative. Something must have happened to keep him from coming.

Fear washed over her and she set aside her mending and rose to her feet. She had to know, had to find out why he hadn't come for her. But how? She could never find the stronghold. She hadn't been lying to Major Holt when she'd told him she didn't know the way. But, if she did know, then she would go to him, would make him explain his reasons for not coming.

The crystal that rested against her breasts felt warm against her flesh, reminding her of the night Spotted Wolf had given it to her. It was all she had left of him now.

A squeaking hinge interrupted her thoughts and she jerked toward the door as it opened. Her uncle strode briskly into the room. He stopped short at the sight of her and frowned. "Is something wrong, Jennifer?"

"Wrong?"

"You look unwell."

"I am healthy enough." Healthy, but not happy. "Would you like tea, Uncle? I have freshly baked cookies."

He cleared his throat. "Yes. That would be good. Perhaps you will join me?"

"I am not hungry."

"Then just sit with me."

"If you wish."

Her uncle remained silent while she set the table with tea and cookies. "I have been considering what that Indian said to you and decided caution was the best policy to follow."

"I don't understand."

"The Indian told you Captain Brady was not to be trusted."

"And you believe him now?"

"No. But I do not dismiss his warning completely. I believe Brady is a just man. Trustworthy. But there is a traitor here, someone supplying information on the rifle shipments. We cannot afford to ignore any lead."

"So what are you going to do?"

"Watch. And wait. If Brady is the man, he will give himself away in time."

"Spotted Wolf said you couldn't trust him."

"I know you trust the man, though only God knows why, but even if he's right, he didn't say Brady was guilty of supplying information to the Comancheros."

"No. He did not. And I'm not so sure I was supposed to give you the information about Captain Brady. But it seemed the right thing to do."

Major Carlisle was silent for a long moment, then, placing his hand over her smaller one, he said, "Jennifer, my dear, I've been meaning to speak to you. You're not the same since you came back."

"No, Uncle. I'm not." She met his eyes with a long look. "I've been wondering about Spotted Wolf." She couldn't tell him about the rendezvous. But she had to know that her uncle had kept his promise of safe passage to the Indians. "Uncle, safe passage was part of the bargain you made with the Indians." Her voice was shaky when she continued, "You did keep your side of the bargain, didn't you?"

"Jenny . . . my dear. There are some things you don't understand. Our assignment here, the reason we are stationed at this fort, is to drive the Indians off this land. To give safe passage for travelers."

She felt a chill crawl down her spine. "You did something," she whispered. "Something horrible."

"I did what any other officer would have done."

"What did you do?"

"I had the Indians followed."

"You went to the stronghold?"

"Not me, personally. But I sent two troopers to follow them. Their riderless horses were recovered later. Along with the ones the Indians had been riding."

"Oh, God," she whispered, feeling the color leave her face.

"I did what I had to do, Jenny. And in doing so I lost two good men."

"You killed four good men."

"I never!" He released her hand, and the eyes that held hers had gone stone cold. "I don't know what happened to you out there. Maybe Major Holt was right in his estimation of what happened." He gripped her arms tightly. "Was he, Jenny? Did that Indian lay hands on you in that way? And did you actually allow his touch?"

"Yes!" she shouted. "I did!"

"Oh, my God!" He jerked back, his hand knocking over the fragile cup and spilling tea across the lacy tablecloth. "Do you have no honor, girl? How can you face me with this? You're ruined! Your reputation will be shot to hell! No decent man will have any part of you now."

Jennifer had known how he would react, had heard about the way rescued women captives were treated. They were shunned by both women and men, treated as though they were lepers, unclean, unfit to be touched.

So far, Jennifer had escaped such treatment. Except for Major Holt. But the reason could very well be because she rarely left her house. And up to now, she had remained silent on that particular subject.

"Did you hear me, Jennifer?" Major Carlisle roared. "I said no decent man would have you now."

"There was no finer man than Spotted Wolf, Uncle," she said coldly. "And you have killed him."

"Don't you understand, girl?" His face was livid, mottled with rage. "You have ruined whatever chance you may have had of finding a decent husband."

"I want no other husband."

"There's only one thing to be done now. Only one way you might have any kind of future."

"And what is that?"

"You have to go back to Chicago. Lord knows if your grandmother will allow you to return when she hears what happened." The rage slowly drained away and he slumped into a chair again. "I'm sorry, Jenny. This isn't all your fault. I brought you here against my better judgment. I should have made you stay with your grandmother."

Tears glittered in her eyes. "Had I stayed there, I would never have met Spotted Wolf."

Major Carlisle's expression hardened. "By God, I'm glad he's dead!"

"Yes. I imagine you are." She almost choked on the words. "But I'm not! And I wish I were!" She could no longer hold back the tears of despair. She ran from the room and threw herself across the bed, her shoulders shuddering as sobs shook her frame.

He was gone. Spotted Wolf was dead. She would never see him again, never feel the warmth of his embrace. Oh, God, how could she stand it?

Twenty-nine

The journey was long and arduous, but the scenery outside the train window failed to hold Jennifer's attention. The clacking of the wheels against the rails seemed to keep time with her thoughts as her mind wandered back to those last days with Spotted Wolf.

They had been wonderful, those days. And she would hold fast to her memories, would keep them clutched to her heart.

She blinked away the moisture that suddenly clouded her vision, silently vowing to hold them back, to be strong when others were present. Only in the privacy of her room would she allow her tears to fall and eventually, she hoped, she would deal with her grief.

Suddenly the train slowed, jerking her to the present as it passed over switches and began to weave slightly.

Brakes squealed, and the lights of the station could be seen through the windows. Then the conductor hurried along the aisle. "Chi-cago! Chi-cago! Chi-cago!"

The train shuddered to a stop; wind whipped coal smoke along the platform. Jennifer joined the people filing off the train, ignoring those that pushed past her as they hurried to their final destination.

Since her expected arrival time had not been determined, there was nobody waiting to meet her. Jennifer left the station, hailed a Hanson cab and waited until her meager possessions had been tied down before she entered the carriage and leaned back in her seat.

Chicago's sprawling stockyards and equally expansive rail yards worked in concert, providing a flow of livestock to all parts of the east and the south. The stockyards had spawned a burgeoning meat-packing industry, as well as tanneries and glue factories. Readily available work had drawn the jobless, and the presence of a large labor force had attracted other industries. During the past three years alone Chicago had tripled in size to a population of over three hundred thousand.

The city, divided into three sections by the Chicago River and its two branches, was also an attractive place in which to live. Its streets were laid out mostly in a grid, with numerous large parks and botanical gardens. Theaters, fine restaurants, yachting clubs and other forms of entertainment were readily available. But the explosive growth of the city had also brought problems.

Most of the buildings were wooden. The thirteen miles of docks along the mouth of the Chicago River were made of wood, as were the paving blocks used on the streets.

Their route took them past Lincoln Park in the north division. The lagoon, known as Swan Lake, had been one of Jennifer's favorite places. It was also a favorite tryst place for lovers.

Soon she reached her grandparents' home. It was a big house, a mansion, set on prime land amidst massive oaks, with enough elaborately trimmed shrubbery to necessitate a full-time gardener. Beds of impatiens blazed with red and purple flowers.

The driver urged the horses toward the majestic circular driveway and stopped in front of broad, flower bordered steps that led up to a deep pillared veranda. There were no flowers in the front windows. All of the drapes were pulled together and the house had a vacant look about it.

It had felt that way before, Jennifer reflected. Empty, lonely, vacant. Just the way her heart felt.

She stepped down from the carriage and slowly ascended the wide steps. She crossed the wide veranda, her shoes sounding loud as they struck against the planks.

Lifting the doorknocker, Jennifer allowed it to fall against the heavy wooden door. The resulting bang was a hollow sound.

Footsteps sounded in the distance, then became louder as they drew closer. Metal grated as the bolt was drawn back, then the door was suddenly flung open.

"Miss Jennifer!" the maid who stood before her exclaimed. "It's good you've come home."

Home.

The word had no meaning to her. This place had never been home to her. Nor would it ever be. Home was a word that meant warmth, love, sharing, and there was little enough of that to be found in this house.

She forced a smile to her lips. "Hester. It's good to see you again."

"And you, Miss," the girl said warmly. "It's been a sad and lonely place since you've been gone."

"Don't let my grandmother hear you say that," Jennifer said.

"No, Miss," the girl said. "I wouldn't dare do that.

I'd be fired for sure." She bent to retrieve one of Jennifer's bags. "Your grandmother has placed you in the big rose room this time. She said you'd like it better here if you had more room." The girl's lips curled into a smile. "Like she thought that was the reason you left before. Because you didn't have enough room."

"Hester!" a sharp feminine voice called. "Who was at the door?"

"Miss Jennifer, Ma'am," Hester called.

Jennifer looked up the stairway and saw her grandmother standing on the first landing. Cornelia Whitcomb was a tall, stately looking woman with steel blue hair styled in soft waves at the sides and pulled back into a soft knot at the nape of her neck. Although she was thin, almost bony, she looked so stern and secure that she appeared much larger. The black dress she wore was ankle length, designed that way to allow her more freedom of movement, and it was secured at the high neck with a diamond brooch.

She descended the stairs slowly, her stone cold gray eyes never leaving Jennifer. "Hello, Jennifer. So you finally came to your senses and returned." She looked with distaste at the brown dress and short cape that Jennifer wore. "Your uncle certainly didn't worry much about your wardrobe, did he?"

Despite what her uncle had done, Jennifer felt the need to defend him. "Uncle Walter stays busy, Grandmother. Running a fort isn't always that easy."

"He shouldn't have sent for you then. And just look at your skin. It's absolutely disgraceful! You're as brown as a hazelnut. Didn't you remember anything I taught you about protecting your skin from the sun?" She looked at the maid.

"Hester. Draw Jennifer a bath. As soon as she's finished with it, rub some lemon oil on her, then

cover every inch of her skin with that special softening cream Andre sold me the last time I visited
his beauty salon."

"Yes'um," the girl said, hurrying past them with
a bag in each hand.

"I'm sorry to arrive in such a state, Grandmother,
but it was a long journey and . . ."

"Yes, yes. We'll discuss it later. Just run along now
and take your bath. And after Hester treats your skin
with lemon water and creams, rest yourself for
awhile. We have some people coming to afternoon
tea."

"Oh, Grandmother. Do you really need me there?
I'm afraid I don't feel up to meeting anyone today."

"Of course I need you there. The whole thing
was arranged for your benefit, Jennifer."

"Your uncle wired me after you boarded the train.
I knew you'd be coming some time today, but not
exactly when or I would have sent Robert to meet
you. But we can't waste a moment of time now that
you're here. You should have been launched into
society a long time ago. But I allowed you and your
grandfather to overrule my good sense." Her eyes
bored into Jennifer. "Not anymore though. This
time I intend to have my way."

A door opened farther down the hall and Jennifer
turned to see her grandfather hurry toward them.
"My dear," Jacob Whitcomb said, taking her in his
arms and hugging her against him. "It's so good to
see you again. The house has been empty without
you here." He drew back and looked at her. "You
seem sad, my dear. Worse than when you left us.
Has something happened out there?"

"Of course not!" Jennifer's grandmother snapped.
"What on earth could you mean, Jacob? Jennifer is
just fine. She is weary from her journey and needs

to bathe and rest. Run along now, girl. There'll be plenty of time to talk to your grandfather later."

"She doesn't look dirty to me," Jacob muttered.

Jennifer and her grandfather exchanged looks, both realizing it would do no good to argue the point because her grandmother would allow them no peace until Jennifer bathed and had softening creams smoothed over her skin.

Standing on tiptoe, Jennifer bestowed a quick kiss on her grandfather's cheek and hurried to the room that had been cleaned and aired for her.

Hester stood over Jennifer's cases, pulling garments out and placing them in bureau drawers. She frowned at a pitifully thin flannel nightgown she'd just removed with tight cuffed sleeves and a high neck. "Lordy, mercy, Miss," she exclaimed. "Your grandmother will have a conniption when she sees your clothes. You don't have a single garment here that you didn't take with you. Didn't you get anything new while you were away?"

"I'm afraid not," Jennifer replied. "But there's not a thing wrong with my clothing, Hester. Every item there is in good repair."

"Maybe so. But you know how your grandmother is."

"I know." Jennifer sighed. "Did you know she has a tea planned for this afternoon?"

"Yes."

"How many people are expected, Hester? I can't bear to think of having to face a crowd."

"I know, Miss. But I expect there won't be many today." She straightened her back, arching her back muscles and began to name the couples who were expected. "The Longs are coming. And the Goodwins, they'll probably bring their daughter, Evelyn along as well. And the Courtneys should be here.

They never refuse one of your grandmother's invitations. And Colin Davenport! I believe that's all. That makes . . ."

"Colin Davenport is coming?" Jennifer groaned. "Oh, God!"

"Now, Miss Jennifer," Hester chided. "Mr. Davenport is a gentleman. He comes here quite often. Always asks about you when he does and he never fails to ask after my own health."

"I know he's nice, but I'm quite aware that my grandmother is trying to make a match between us." She looked hopefully at Hester. "I don't suppose he got married while I was gone?"

"No, Miss," Hester said with a smile. "I don't believe he did. But it wasn't for want of enough young ladies. They're always throwing themselves at him." She rolled her eyes. "You should see them. Anytime he's in a room you can tell, because all the young ladies are crowded around him like bees to a honey pot."

"Too bad one of them didn't catch his eye."

"Maybe he was just waiting for you to come home, Miss."

"I hardly think so, but I imagine that's what my grandmother believes."

"She just worries about your future, Miss. It's not really her fault. You're the only granddaughter she's got and the only one she'll ever have now that your ma is gone." She clapped a hand over her mouth. "Miss! I'm so sorry. I shouldn't have mentioned your ma."

"Of course you should have," Jennifer said quickly. "I have learned to accept my parents' death, Hester. It bothers me more if they are never mentioned. It's as though my grandmother pretends my mother never existed."

"Maybe it makes losing her only daughter easier," Hester said softly. "But anyways I better watch my tongue around your grandmother. She'd have my hide and probably my job too if I go talking about your mother where she can hear me."

"Surely you wouldn't be let go for such a trivial thing."

"Don't place any bets on it. I'll go draw the water in the bathtub now, Miss." Hester had learned that Jennifer would refuse help with that chore. "Just call me when you want the lemon and glycerine cream rubbed on."

"Thank you, Hester," Jennifer said.

After gathering up fresh clothing, Jennifer entered the water closet down the hall from her room. It was an ample source of pride for the family. The white porcelain bathtub with claw feet set on glass balls had ample room for even the largest body.

As Jennifer sank into the steaming water, she decided there were certain advantages to civilized living that she had missed.

Later that afternoon, Jennifer stood beside her grandmother to receive her guests. The Longs came first. Then Geneva Goodwin and her daughter, Evelyn, a teenager with a profusion of golden curls that sprang around her piquant face.

"My dear," Cornelia said warmly, clasping the hand that Mrs. Goodwin had offered between both her own. "Where is that rascally husband of yours?"

"He's away at the moment," Geneva explained.

"I wanted my granddaughter to meet him." She looked at Jennifer. "He's in politics, Jennifer. We're hoping he'll be our next senator. If the women were able to vote, that office would most certainly be his."

"So glad to meet you, Mrs. Goodwin," Jennifer murmured, meeting the dark haired woman's gaze.

Geneva smiled at her. "It's nice to meet you too, Jennifer. I hope we'll be seeing a lot of you in the future. Evelyn does tend to get lonesome here in Chicago."

"Are you new here then?"

"Yes. We've only been here a few months now. I hear you've only just returned from west Texas. Did you like it out there?"

"Of course not," Cornelia said quickly. "What civilized young lady would like living in such a horrible place? Jennifer is quite excited about being home again. Aren't you, my dear?"

"Oh, quite," Jennifer muttered. "So much that I'm afraid the excitement might be too much for me."

Geneva laughed suddenly. "We're originally from Texas," she said. "I was raised down on the coast. And my husband, Clifford, has been across the state and back again. He used to be a wanderer, I'm afraid. Until I put my brand on him."

"Really?" Jennifer said. "I would love to meet him. Where did you live on the coast? My father's farm was near Washington on the Brazos."

"I was raised in Houston," the woman said with a smile. "But that's not too far away from there."

The girl beside them moved restlessly, and Geneva stepped aside and said, "This skittish filly here is my daughter, Evelyn."

"Momma," the golden-haired girl chided. "I'm not skittish, nor am I a filly. But I don't think it's appropriate to keep standing in the doorway since other people are arriving."

"By other people she means Colin Davenport," Geneva Goodwin teased, her lips curling into a wide smile.

"Mother!" Evelyn snapped. "Please don't tease

me when he can hear you. Colin will think I'm just a silly child and you know you're going to bring me out in society next spring."

Mother and daughter moved into the parlor to allow their host and hostesses to greet the newcomer.

"Colin!" Cornelia exclaimed. "How good of you to come on such short notice. Look, Jennifer, my dear. Here's Colin Davenport. You remember him, don't you?"

"Of course." Jennifer couldn't help comparing Colin Davenport to Spotted Wolf. He was an inch or two shorter than the warrior and slimmer in build.

"And why wouldn't I come?" he asked, his eyes on Jennifer. "Jenny! It's great to see you again. You haven't changed a bit!"

"According to my grandmother, I've ruined my complexion by staying too long in the sun."

"Jennifer!" Cornelia's voice let Jennifer know she felt her words were scandalous, as though her granddaughter had been vulgar.

After the greetings were made, Colin Davenport asked her to show him the garden.

"That sounds nice, Colin," Jennifer said, feeling grateful for his suggestion. It would meet with her grandmother's approval. "But we must ask Evelyn Goodwin to join us or she will be left alone with the married couples."

"Must we?"

"Yes. We must."

When approached, the young girl quickly accepted the invitation and followed them out to the garden, leaving the others to their own devices.

Thirty

It was more than a month after Jennifer left the village before Spotted Wolf was well enough to travel. During his recuperation, he thought about her constantly.

Images of her beautiful face formed in his mind; her delicately molded features, her large blue eyes, her shining copper curls. Even the expressions that had mirrored her changing moods were indelibly engraved in his memory.

Nothing would ever be the same, he reflected. He had loved her since the moment she'd stumbled over him on the mountain. But he'd been too blind to realize that, too stubborn to admit it.

What had she thought when he hadn't been at the rendezvous? he wondered. Had her feelings for him changed since they parted?

He would know the answers to his questions soon, he reasoned, because he was leaving for the fort tomorrow. And, if her feelings were still the same, then he would bring her away with him, would take her for his wife.

He delved in the reed trunk where he kept the fringed buckskins that Star Woman had made him for the season of the long cold. Many white men wore such clothing. He would enter the fort and he would see Jennifer once again. If she was as miserable as he, if her feelings for him had not changed, then he would take her away from there. And Heaven help the man who stood in his way.

Several days later he rode into the fort unheeded. No demand was made for the rifle he carried in the crook of his arm, no alarm was given because an enemy had come among them. The young trooper posted as guard accepted him for what he appeared. A trapper or a mountain man. Nobody to concern them.

He made straight for the Suttler's store since that was the usual place to learn the latest news.

Pushing the door open, he entered a room that was stuffy and smelled of stale tobacco and leather. He looked around correctly identifying jugs of sorghum and barrels of rice, beans and flour. Stored beside those items were barrels of nails and tables piled high with bolts of material, ribbons, and scented soaps.

The soaps reminded him of the yucca root Jennifer had used to bathe herself the first night they had made love. How could she possibly prefer a life with him to the kind of life she led here?

His gaze roamed farther, taking in the harnesses and traps hanging on the wall beside pots and skillets and rifles and other items too numerous to name.

"Help you?" the middle-aged man leaning against the counter asked. He was a tall man with bright blue eyes and a head as bald as a newly laid egg. A canvas apron covered his shirt and tie.

"Do you have ammunition for my rifle?" Spotted Wolf asked.

"Springfield, ain't it?" the clerk said, eying the rifle the buckskin-clad man carried so easily. "Forty five-seventy is what you'll be needin'. Comes a hundred to a box. How many boxes you need?"

Since he had just bought plenty of guns and ammunition from the Comancheros, Spotted Wolf held up one finger. The clerk reached on a shelf behind the counter and took down a box of ammunition. "That'll be four dollars!"

Spotted Wolf dug in his pocket and pulled out four silver dollars. "How much for the yellow ribbon?" he asked.

"Nickel a yard," the clerk replied. "Finest satin ribbon this side of Missouri. Guaranteed to please the ladies. Want me to cut some for you?"

After mentally calculating the white man's way of measuring, Spotted Wolf replied, "One yard should be enough."

The clerk whistled as he measured out the ribbon, and when he was done he laid it on the counter beside the ammunition. "Need anything else?" he asked cheerfully.

Spotted Wolf thought a moment, then decided the chance was too good to pass and named several items that were hard for the Comanche to come by. Then he said, "I could use a glass of whiskey too." Although he had no use for the white man's liquor, he knew that it gave him an excuse to linger awhile and make conversation.

The man reached for a tankard and filled it with amber liquid. "There you go," he said, placing the bottle on the counter. "Just help yourself when you're ready."

"Nice fort," Spotted Wolf said. "It should offer good protection." He deliberately imitated the drawl of the old white trapper that used to come to the village to trade goods.

"Nice enough," the clerk agreed. "And the size of it keeps the Injuns from causing us trouble."

"What man is in charge?"

"Major Carlisle. Good man too."

"Carlisle?" Spotted Wolf pretended to think about that for a moment. "His name has a familiar sound." He lifted his glass and took a sip. The liquid burned his throat. "Does he have a daughter?"

"No daughter," the clerk grunted. "Got a niece though. She lived with him until a short time back."

Spotted Wolf's gut tightened. "She is no longer here?"

"Nope." The man leaned closer. "Got herself stole by the Injuns awhile back. When she come back he sent her off to the East quick enough. Guess he couldn't live with the shame of what happened to her."

A muscle twitched in Spotted Wolf's jaw and his grip tightened around the glass. He wanted to wipe the smile off the man's face, but managed to restrain himself. Nothing would be accomplished by winding up in the white man's jail.

He drained the glass of liquor and gathered up his goods and with a nod at the clerk, left the store. There was a sour taste in his mouth and a pain in his stomach. His journey had been in vain.

He stopped beside the hitching post where he'd left his mount and fastened the supplies to his saddle. The day was miserably hot, made hotter by his disappointment in finding Jennifer gone. He took off his hat and wiped the sweat from his brow.

Hearing a gasp, he jerked around to face a young, freckle faced woman. She was staring at his hair. "It's you, isn't it," she whispered, her gaze meeting his eyes. "You're him. The one who . . ."

"Do I know you?"

"No. But I know you." Her hands were clasped between her breasts as though for protection. "You're the one that . . ." She broke off and her eyes widened even more. "You came to find her, didn't you? But you're too late. Her uncle sent her away."

The sounds of boots against the plank walk caught their attention. "If you want to know about Jennifer, then meet me behind the stockade after dark." She hurried away, leaving Spotted Wolf staring after her in confusion.

With several hours to kill, Spotted Wolf went to the livery and rubbed down his horse, gave it hay and water and went to the store again. He bought fresh bread and ham and seated himself at a table and ate. The clerk was inclined to talk but the warrior was silent to discourage conversation. It seemed an eternity before Spotted Wolf could leave and meet the woman.

Finally it was time.

She was waiting for him in the shadows cast by the building. "I didn't know if you would come."

"I was not sure I would. But I could not take the chance you were telling me the truth. What do you know about Jennifer?"

"She thought you were dead. She went back East, to live with her grandmother in Chicago."

"She thought me dead?"

"Yes. Her uncle told her that you'd been killed. Why didn't you come for her sooner? She was heartbroken."

"I could not. Her uncle sent men to slay me. But I lived through the attack. I was severely wounded, unable to ride."

"You should have sent her a message."

"She should have waited for me."

"Do you know what it was like for her here? Her own uncle was ashamed of her, of what you had done to her."

"I only loved her."

"I'm sorry. For both of you."

"I do not need your pity," he said coldly. "I only need directions to Jennifer's people."

"You can't go there."

"Why not?"

"Well . . . you're an Indian."

He nodded his head. "Yes. I am that. But Jennifer is my woman."

"It's no good, you know," she said softly. "She couldn't have any kind of life with you."

"That is for her to decide."

"But how would you travel? It's more than a thousand miles to Chicago and there are more than three hundred thousand people living there."

Her words struck him like a hard blow. How could he find Jennifer in a place like that? A place where so many people lived. It seemed an impossible task, but he must at least make the attempt. Unless there was a way of contacting her and having her come to him.

"The telegraph wire," he muttered. "Could a message be sent to her so that she would return here?"

"She couldn't come. Even if she wanted to."

"How can you know that?"

"Jennifer has no way of returning. It takes money to ride the train and I don't believe her grandparents, at least her grandmother, would give it to her knowing she'd leave them again."

"I cannot give up and leave her there either."

"Why not? Why don't you just leave her alone, allow her to find happiness with someone else, a man from her own race? Don't you see how selfish it would be for you to take her back to the life you lead? She would find more pain than happiness in such a situation."

"Perhaps you are right," he said. "The Comanche people are facing great difficulties at this time."

"I know. She told me how Colonel MacKenzie is hunting your tribe, constantly pushing the Comanche farther West. I sympathize with your plight, but you should leave Jennifer alone. In time she will find someone else and make another life for herself. Allow her that chance, please, I beg of you."

The woman might be right about Jennifer's chances of happiness with him, but Spotted Wolf knew he must see her once again. That he must hold her again.

Perhaps then he could find a way to say goodbye forever. He wondered though, if he ever could.

Thirty-one

Spotted Wolf strode down the boardwalk, heading for the hitching post where he'd left his mount. As he approached the Suttler's store, a tall man wearing buckskins similar to his own stepped out onto the boardwalk. When he saw the warrior, the man stepped back a pace.

"Sorry," the stranger muttered. "Didn't see you coming."

Spotted Wolf's gaze narrowed on the man. There was something familiar about him, something he couldn't quite place.

He strode quickly toward his mount and untied the reins from the hitching post, feeling a sense of uneasiness. He slid his gaze toward the stranger again. The man was still watching him. Spotted Wolf felt the hair at the nape of his neck rise. Was the stranger suspicious of his identity?

Droplets of sweat collected beneath his sweatband and he took off the hat to wipe the moisture away. Then he fiddled with the saddle as though believing the strap had loosened, throwing another covert look at the stranger whose gaze remained locked on him.

Alarm swept like a current through his belly. What had he done to arouse the stranger's suspicions?

Should he ignore the other man and hope he would be allowed to leave the fort unchallenged, or should he confront him?

Their eyes met and held and Spotted Wolf suddenly felt a sense of familiarity. Had they met at some time or another? The stranger seemed to hold no enmity, seemed only to be confused.

The decision was suddenly taken out of his hands as the man strode toward him, determination in every step he took. And as he drew closer, the sense of familiarity deepened.

Even before the man stopped beside him, Spotted Wolf identified him.

It was Pecos Smith.

His lips formed the name, but before it could be uttered, the stranger spoke. "It *is* you, Johnny! I don't believe this!" He clasped Spotted Wolf on the shoulder while his gaze bored into him. "It's been a long time, boy. Years since I last saw you. But what luck! Serena will never believe I found you so easy. What in hell are you doin' here anyway?"

"It's a long story, Pecos," Spotted Wolf said.

"I've got plenty of time, boy. In fact, you're the reason I'm here."

"Me?"

"Sure. Is there some place we can go to talk?"

"Not here," Spotted Wolf muttered. "Too many bluecoats around for my satisfaction."

"I imagine so." Pecos lowered his voice. "I heard you were with the Quohadi Comanche now. Heard tell, too, that Quanah is your war chief now. But it was hard to believe, him being so young."

Spotted Wolf nodded. "It is true."

He had no hesitation in revealing that information to Pecos. Although he had not seen him for twenty years, Pecos was well known among the Indians, had been raised by the Comanche. It was the reason Spotted Wolf's sister, Serena, had hired Pecos to guide her to Buffalo Hump's camp where her brother had been living with the Comanche, believing himself to be of their blood.

"I need something to eat before we ride out of here," Pecos said.

"I have plenty of food in my saddlebags," Spotted Wolf said. "It would suit me better to leave this place now. Before they discover who I am."

Pecos laughed abruptly. "I imagine it would. Okay, boy. I'm ready to ride when you are."

Several hours later they sat beside a swift flowing stream among the remains of their meal.

"Are you going to tell me what you're doing here?" Spotted Wolf asked.

"Yeah. I've been working up to that."

"Is Serena all right?"

"Yeah. She is. But she'd be better if you'd come back with me."

"You know I cannot leave the People to fight alone," Spotted Wolf said bitterly.

"She took it hard when she had to ride out of that camp without you, Johnny."

Spotted Wolf had refused to acknowledge his White Eyes sister, had told her he was a Comanche, that he wanted no part of her world. Although he had never regretted that decision, he did feel regret that he would never know her.

"I have no memory of her before she came to the village," he said. "I was too young when the Comanche took me. But they raised me, as they raised you. They are my People. There have been many times I have wanted to go to her and tell her I am sorry my actions added to her pain. It cannot have been easy for her."

"No. It hasn't been easy." Pecos studied Spotted Wolf for a long moment. "You said you wanted to go to her and apologize. You could do that, you know. And at the same time you could help the Comanche."

"What do you mean?"

"A few weeks ago I was contacted by a newspaper back East," Pecos said. "They've been doing some stories on the plight of the Indians out West. The reporter who contacted me had something definite in mind. I met him when his paper was doing a story on Cynthia Ann Parker. That's the reason he knew I had lived among the Indians. He wanted me to go on a tour, wanted me to speak before large groups of people, to obtain names on petitions, speak out against the brutal treatment of the Indians." Pecos's eyes glittered with excitement.

"And it just might work, Johnny. If we could get enough names, we could go before Congress. They would have to listen to us then, would not be able to dismiss the plight of the Indians. They must be convinced the army is handling the situation wrong, that peace must be obtained, whatever the cost."

"It sounds good," Spotted Wolf admitted. "Do you think they will listen to you?"

"Not to me," Pecos said. "To you!"

"Me?" Spotted Wolf exclaimed. "The White Eyes would not listen to me. I could not speak to them as you could."

"Yes, you could! And the newspaper was wild about the idea. The reporter was positive it would work, Johnny. Just think of it. The newspaper will arrange everything, for tutors to teach you the things you'd need to know to make the easterners sit up and take notice. The paper will pick up the tab on all expenses. You'll be going to every major

city in the United States. Just think of it. The chance
of a lifetime. And better yet, my family will be along
with you on the tour."

"I could not desert the People, Pecos. You know
that."

"You won't be deserting them, Johnny. You'll be
helping them more than if you were supplying them
with one more warrior. More battles have been won
with words than weapons, my friend."

"This tour you speak of. You said it will take us
to every major city?"

"Yes. And the *Chicago Tribune* is paying for everything."

"I will consider your words, Pecos," Spotted Wolf
said. "And perhaps I will accompany you on this
tour. But first I must return to the village and speak
with the elders. They must all agree with your plan."

"Of course," Pecos said. "So what are we waiting
for? Your sister is anxiously waiting for me to bring
you home."

The two men mounted and rode away.

Jennifer walked with Colin beside the lagoon at
Swan Lake in Lincoln Park. It was barely dusk; he
had induced her to walk with him after days of staying in her grandparents' home.

At this time of day there were many couples boat-
ing, a favorite pastime for most young courting couples.

They could still see the pale green of the slopes
ahead and the verdant foliage on the trees surrounding the lake. Most of the houses were scattered enough to foster a sense of peace.

The soft air was deliciously moist and cool at this
time of day, the wind blowing off Lake Michigan,

carrying the miasma of smoke from the factories away from them. They strolled along a quiet lane. They had not spoken for a long time, but after awhile Colin broke the silence.

"You've changed since you've been away, Jennifer." He took her hand in his. "You're quieter, and you appear unhappy. Do you still miss your parents so much? It's been almost a year since they passed away."

She felt ashamed. If the truth be told, she didn't think about her parents as much since she'd been abducted. For a time, her own safety had totally consumed her. That had been replaced by her deep feelings for Spotted Wolf. Now the hurt was so fresh that he was all she could think about.

She realized Colin was still waiting for a reply. "I guess I'm just finally growing up, Colin."

"Are you really? Then perhaps you're ready for me to say what I've been longing to say since the first day we met."

"No, please."

"No? But you don't know yet what I was going to say to you."

She couldn't help but know. Ever since she'd come back to her grandparents, Colin had made his feelings known in so many different ways. "I don't want you to be hurt," she said softly.

"Then you don't care for me."

Selfishly, she wanted his companionship. For that reason she didn't say anything to dissuade him. "I'm not really sure how I feel, Colin. I need time." She met his eyes. "Would you allow me that time?"

He smiled at her. "Yes. At least you have given me hope." He squeezed her hand. "You can have all the time you need, dear one. All the time in the world."

Jennifer knew it would take all the time in the world to forget Spotted Wolf. If she ever could.

Pecos was eloquent when he spoke before the council and he managed to convince every man there that the best thing for the Comanche was for Spotted Wolf to go on the proposed tour.

Star Woman was sad when they parted, knowing, as he did, that it was unlikely they would ever meet again. He stood beside his horse just before leaving the village, and despite the onlookers, he kissed her on the forehead.

"Goodbye, little mother," he said sadly. "You will always have a place in my heart."

"And you will always have a place in mine," she whispered, blinking back the tears that threatened.

"Coyote Man has promised me he will see to your needs," Spotted Wolf said. "You will not be neglected."

"I never thought I would." She twisted the lace of her doeskin dress. "I have never told you how much joy you brought into my life. And I want you to know now."

"You do not have to speak the words."

"Nevertheless it makes me feel better to speak them. You took the place of my own son who was killed in the battle at Pease River. Without you, I would not have found the will to live."

"Do not be foolish," he chided.

"It is true."

He frowned at her. "I hate leaving you this way."

She smiled at him. "But you must. Your happiness lies somewhere else, Spotted Wolf. You are going to the world of the White Eyes. You will find Jennifer there."

"I hope you're right. But she has traveled far away."

"Nevertheless you will find her."

He rode away from her then, praying that she was right, knowing that, even after he reached Chicago, it would be hard finding Jennifer in such a large city.

But somehow he must do so.

Thirty-two

The house where Pecos and Serena lived was built in a colonial style, with a huge, circular drive that wound through flower beds and large oak trees. Pecos dismounted beside the hitching rail and handed his reins to a boy who appeared to be waiting there for just that purpose.

"The missus will be glad you're home again," the boy said, his smile wide and happy. His gaze flickered between the two men.

"Not as glad as I am to be back, Josh!" Pecos mounted the wide steps to the porch and lifted the brass doorknocker to pound on the front door.

Footsteps sounded from inside, the door was suddenly flung open and a large black woman stood glaring at them. "Lawdy, mercy!" she shouted. "If it ain't Mr. Pecos come home again!" She motioned them inside with a large hand, her gaze lingering for a moment on Spotted Wolf.

"I guess you be the brother," the woman said. "Humph! Don't look like no wild man to me." She turned away from them and yelled. "Miz Serena, Ma'am! That man of yours done come home again!"

"Why don't you just holler for her, Josey?" Pecos asked dryly.

"Why Mr. Pecos, I done thought that was what I was doing." She frowned at him. "Reckon I didn't holler loud enough though or she'd of come on the run."

Hurried footsteps sounded upstairs and a head covered with fiery red curls dipped over the bannister. "Daddy?" a high, girlish voice cried. "Is it you? Are you back already?"

"Damn straight it's me!" Pecos shouted. "And I am back."

The girl, who appeared to be in her mid-teens, squealed and raced down the curving stairway in a flurry of skirts. Halfway to the bottom she threw her leg over the bannister and slid the rest of the way down, landing nimbly on both feet.

Laughing, Pecos picked her up and swung her around. Spotted Wolf could see the affection they had for each other and somehow that made him feel the loneliness of his own situation even more.

When the girl's feet were firmly on the floor again, she turned her attention to the warrior waiting quietly beside her father.

"Hello." Her green eyes were bright with laughter. "Are you my uncle? The wild Indian Daddy was hoping to bring home with him?"

"I guess I am." He wondered what he was expected to do. The Comanche were formal people, unaccustomed to showing their feelings to others, yet it was obvious these people were not.

"This young lady is my daughter, Spring," Pecos said dryly. "But I suppose you've already guessed that."

"Are you going to kiss me?" Spring asked pertly.

Spotted Wolf was taken aback by the suggestion and looked to Pecos for instruction.

"It *is* customary," Pecos said, his eyes twinkling

with humor. "But I'm not so sure she deserves it since she requested it."

"Daddy! He doesn't know how to act yet. I'm just helping him over the rough spots." She closed her eyes and lifted her face for her uncle's kiss.

Feeling terribly awkward, Spotted Wolf gripped his niece's forearms and bent to kiss her mouth.

"On the cheek," Pecos growled.

Spring's eyes popped open and she glared at her father. "Da-a-addy! If you hadn't said anything, he wouldn't have known!"

Spotted Wolf's lips twitched as he placed a chaste kiss on her cheek. She sighed with disappointment. "I wanted something to tell the girls," she pouted. "I wanted to tell them a wild Indian kissed me." Suddenly she brightened. "But I don't have to tell them it was on the cheek, do I? They won't know that unless I tell them."

"I think you'd better tell the truth, though," her father said. "Don't you?"

"I guess so."

Spotted Wolf had been listening to the exchange with amusement. Spring was obviously a lively young lady who kept Serena and Pecos on their toes.

Suddenly the hair on the nape of his neck stood on end. He had a sense of being watched. He lifted his head and saw a woman standing at the top of the stairs. She was small in stature and her thick, auburn hair was braided and wound around the crown of her head. She wore a dove gray gown with a high neck and at the moment both hands were clasped together over her heart.

She descended the stairs slowly, as though her legs were trembling and to go any faster would put her off balance. And all the while her gaze was focused on him.

Serena.

Even though twenty years had passed since they'd met, he could detect very little change in her outward appearance. His legs seemed to move of their own accord, without direction, as he strode to the foot of the stairs.

She stopped on the bottom step and looked up at him. "Johnny?" her voice quivered, as though she could hardly believe what her eyes showed her.

"Serena."

Spotted Wolf spoke her name and, as though a dam had broken, she could not stop the flood of tears. "Oh, God," she whispered. "It *is* you, Johnny."

When she flung her arms around his neck and pressed her head against his shoulder, he looked helplessly at Pecos, wondering what he should do, wondering how he could stop her tears.

But Pecos only stood there, watching quietly.

Silently cursing his brother-in-law for refusing to comfort his sister, Spotted Wolf closed his arms around her and patted her silky hair. "Do not cry, little sister," he murmured. "Do not cry." He continued repeating the words and his soothing pats until she pulled back and gazed up at him through moist eyes.

"Just look at me," she laughed shakily. "I've waited years for this to happen and then when it does, I start blubbering like a complete ninny." She smoothed her palm over his cheek. "Welcome home, Johnny. My dear, dear, brother."

As though unwilling to be ignored any longer, Pecos took his wife into his arms. "How about welcoming me home too?" He dipped his head and kissed her soundly. "Well, now that that's all over, what're we having for supper?"

It was just the right note to set everyone laughing. And, as though she'd just been waiting for the hellos to be over, Josey entered the room again, carrying a large wooden spoon with a long handle. "Supper's on the table! And if you all don't come get it right now, I'm gonna throw it out to the hogs."

"Don't you dare throw my apple pie out, Josey!" Pecos said.

He aimed a swat at the woman's ample bottom and Josey squealed and jumped out of the way. Turning quickly, she waved the large wooden spoon threateningly. "You keep your hands to yourself, Mr. Pecos!" she snapped. "Lessen you wanta feel this spoon up the side of your head. An' how you figure you gonna get apple pie anyways? Maybe I didn't make one."

"Then what kind of pie did you make, Josey?"

"Never said I didn't make one. Just said maybe I didn't."

"Will you two stop arguing and give me a chance to talk to my brother?" Serena complained.

"And have you start blubbering all over again?" Pecos asked. "Not on your life. He's here now and he's not going anywhere. At least not for awhile. Give the poor man a chance to adjust before you start badgering him with questions."

Spotted Wolf was glad of Pecos's intervention. Things were so different here than what he was used to; he found them almost overwhelming.

Spotted Wolf had had little to do with white men in the past, other than a few trips into town occasionally to gather information that would help them in their fight against the invaders. That was the way he had learned about the legalities of land titles, while he was trying to find legal loopholes hoping to use the White Eyes' own laws against them. The lawyer he'd consulted had been of little help though.

The laws were obviously made for the white man, not for the Indian.

Perhaps though, they had finally found a way to help the People. He certainly hoped so.

The dining table was long enough to seat more than a dozen people and it was set with platters of every kind of food imaginable.

"You sit next to me, Uncle Johnny," Spring said quickly, pulling a chair out for him. "And you're supposed to hold my chair until I sit down and then help me push it under the table."

"Spring," Serena chided gently. "There will be enough time later for Johnny to learn all that. This first meal together will be free of lessons." She looked at her brother. "You are going to stay with us, aren't you, Johnny?"

"Yes," he said. "For awhile."

"I am so glad," she murmured, and her eyes became moist again.

"Stop that, Serena!" Pecos said gently. "Don't go to pieces on us at the supper table." He seated Serena, then took his own chair at the head of the table. "It was as confusing for me in the beginning, Johnny," he said. "All this stuff that's considered manners is a lot of hoopla, but it's something I had to learn to keep from standing out in a crowd."

"I too will learn whatever is necessary," Spotted Wolf said gravely.

"We will help every way we can, Johnny," Serena said.

"Yes," Spring chimed in. "Mother and I are going on the tour with you and Daddy. It will be such fun! The girls are all terribly envious of me." Her green eyes widened dramatically. "Just wait until they know you really came. We didn't think you would. Mother said . . ."

"Spring!" Serena said sternly. "Stop bothering your uncle and attend to your meal."

"Yes, Mother."

Spotted Wolf would never forget that first night with them. Being quite unused to such exuberance he was stimulated by their laughter, by the women's constant chatter while Pecos looked on his family with indulgence.

It was something he wanted for himself, he realized. Desperately. If he could have a family like Pecos had, a wife who looked at him with love in her eyes, a daughter, a miniature copy of her mother, who would brighten his days with laughter, perhaps even a son he could teach the ways of a man, then he would be satisfied.

But without Jennifer, his dream was impossible.

Perhaps he was wishing for too much. Perhaps he would never see Jennifer again. That thought brought him new pain.

How could he even contemplate a life without Jennifer?

He was afraid he would be unable to find her, yet he must make the attempt.

He blocked thoughts of Jennifer from his mind and concentrated on his meal, on the platters piled high with meat and vegetables of a sort that he'd never eaten before.

True to her word, when the platters had been cleared away, Josey brought in a hot apple pie. And when it was finished, every piece on the plate having been eaten, they left the table and went to the drawing room to make plans for the tour that would set him on a different path of life.

Thirty-three

Crosby's Opera House was on Washington Street, next door to the St. James Hotel. It was considered the city's most magnificent entertainment hall, with its profusion of draperies, painted ceilings and intricate carvings. Its magnificence and beauty, Jennifer had been told, was equaled by no other in the country.

It had been closed most of the summer for renovations and was scheduled to be officially reopened on October 9th. Colin Davenport had tickets for that gala occasion, he assured Jennifer; Theodore Thomas's symphony orchestra was to start a ten-day series of concerts.

The theater was used for other events as well, Jennifer learned. In 1868 the Republicans had held their Presidential convention there, nominating the Civil War's Northern hero, General Ulysses S. Grant.

Tonight's events were not nearly so prestigious, yet the hall contained a large crowd, some of them probably drawn by the desire to be the first to see the lavish changes that had been made.

Jennifer followed the usher down the aisle until they reached the sixth row. He stopped and looked at the tickets Colin had given him to make certain of the location, then pointed at two vacant seats in the middle.

Colin went first to make way for Jennifer, and the other patrons rose obligingly, pushing their seats back in order to allow the newcomers to reach their places. When they were finally seated, Colin turned to Jennifer. "I tried to obtain aisle seats but it was impossible. Those seats sold out first."

"These are fine, Colin," she assured him, settling herself in the seat before taking in her surroundings. "It's a beautiful place," she commented. "Would you just look at those mirrors! They appear to be made of gold."

"They almost could be," he replied. "According to the *Tribune,* Albert Crosby spent more than $80,000 for new carpets, bronzes and those ornate mirrors that you're admiring. That little news item is probably responsible for there being so many people here tonight; everyone wanted to be the first to see the renovations. I'm sure the speaker will be gratified to find such an audience."

Jennifer asked, "Who is the speaker tonight?"

"I really don't know, Jenny," he replied. "But I thought the subject might interest you." He opened his program and held it closer, squinting in the dim light cast by the gasoline lanterns hanging from the walls. "It says here a committee has been formed to make known the plight of the Indians in the West."

Jennifer fingered the crystal that hung around her neck, wondering at her utter lack of feelings. Had she conditioned herself so much that even the mention of the Indians could make her feel numb?

"Does it say who formed the committee?" She wasn't sure why she asked the question, only knew that she was curious about it.

"The *Chicago Tribune* was responsible for the formation. The list of people involved is enormous though. There's a man named Jenkins and another one named Smith listed here. And there's a notation by Smith's name that says he was raised by the Indians. I read something about him in the papers yesterday, but I can't remember exactly what it was. Guess it wasn't important."

"Is Smith the speaker?"

"No. I don't think so. Let's see." He scanned the program. "It says a man named Warner is the speaker. John Warner."

"Did the newspaper say what tribe the man lived with, the one named Smith?"

"No. I wouldn't have known the difference anyway. I'm not that familiar with Indian tribes. I suppose you are though."

"What do you mean by that?" she asked in a cool voice, tightening her grip on the crystal. Did he know what had happened to her?

He looked at her in surprise. "Just that you are probably more knowledgeable, having been raised in the West."

"Oh." Jennifer knew she'd have to be more careful in the future. She'd thought for a moment that someone had told Colin about her past. But they couldn't have. She was almost certain her relatives hadn't given it away.

"Look!" Colin said, squeezing her hand to gain her attention. "The program is about to start."

Jennifer watched several men file out on the stage and take the seats that had been arranged near the center of the stage, while another stopped behind the podium. He held up a hand and waited.

"For those of you who don't already know, my name is Peter Jenkins. I am employed by the *Chicago Tribune*. He cleared his throat. "I am employed for the specific task of learning more about the plight of the Indians in the West." He leaned on the podium and gazed intently at the audience, seeming to touch on each person with his eyes.

"What I found was simply appalling! No one, no matter their color or race, should be treated in the manner that the noble red man has been treated. This land was theirs before the white man arrived on these shores. It was theirs!" His fist struck the podium. Jennifer had been completely mesmerized by the power of his voice and the words he spoke.

"What have we done? We came to this land and we wanted it. So we took it!" His fist slammed against the wooden podium again. "We brought our armies and we forced the Indians West. And when this land became crowded, we looked toward the West where there was still plenty of land to be found. No matter that it was already occupied. We wanted it, so we set about taking it. Just like we took this part of America. When do we stop this madness?"

He bent over the podium, and lowered his voice. "When? Do we continue until there are no Indians left alive to resist? Can we, who claim to be a civilized race, continue to deprive a noble people who want nothing more than to be left alone?" He straightened himself. "I think not. Such actions condemn us." He waited a long moment, allowing the audience to consider his words. "We have a man here tonight who spent his early years among the Indians. He will speak to you now. I give you, Pecos Smith."

The audience applauded loudly as Peter Jenkins left the podium and seated himself in the row of chairs at the back of the stage.

Another man took his place behind the podium.

"That's him," Colin whispered. "The man I told you about. The one that was raised by the Indians."

"Shhhhh," she whispered, her gaze never leaving the tall man who stood at the podium.

"Good evening," Pecos Smith said. "I'm afraid I'm

not much of a speaker. Quite unlike Peter Jenkins. But I intend to do my best to help you better understand the Indians. My qualifications are of the highest since, as Peter pointed out, I spent my early years among them." He leaned over the podium as though to make a point.

"In the past few years, many stories have come out about those early years of mine. It's been told that the Indians rode in, killed my parents, took their scalps and rode away with me. That is absolutely untrue. My parents were killed, but not by Indians as it was reported. They were killed by renegades who set the cabin afire.

"The Indians found me wandering beside the Pecos River, too young to speak my name, and took me with them, called me Pecos. The Smith was added later when I left the village and made a home with the people whose blood flowed through my veins.

"Now you might be saying that, considering my age, which I'm not telling . . ." the audience laughed obligingly, ". . . that the Indians' motives have changed considerably. But tell me this. If their motives have changed, if the Indians are now motivated by revenge, who could really blame them?" He stared down at his audience.

"But they have not changed. The Indians want only to live in peace! And yet will they be allowed to do so?" He paused for a long moment, then answered his own question. "No! They will not! Something has to be done about it before more lives are lost. And that is why we are here, ladies and gentlemen. We're trying to do something about it.

"When the *Tribune* contacted me to speak out for the Indians, I informed my wife. It was her idea, motivated by love for her brother who had been lost to her for more than twenty years, to attempt to persuade him to join us in our endeavors."

"He must be talking about John Warner," Colin whispered. "I wonder how he fits into all this. Frankly I'd like to hear Smith. He could talk about his life as an Indian."

Jennifer glared at him. "Shush, Colin!" she hissed. "I want to hear this."

"Sorry," he mumbled.

Jennifer looked at the podium again, frustrated when she realized she'd missed the end of Pecos Smith's speech. He had left the podium and resumed his seat and another man had taken his place.

She watched the newest speaker, wishing the light was brighter so she could see him better. She wondered who he was. Pecos Smith had probably given his name before he sat down again, but, with Colin distracting her, she had missed hearing it.

The man at the podium was tall, widely built, and his hair was dark, slicked back off his forehead. He appeared almost embarrassed to find himself on the stage and she felt sympathy for him. He was obviously unused to having so many eyes focused on him at once.

He stood there for a long moment as though he didn't know exactly how to begin and the audience moved restlessly.

"I . . . I . . ." He cleared his throat. "I find this role of speaker hard. And, although I have spoken before many large groups during the past several weeks, I still find it hard to begin." He took a deep breath. "But I must. I need to make you understand what is happening out West, because the fate of the people rest on your shoulders."

Jennifer stiffened, realizing his voice sounded familiar. She looked at him closer, but he appeared no different from the others who were seated behind him. He was dressed in the same manner, three piece suit with a gold watch chain as thick as her finger crossing his high-buttoned braided black vest.

She moistened her dry lips, and her heart picked up speed, sending blood surging through her veins.

Of course she was imagining things. He bore no resemblance to Spotted Wolf. None whatsoever. It was just that his voice sounded so much like the warrior's that it brought back painful memories, memories that she'd tried so hard to keep at bay.

"He's right about one thing," Colin whispered. "He's sure not any kind of a speaker."

Jennifer gave him a withering stare and Colin's face colored. "Sorry," he mumbled again.

Turning back to face the podium, Jennifer listened to the speaker, trying to convince herself there were differences between his voice and the one she remembered so well.

"Unlike Pecos," the man at the podium said, "I was not found wandering beside a river. The Comanche took me in a raid when I was a very young boy. I grew up among them, lived with them until a few weeks ago."

Jennifer sat up straighter, and her heart beat like a hammer, sending blood thundering through her veins. It couldn't be him . . . it couldn't!

"I know the Comanche." His voice rang out. "I *am* a Comanche. The white man knows me as John Warner. But to the Comanche I am Spotted Wolf!"

Spotted Wolf! Oh, God, it was him. He was here! Her relief and joy were almost overpowering.

"We have but one goal," Spotted Wolf thundered. "And it is to remain free. We want only to live our lives as we have always done. It is not our desire to slay the white man." His voice droned on. "We do what we must. The soldiers are determined to take our land, to send us to their reservations."

Jennifer's eyes were glued to the man standing behind the podium. She could hardly believe he was there, standing so close to her. And yet he was! Oh, God, how had it happened? He was here, in Chicago! Standing there alive and well when she had thought him dead!

A sudden thought occurred to her. Why hadn't he kept their appointment on the mountain? She had been so certain that death had kept him away, yet there he stood, alive, well. And, dammit, as healthy looking as any man could wish for.

Had he merely changed his mind about meeting her? That thought hurt, piercing as deeply as a sharp knife.

Fool, her heart cried. He loves you. Give him a chance to explain. "Something might have happened to keep him away," she muttered aloud. Even though death hadn't taken him, something else might have caused the delay. She must give him a chance to explain. Her heart demanded it.

"Did you say something, Jennifer?" Colin whispered.

"No! Yes. I have to leave, Colin," she said quickly. "Right now."

He looked concerned. "Are you feeling ill?"

"Yes." She grabbed at the excuse. "I feel nauseous. It must have been the fish the cook made for dinner." She rose to her feet and shook out her long skirt. "You stay here, Colin. I'll meet you in the lobby when this is over." She turned to the gentleman seated on her left. "Pardon me. I must leave now."

With a heavy frown, he straightened himself and raised the bottom of his seat to give her more room. Jennifer hardly noticed the frowning patrons as each of them lifted their seats and stood back to allow her to pass.

Her excitement at seeing Spotted Wolf again pulsed through her veins as she left the hall and hurried up the stairs where the dressing rooms were located. She felt dismayed when she saw the crowd that had already gathered near the stage, apparently hoping for a chance to speak with the warrior.

Crossing to an usher, she said, "I need to see Spotted Wolf . . . uh, Mr. Warner."

He snorted. "Yeah lady. I 'spect you would. But by the looks of that crowd, you'll be lucky if you get within shouting distance of him."

"But I *must* speak to him. It's terribly important."

"That's what all them other folks said too. Most of 'em newspaper reporters wanting his life story."

Her lips tightened. How could she talk to Spotted Wolf if she couldn't get anywhere near him? Perhaps if she sent him a note, it could be arranged.

Digging in her reticule for pencil and paper, she wrote a short note to let him know she was waiting to see him.

Returning to the usher, she handed him the note and added a large tip to insure it would be delivered. "Would you make sure Mr. Warner receives this?" she asked.

He shoved the money and the note into his pocket. "Sure thing, lady."

"Is there somewhere I can wait in private?" she asked.

"Afraid not. You'll have to make do with the lobby."

"Thank you," she said stiffly.

Descending the stairs again, she seated herself on a cushioned bench in the lobby. The drone of voices was a distant hum, heard vaguely through the closed doors. Finally the sound of applause could be heard and then the wide doors opened and the crowd emerged.

She pressed herself against the wall near the stairs to make sure the usher could find her when he brought the reply. Colin found her still waiting when he emerged from the Concert Hall.

"Are you feeling better now?" he asked, peering into her face.

"A little," she replied, glancing anxiously up the stairs at the crowd still gathered there. "But I would like to wait awhile before we leave. Just to make sure my stomach has settled."

"Certainly." He seated himself beside her and patted her hand. "What did you think of the speakers? John Warner wasn't exactly what I pictured." He continued to speak but Jennifer paid no attention to him, her thoughts focused on the crowd upstairs that was finally beginning to thin.

They were still waiting an hour later. The crowd had departed and the Opera Hall seemed empty now. Jennifer spotted the usher she'd given the note to and stood up quickly. "Wait for me, Colin," she said. "I'll be right back."

Hurrying to the usher, she said, "Did you give him my note?"

"Your note?"

"Yes. The note I gave you for Mr. Warner." Was the man dense? "I've been waiting here to see him."

His expression cleared. "Oh, yeah. That note. Sure. I gave it to him."

"What did he say?"

"Said he didn't have time to talk to nobody. He was tired and in a hurry. He went out the back way a long time ago."

"He didn't have time to talk to me?" she whispered, her face blanching.

"Nope. Sorry lady. I guess it was important to you. But them reporters have been hounding him ever since he got to town. Avoiding them wouldn't do his cause no good, so he ain't had much rest lately what with one thing and another. He'll be around town for awhile though and you might have more luck some other time."

He blurred before her eyes. She couldn't see, could hardly even think. Her actions were automatic as she turned away from him. "It doesn't really matter," she muttered. "I guess it wasn't so important after all."

Her ears rang, her heart thundered. Everything was seen through a mist as she hurried to the Ladies Room.

She fingered the crystal pendant Spotted Wolf had given her. It felt hot to the touch. According to Spotted Wolf, it was a healing stone. Had he given it to her, hoping it would heal her broken heart after he cast her aside?

Her eyes brimmed over and she wiped away the foolish tears, silently cursing herself for the fool that she was. Then she cursed him. "Damn you, Spotted Wolf! You could have faced me, could have told me you didn't love me, that you no longer wanted me."

Grimly, she straightened herself. She would waste no more tears on him. Not one drop.

As she emerged from the Ladies Room, she tore the crystal loose and flung it across the hall. Then she joined Colin, unaware of the man who'd only just emerged from a room farther down the hall.

Thirty-four

Spotted Wolf stopped short at the sight of Jennifer. He could hardly believe his eyes, and for a moment was struck speechless. He had been searching for her since he arrived in Chicago, but his search had been fruitless. Now, here she was. She had come to him.

Even as that thought occurred, she walked away from him without acknowledging his presence and joined a tall man in the central hall.

"Thank you for waiting, Colin," she said, her voice carrying clearly.

"I'd wait for you forever," the man she'd called Colin replied.

Spotted Wolf frowned. Who was he, this man who claimed he'd wait forever for her? What was his relationship to Jennifer?

Desperately needing an answer to his question, Spotted Wolf waited silently until they left the Opera House, and then he followed.

The house was quiet when Jennifer entered, and she felt grateful for that fact. She intended to go directly to bed. Only in sleep would she find peace from her turbulent thoughts, from the memories that plagued her. But it was not to be. As she reached the stairway, her grandfather opened the door to his study.

"Now isn't this a pleasant surprise?" He smiled and took her hand in his. "I was just reading a letter from your uncle."

"Oh." She pretended interest that she didn't feel. "How is he?"

"He is doing well. Told me to tell you his watch on a certain captain . . . I forget the name . . . proved useful." He paused. "You can read the letter if you wish."

"Not right now, thank you. I'm rather tired."

"You do look weary, my dear. Go on up and rest yourself."

She mounted the first step, then paused. "Was the man he mentioned named Brady?"

"You know, I think that was the fellow's name. You knew him, then?"

"Just slightly. Uncle Walter thought highly of him."

"Not anymore. Seems the fellow was caught selling information."

So Spotted Wolf was right.

"Good night, Grandfather. I'll see you in the morning."

"Good night, my dear."

She climbed the stairs and entered her bedroom. The maid had left the light on and the window open to allow fresh air into the room.

After donning her nightgown, Jennifer crossed to the window and looked down on the well-kept lawn below. The moon was full, bathing the night in its pale light. A flicker of movement caught her eye, but it was quickly gone. Probably a cat, she thought, turning away from the window.

She went to her bed, but sleep eluded her. Her mind brought forth memories of Spotted Wolf, of the first time she saw him, pale and sick from rattlesnake venom. She had no idea that he would come to mean so much to her, that he would be the cause of so much heartache.

Sighing, she tossed restlessly. His expression had been so tender, so caring, when he made love to her that first time. Had it all been a lie? Had he been pretending all along?

Those thoughts plagued her long into the night, but finally she fell into a restless sleep. She dreamed he came to her. He made no sound as he spanned the distance between the open window and the bed. Then, his face bathed in moonlight, he stretched out beside her and gently caressed her throat.

Jennifer moaned softly, leaning into the caress. He smiled and unbuttoned her nightgown, pushing it away from her shoulders, replacing it with his lips.

She felt the sweetest pleasure at his touch and hungered for more. The man in her dreams seemed happy to oblige. He pushed the nightgown farther down her body, easing the flannel from her arms until her breasts were completely exposed. Then he cupped the swelling peaks in his palms and gently caressed her flesh.

Her hips surged toward him, and she moaned again. "Spotted Wolf," she whispered, giving herself over to the dream. "Don't torment me so. Make love to me. Please."

As though he had only been waiting for her plea, his mouth closed over one taut nipple while his fingers worked magic on the other one, and she moaned again, her hips moving against him, eager for him.

Suddenly he lifted his head and kissed the side

of her neck. His voice was rough when he spoke, his breath whispering against her ear. "What about the other man, Jennifer? Does he make love to you? Does he touch you like this? Does he make you feel the way I do?"

His words jerked her into awareness and her eyes opened and she stared up at the man who was stretched out beside her.

"Spotted Wolf!" Her gaze flickered back and forth, taking in her surroundings. "I wasn't dreaming. What are you doing here? How did you get in?"

"I came through the window," he replied. "Now answer me, Jennifer. Have you found another man to take my place?"

"I don't know what you mean!"

"I saw you!" he snarled. His fingers dug into her arms. "I saw you with him. He kissed you before he left."

"Kissed me? Do you mean Colin?"

"Is there more than one man who takes such liberties?"

"How do you know about Colin?"

"I followed you from the Opera House, Jennifer. I saw you with him."

The Opera House. Suddenly memories slammed into her. He had ignored her note to him, had left her waiting at the rendezvous without a word of explanation. Now she owed him none.

"Release me!" she snapped, struggling to pull her nightgown over her breasts. "You have no right to be here. No right to question me. No rights at all where I'm concerned. You didn't even have the decency to reply to my note."

His hands dropped, allowing her to cover herself. "What note?"

"The one I sent to you at the Opera House."

"I received no note."

"You did. The porter told me he gave it to you. That you had already left the Opera House."

"He lied."

"He would have no reason to lie."

"I was at the Opera House, Jennifer. I followed you home. If the porter lied about one thing, then why not another?"

"He would have no reason."

"Unless he forgot to give me the note and didn't want you to know. Did you give him money?"

"Yes." She realized Spotted Wolf might be right. The porter was afraid he would have to return the money if he admitted the note had not been delivered. "That explains the note. But not why you didn't come for me? Why are you calling yourself John something-or-other?" Her voice rose hysterically.

"Why didn't you tell me who you were? You told me you loved me and I believed you. You told me you would meet me on the mountain and you didn't come." Her fingers clenched, digging into her palms.

"I could not."

"Why not? You broke your promise to me. Do you know how long I waited? Do you? All night long. I just sat there in the dark, waiting. And you didn't come."

She struck him then, lashing out with both fists, wanting to hurt him as he had hurt her. She realized that she was crying and silently cursed herself for her weakness, but could do nothing to stop the tears from flowing.

His eyes blazed down at her and he gripped her waist, pulling her against him, holding her tightly as she sobbed. And gradually, his close touch helped to ease her pain.

"Hush, hush," he rasped harshly. "I couldn't come, little one. I would have done so had I been able. But I could not."

She pulled away from him, lifting tear-drenched eyes. "Why? What reason did you have for leaving me alone like that, waiting, wanting you so?"

His mouth covered hers in a kiss of passion, so fierce and tender that it took her breath away. Then, he lifted his head. "I was attacked on the way back to the village. By the time I recovered and went to the fort, you had gone." He told her about meeting Clara, who had told him Jennifer's destination, then about Pecos's offer.

"It was easy for him to convince me to make the tour," he said. "It was the only hope I had of finding you." The timbre of his voice sent ripples down her spine and she searched his eyes, discovering secrets, unvoiced longings.

"Is it true then?" she asked. "Do you still love me?"

"I would die for you," he said fiercely.

His lips found her cheek and brushed it, then his teeth bit gently into her earlobe.

"Does this mean we have a future together?"

"It means I want you for my wife," he said tenderly.

"And I want you for my husband." He kissed her throat, then moved his head lower, but she stopped him. "Where will we live?"

"Anywhere you desire."

"How long will your tour last?"

"I am not certain. We are accepting every invitation that arrives. The more people we reach, the more names we acquire on our petitions, which increase our chances of helping the People. Those petitions will be carried to Washington.

"And we are hoping your white leaders will listen to us when we explain the plight of the Indian people, that they will make laws that will allow us to live in peace on our own lands." He sighed deeply. "Even with all the names we gather for the petitions, your government may still refuse to listen, but at least we will have tried."

"It is all you can do."

"Would you like to live on your farm when the tour is over?"

"There will be trouble if we move back."

"Not when that neighbor of yours learns he will have Pecos and the Comanche to deal with now, instead of one lone farmer."

"Pecos would help us?"

"Yes. He is family. And so are my Comanche brothers. Also, the farm is only a few miles from Pecos's and Serena's home. It would be good to live near them."

She agreed with him. She would live wherever he wanted, as long as they were together.

They continued to talk way into the night. And then they made love. And when they reached their peak, he put his hand over her mouth to quiet her cries of ecstasy, afraid she would awaken the household. Afterward, when they lay quietly together, they made plans for their wedding.

"It must be soon," he whispered. "I cannot wait long to have you beside me."

"Neither can I," she replied softly.

"I suppose it won't be as simple as leaving horses at your door."

"No. A wedding requires more than that. And you

must first ask my grandfather for my hand in marriage."

He raised a dark brow. "And if he refuses?"

"Then we will follow your custom. Just bring the horses and carry me away with you."

"Are you certain we cannot skip the grandfather part and just leave now?"

She laughed again. "My grandfather is not an ogre. It is my grandmother who will object."

He looked worried. "You will not allow her to change your mind."

"No. Never. Whatever happens, we will be married before the week is out."

And they were.

It was a beautiful wedding, even if it was hurriedly prepared. But it made them man and wife, and it was all either of them wanted, just to be joined together for the rest of their lives.

And they were.

AUTHOR'S NOTE

Quanah continued to fight for his people. But Bad Hand MacKenzie was determined to win the battle whatever it took.

By winter, little groups of Comanches and Kiowas began to surrender. But it was June 2, 1875, before Quanah entered the reservation, leading his band of half-starved and ill clad people. Bad Hand MacKenzie was at Fort Sill headquarters when Quanah enrolled, and the two enemies came face to face. But it was a brief, uneventful meeting; they were both too proud to reveal their feelings.

Quanah began his second life then, at the age of thirty. He spent the next thirty-five years traveling the white man's road, a model of citizenship. He disproved the theory that Indians could not adapt to change, initiating change whenever it promised to benefit the Comanches. He met with his mother's people, mastered their language and eventually became a major shareholder in a railroad. He was at ease lobbying for Comanche interests in Washington's corridors of peace, yet nothing ever tempted him to forsake his Comanche heritage and, upon his death in 1911, he was buried in the full regalia of a Comanche chief, beside his white mother, Cynthia Ann Parker, the woman the Indians had named *Nadua*—Keeps Warm With Us.

ROMANCE FROM JO BEVERLY

DANGEROUS JOY   (0-8217-5129-8, $5.99)

FORBIDDEN   (0-8217-4488-7, $4.99)

THE SHATTERED ROSE   (0-8217-5310-X, $5.99)

TEMPTING FORTUNE   (0-8217-4858-0, $4.99)

Available wherever paperbacks are sold, or order direct from the Publisher. Send cover price plus 50¢ per copy for mailing and handling to Kensington Publishing Corp., Consumer Orders, or call (toll free) 888-345-BOOK, to place your order using Mastercard or Visa. Residents of New York and Tennessee must include sales tax. DO NOT SEND CASH.

ROMANCE FROM JANELLE TAYLOR

ANYTHING FOR LOVE   (0-8217-4992-7, $5.99)

DESTINY MINE   (0-8217-5185-9, $5.99)

CHASE THE WIND   (0-8217-4740-1, $5.99)

MIDNIGHT SECRETS   (0-8217-5280-4, $5.99)

MOONBEAMS AND MAGIC   (0-8217-0184-4, $5.99)

SWEET SAVAGE HEART   (0-8217-5276-6, $5.99)

ROMANCE FROM FERN MICHAELS